NAILBITERS

The Project Collusion Series: Book 1

M.K. Williams

Printed in the United States of America

First Printing, 2015

Cover Design: Nora Gecan
Publisher: MK Williams Publishing, LLC

Library of Congress Control Number: 2015913965
ISBN
978-0-9967414-8-4
978-1-952084-07-2
978-1-952084-17-1

Second Edition, 2020

Mary K. Williams

1mkwilliamsauthor@gmail.com
1mkwilliams.com

All Persons Fictitious Disclaimer:
This book is a work of fiction. Any similarity between the characters, companies, and situations within its pages and places or persons, living or dead, is unintentional and co-incidental.

DEDICATION

For JMW

OTHER WORKS BY M.K. WILLIAMS

FICTION

The Project Collusion Series:

Architects

The Feminina Series:

The Infinite-Infinite

The Alpha-Nina

Other Fiction:

The Games You Cannot Win

Escaping Avila Chase

Enemies of Peace

NON-FICTION

Self-Publishing for the First-Time Author

Book Marketing for the First-Time Author

How To Write Your First Novel: A Guide For Aspiring Fiction Authors

Going Wide: Self-Publishing Your Books Outside The Amazon Ecosystem

Author Your Ambition: The Complete Self-Publishing Workbook for First-Time Authors

TABLE OF CONTENTS

PART ONE

To Err is Human

"The theoretically interesting point is that what seems to be a preponderantly masochistic people have developed sadistic specialists."
- *Body Ritual Among the Nacirema.*
Miner, Horace (1956)

I was trying to remember what had happened to get me to that point. Sweating, heart racing, trying to stay silent and appear calm as the car slowed down. I could just barely make out the figure standing on the shoulder of the road not ten yards away. I knew that we would have to be questioned and if the answers weren't acceptable- well I wasn't exactly sure what would happen then. Potentially we would have been killed on the spot, but I knew that torture was much more likely. My eyes were already shut behind the protection of my sunglasses, but I squeezed them tighter hoping to transport myself back in time. Mentally this worked, physically it didn't.

It hadn't even been three weeks, but everything had changed. Absolutely everything. My first thoughts brought me back to an easy evening in early spring. The air was cool and the night was silent except for the few crickets brave enough to come out before April. I was one of those few lucky souls that never experienced allergies. Not cats, not dogs, not strawberries, not peanuts, not pollen. Nothing. I was lucky enough to be enjoying a quiet evening laying in a green, green meadow and counting the planes flying overhead. Breathing easy, I was taking in that moment. I had not known at the time that it would be the last clear moment.

Now I can't even remember what it was like to see the cool blue-gray of the sky as the rain clouds had formed over the firmament, but no precipitation had yet to accumulate. The bright green grass looked much darker in the low light of the evening, and it smelled sweet. I can now tell you that was the last night I was able to breathe easy. We now know that it was at 2:00 am the next morning that the invasion had begun.

From what we now know, or have reasonably inferred, there had been sleeper cells in critical population centers for years. Maybe even longer. I had the fortune of never stepping into these areas. Although I wonder if I had ventured there sooner if my allergic reaction would have given *them* away.

I thought whatever intergalactic spores they brought with them, I was allergic to. Other people had to deal with ragweed, and I had to deal with cosmic residue. I don't know if other people had this allergy, surely I wouldn't be the only one. As our population had quickly dwindled, it might be realistic that I could be the lone human with this problem.

The following weeks were a blur. Literally and figuratively. Everything happened so fast. It hurts to think back on it all because it is still so fresh, but yet it seems to be as far away from me as anything else once familiar. As I sat four thousand miles away from "home" in an arid desert, the space between now and then felt like an infinitely expanding plane of existence that will never be crossed. But in this timeframe, this void, everything was gone. My house, my town, my life. A few of us from Cherry Lane had escaped, but I don't know where they are now. They invaded and since then there had been no normalcy, no regimen, no organization, nothing but fear and anxiety. No answers.

And of course, I was in the center of it all wincing and sneezing. Unlike most allergies, mine settled primarily in my eyes. My throat was spared the inconvenience of phlegm, but my eyes burned. They had been burning for weeks now. I was able to find some eye drops a few towns back and sold what is not proper for a lady to sell in order to take three 16 oz. bottles with me. But I was desperate to see. After the first week of screaming and bleeding and running, I realized that the invasion and my sudden onset of ocular difficulties were related. Especially when they were closer, it got worse.

Now in this moment, I knew who was waiting for us several yards away, I didn't have to look, not that I could. My eyes were welling with water. And the sunlight that surrounded the car was like a fire waiting to engulf my irises. I kept squeezing my eyelids tighter and tighter until my tender eyeballs begged for oxygen. I tried to allow my other senses to take over.

I could hear Don in the front seat hurriedly moving something and this brought me back to the present. Becca was searching for something in the glove compartment. I knew that the gun Don had stolen from Becca's father's safe was in the glove compartment and I was dreading what a fumbled attempt to grab at it could mean: an accidental firing of a bullet into my gut. I opened my eyes slightly. White light pierced my eyes like a javelin. I wanted the two of them to think I was still asleep. I wanted this to be the dream, but unfailingly, this was the reality that continued to greet me every time I left my slumber.

"Hurry Becca, give it to me," I saw her nimble hands grab the handle and she picked it up, holding it like it was a dirty diaper.

"Put it down, do you want to get us all killed?" Don yelled at her. He grabbed the gun by the chamber and shoved it between his seat and the cup holders. Don was always yelling at Becca, which under any other circumstances would cause me to instinctively tell Don to fuck off and stop yelling at my friend, but knowing the severity of our potential situation I could understand why he was so angry.

I felt the car stop and heard the empty fast food containers, pilfered and picked-over, on the floorboards shift slightly. I made the painful decision to look up above the rims of my shades and could see a figure standing right outside of the driver's window. I looked quickly over to Becca whose face said it all. It was one of *them*. I could see something dark moving in the distance coming up to her window as well.

We'd been driving for three days after a week in hiding in the Smoky Mountains and were halfway through Texas at that time- which meant we were in the middle of nowhere. No cars behind us, no cars ahead of us. The only thing we could have run into out here was the one thing we were running from.

I shut my eyes and tried to remember my last peaceful evening. The memory was slipping away, receding like a quick tide. I could feel sweat above my lip and on the sides of my arms and on the back of my neck. My mind was taken away from my hypersensitive evaluation when I heard Don explaining that we were traveling to find work. It seemed that explanation wasn't sufficient. I kept my eyes closed, maybe too tightly because I didn't want to see what was happening; I wanted to remain invisible in the backseat. I wanted all the dust we had stirred up on the open land to cover me so I could sink into the earth and be hidden from all: humans and otherwise.

I heard Becca make a high-pitched sound. I could tell she was crying because she had a tendency to only make that sound when she cried. I also heard her sniffle through a congested nose. I convinced myself to open my eyes so I could see what was coming before it happened.

The instant I opened my eyes I knew it would go from bad to worse. And it did. I looked at Becca and she must have sensed that I was awake because she moved her eyes to look at me. The figure that was standing outside of Don's window shifted its weight and was now peering into the back seat at my curled up body. I couldn't pretend to be asleep anymore, so I sat up. The car door to my right flew off and the figure that had been approaching the passenger side of the car, that had managed to avoid my attention until that moment, was gripping my arm. Soon I flew through the air. Becca screamed and Don must have decided it was time to start shooting. I heard three loud pops before I hit the ground eight feet from the car.

When I came to, I could hardly see anything because my eyes were swimming in tears. I didn't know how long I had been knocked out from the drop, but my entire head hurt. After a few seconds, I started to make out the shape of the car in the distance. I knew I didn't want Becca or Don to be dead or taken, my survival instincts kept telling me that I shouldn't be alone.

I tried to focus hard on the car, thankfully the wind had died down and the thin dust that kept getting in my eyes, my poor battered and abused eyes, relented for the moment. One of the dark figures was still by the car and I could see that something was now on the ground. I heard Becca's voice and it sounded like she was a mile away. She was really only three feet from me; she was being dragged by the brut figure that had thrown me. I screamed out for her and I could barely hear my own voice as the sound of my heart pounding had drowned out all other sounds.

I tried to crawl closer to her with no plan of how I could somehow free her and take off, but I crawled anyway. My left leg felt heavy and uncoordinated which I assumed was from a dislocated patella. "Becca," I kept calling. The large figure that was by the car started making its way over to us and I found a rock on the ground. A small one, but it was all that I could grasp in my hands except for clods of dirt and dried grass.

As I inched closer to my friend, I could see that she was covered in blood, soggy and saturated in it. My screams intensified at this point, but my mind couldn't connect the blood with her complacent gaze. She was in shock, I was in a panic, and both creatures were cool and menacing as ever.

The handler dropped Becca and turned to me, it grabbed me by my hair and forced me to sit on my knees. The pain in my left leg stung like a hundred bees at once and I yelped in pain. My hand reflexively released the measly rock I had grabbed. And an indecipherable command that sounded something like "Granphundula hexo" was grumbled at me. I kept my head down and tried to obey as best as I could, though I couldn't comprehend what it wanted me to do. Would obedience save me from death or mutilation?

On our way driving west, the three of us had passed through an abandoned suburb. We decided to spend an hour scouring for food before continuing on our way. One of the homes we went into had the windows busted and the door kicked in. A similar scene to the other houses on the block, only this house smelled rancid and there were flies everywhere. I found the bodies in the bathroom first, and I couldn't keep this memory from my mind. It was gruesome and bloody and thinking back on it, a thorough investigation of the types of wounds would have served me well, but the knowledge of what to expect next would have only left me more petrified than I already was. This image was now plastered in my mind. I didn't want to become maggot food.

I turned my head slightly to the right to see Becca. She had her head down too and blood was dripping from her hair onto the ground. While the two figures were convening a few yards away, I made an attempt to whisper to Becca.

"Are you okay?"

She didn't move.

"Becca, are you hurt?"

She still didn't move. I looked back at the car and realized that there were only four living beings on the side of the road. The shape that I had seen on the ground next to the car was Don. I squinted for a better look and I was horrified and relieved at the same time. Don had been on his way to becoming a human mercenary. Seeing his body, I knew that worst tragedies had already occurred; his death would not be any more significant than the rest.

I thought for a second that I was saved. Don was dead, his legs and torso and arms all attached, unmoving because the upper half of his head was gone. Only the lower mandible was apparent at the top of a neck that was no longer needed. I was horrified at the site of his body, but wildly excited to be free of him.

Should I run to the two figures who had freed me from Don? A cold realization settled over me. I had traded one prison for another. At best they would decide to leave us on the side of the road, in which case we could starve within days. I might have welcomed the crows that would circle so that they could take me away piece by piece.

The figures started to move toward us again. I tried to look up to finally see what *they* were- what did *they* look like? *They* were so dark and I couldn't tell if it was what *they* were wearing or just how *they* were; their species. With each step that they took towards us my eyes filled with reactive water, trying to wash as much of the allergic agitators out of my eyes as possible, but leaving my vision completely compromised. Too tall to be human, and too calculated and evil to have any trace of humanity within them, these figures were slowly stalking us all. *They* stood behind us and slung a thick and stiff cloth over our heads. I tried to ascertain the material. Canvas maybe? Raw canvas, hard and firm and unforgiving against my skin. Sitting there blindfolded and hunched over, my senses began to pick up on everything that they could. My hearing was still dulled, but any faint sound made my head jump. I had expected to hear the pop of a gun and then darkness. I wondered how long those interminable seconds would stretch on for.

Then I heard a loud bang and felt a rush of heat on my face, heat that had pushed through the fabric. It was too hot to be a breeze on the plains. *They* must have set fire to the car and the extra gasoline exploded. I was glad that my hearing was already impaired from earlier. One of the figures pulled me up and started moving me. Every other step was torture. Right foot down, ok, left foot down, and I was in pain. I could feel my body favor this side and placed my weight on my right hip. We could have been walking for hours; we could have been walking for twenty minutes. I wasn't sure, but I knew I was in pain. I heard the sound of metal moving and scraping along the hard dirt of the ground. Then I felt cool air hit my face and a sweet and evaporated stench burn my nostrils.

They had pushed us into our seats, or at least I felt *them* push me. I heard another low female grunt next to me, what I assumed was Becca's voice. The seats felt plastic and were seated low, my feet were flat on the floor of whatever vehicle we had been placed in, but my knees were high above my thighs, an uncomfortable angle to maintain for a long time.

And it felt like a long time. I could feel the occasional jostle as the vehicle hit a pothole or a rough patch of road. *Shouldn't we be flying in one of their hovercrafts?* I thought to myself, a sick daydream of when we thought aliens were only nonsense and their unimagined technologies were fantasy. I amused myself and kept my mind alert by running through the capitals of the fifty states, then the U.S. Presidents in order, then the parts of the periodic table that I could recall, then the U.S. Presidents in reverse order. My mental games helped me to stay focused yet detached, but my eyes continued to weep under my black hood. Those *things* were still close enough to continually trigger a reaction. The pain in my knee began to dull, no doubt as water from my body was rushing to the area, but each slight bump in the road shot an unforgiving pain through my left leg.

Finally, we stopped. It must have been an hour, given my deliberate pace in my mental exercises; I tried to calculate the exact minutes I had wasted, but eventually lost track and was left with a guesstimate.

My right arm was grabbed. I tried to sense if *they* had hands, did it feel like a palm with five fingers around my arm, or was it something different? I was trying to discern what shape *their* hands might take under *their* mesh gloves, but once I was pulled up to my feet, my knee quivered in electric pain, distracting me from the finer details of my tactical senses. I couldn't stop myself and let out a sharp whine. I sounded like a scared little girl, and at heart I was, but I had not intended for *them* to ever know that.

I heard a grunt; my arm was tugged indicating that I should walk forward. I hobbled forward; my captors would have to accept this compromise as my ability to walk was significantly impaired. I caught my own thought and tried to remind myself that these weren't humans, *they* had no empathy or ability to compromise. These were non-humans, aliens with no capacity for mercy. From what I had seen of their destruction to date *they* had no emotions and certainly were more ruthless than any gang-banger, mob-boss, drug-fiend or fascist dictator. I wondered if *they* were robots. The evil I had already witnessed was out of this world. I chided myself for thinking I could force them to compromise; there would be no middle ground here. Gene Roddenberry had penned it accurately all along, resistance is futile.

We had arrived at some kind of routing station. That was what I named it in my mind; with no other information available to me it had to be a routing station. The other option was that this place would be my morgue, so I decided it had to be a routing station. I could see some light through the black fabric over my head. I could make out the shining white tile below my feet and the narrow lines that I was able to recognize as the reflection of the fluorescent lights bouncing back up from the tile. I occasionally saw dark rectangles in my peripheral vision, some longer than others. I wasn't sure if they were other people, like me, waiting on benches to be marched off further down the hallway or if they were aliens, standing guard.

The hallway felt impossibly long as I fought to walk in a straight line. I hoped that my knee was bleeding and that I would lose consciousness soon. That wish was not granted.

I heard the one that was holding my arm make a noise. A grunt and then a jumble of gargled words, the one that was behind me responded with equally odd sounds. I could hear the sounds, but they made no sense to me at all. We stopped and for a moment I thought we had arrived at the next spot where I would sit and be quiet. I shifted my weight onto my right leg and gave my left knee a slight reprieve. I tried to bend it, a mistake because the pain caused me to immediately bite my lips and furrow my brow. I flinched.

The thing holding my arm sensed it and gave me a quick tug. I was forced off balance and had to throw my left foot down to keep from falling. The pain was intense, but at least I could still feel. For all the confusion that was flooding my mind, I knew that if I was in pain that it meant the limb was still functioning like it was supposed to. If it had gone numb, then I would have had to start calculating my odds of survival with only one leg.

Whatever these *things* were, they seemed to be amused by our human pain. *They* were un-phased by our suffering. *They* were cold, emotionally. Physically I could feel my arm sweating beneath the grip of the guard who was escorting me. *They* were warm-blooded at least.

In all of my observations, I never once made a conscious effort to consolidate all of this data. I just needed something to focus on. My mind was fragile after weeks on the run, and the trauma of this new reality had yet to dissipate. I made sense of it all by asking myself questions. "What do they look like?" "What are you smelling?" "Who else was there?" "Where are you now?" It seemed to be the only normal thing I could do, although it was bordering on psychotic.

I could hear the labored respiration of the thing pulling me along. For some reason, I kept thinking of *it*, as a *he*. I had only seen *them* at a distance, but now being so close and with my eyes covered, I still had yet to get a clear view. From afar *they* all looked uniform. No variation, no differences indicating age, gender, rank, or any other classifying system that was familiar. That's what we humans like to do; we like to classify. Safe/dangerous. Male/female. Fit/weak. We may not like where we are labeled, but we find comfort in that norm.

My escorts stopped. I heard my own breath catch. After several weeks of consistent cortisol rushing through my system, on edge, afraid, on the run, I was jumpy. I was always waiting for the next massive change, but yet never prepared for it. I could hear the voice of another one of *them*. Hoarse and impossibly deep, the tone of *their* voice sent chills up my spine and a piercing whine through my teeth. They sounded like the anonymous bad-guys hiding behind voice modifiers that were never revealed in scary movies. I had once heard that this was the trick that Hollywood used to get audiences to feel the fear. It's not seeing something scary that would terrify the audience; it's not being able to see the villain. I can vouch for the method, hearing the gruff voice, but not being able to see *what* it came from was a new horror.

The one that was holding me responded. This voice was much closer to my ears. I tried to listen for a familiar sound, a hint of some language. But I couldn't make one out yet. *They* were speaking fluently, quickly. My ears couldn't keep up with the pace of *their* dialect.

Finally, after *their* brief exchange, I was led to my right and into a room. In a swift move, the bag was removed from my head and I was pushed down onto the ground. The door slammed behind me before I had the chance to turn around and see *their* figures.

There was one cold light illuminating the room. It shone onto a lime green linoleum floor. I staggered to my feet, disoriented and took a deep breath. The air conditioning must have been recycling the allergens or cosmic dust on the exo-suits of the aliens out of that room. I could inhale deeply and exhale with no impediment. My eyes cleared within seconds. The relief of clear passageways for air, after even a brief amount of time without it, was pleasing. Like when a cold finally clears, you only appreciate the basic ability to breathe because you had taken it for granted until it was hindered.

I tried to discern what kind of a room I was in next. No rest for my weary limbs and mind.

The light was very focused and much of it did not extend beyond the almost white circle on the floor. I tried to navigate around this circle, slowly moving outward. I couldn't see very clearly, which meant I was vulnerable if something was lurking in the shadowy corners of the room. On my seventh timid step, I came to an abrupt stop. My hip swung into a metal table. I came close to losing my balance, but recovered by placing my hands forward onto the cool metal surface. I thought I had my footing, but the metal in front of me began to slide forward, and I began to move forward again, my weight pushing the metal even further away, my center of balance unable to reach equilibrium. In a fraction of a second, I pushed myself back with all the force that I could muster and landed on my feet in a low squat before standing back up. I heard the metal table stop as it crashed into something else in the darkness of the room. I walked slowly towards this sound.

The din of the metal hitting against the clapboard cabinets drew me in further into the darkness. Now fifteen feet from the narrow circle of light I seemed to have found the edge of the room. I felt around to better determine what I was standing next to. I could tell that the metal table was on wheels, I could feel nothing on the top of the cabinet, but it was long. I stretched out both of my arms and tried to feel for an edge with my fingertips. Fully extended and bent over I could feel nothing but more of the same surface. It might have extended across the length of the room. I made the snap judgment that it did. The cabinets spanned the length of the room.

I crouched down gently, trying not to bend my left leg, and began to gently pull at the thin metal handles on each cabinet. They swung easily on their hinges to open and stayed open without drafting back to stasis. I felt around. Nothing in the first cabinet. The second had a stack of what seemed to be paper-like fabric, thin and flimsy and easily ripped. The third had lots of small boxes of various sizes. I grabbed two, one in each hand and walked unevenly back under the light to read them.

The first box, in my left hand, was wide, and I could barely fit my fingertips around to grip it. The label indicated that it contained one hundred sterilized gauze pads. The second box, in my right hand, was small, and the top of the white and blue packaging stated twenty-five packages of topical cyanoacrylate. Liquid stitches, gauze, spotlighting and a gurney- I was in an operating room. I was in a medical arena.

The usual safety that would accompany a hospital, the assurance that doctors are there to help and heal, never filtered into my system. My heart began to race. This hadn't been a convenient stopping point for my captors to bring me here. It was part of a very calculated plan. Here is the room where I would be analyzed, studied, dissected and potentially discarded if I didn't survive the mutilation.

It wasn't my darkest fears that were fueling this worry. It was the reality that I had seen. That home that we had stopped at, when Don still had his head and Becca was still by my side, I had witnessed the gore. The women's bodies severed; their ovaries piled into a bathroom sink while their lifeless corpses stared up at me blankly. They appeared to be stacked up, as though *they* were rifling through each body looking for something specific, and when *they* didn't find it, *they* threw out the rest. Don had to pull me away as the silent shock began to rattle my body. The stench of the decomposition had burned my nose, the hum of the maggots had tickled into my ears, and the writhing and squirming motion of the bugs was engraved into my retinas. The memory boiled up to my mind as I clutched the packages in that dark hospital room. My hands began to shake. I had to pull myself away from that memory, just as Don had done weeks ago.

I started to react. I might have minutes or seconds, or maybe hours until they came back in to do whatever it is that they planned to do. I had nothing on me but my clothing, the same clothing I had been wearing for a week. Don and Becca had pawned some of our electronics for fresh clothes and food as we made our way across Tennessee. The cell phones had stopped functioning completely within the first few days of the takeover, the batteries burned and no available electricity to charge them with. While the technology could have been valuable, none of us knew how to manipulate it, and we had to eat. The clothes we had been wearing for the previous two weeks stunk of dried sweat, and each of us had some blood on us. Don had tried to save a baby on the first day, but his efforts had been useless. Her blood on his t-shirt was at first a badge of mourning, then of intended vengeance, but after two weeks it was only a reminder that life would never be the same.

Becca had narrowly escaped the clutches of one of *them*. Her leg was scratched pretty badly, and fortunately, we had been able to make sure it was healing without infection. But the shorts and tank top she had started running in would not sustain her on our journey.

I had been running when someone next to me, a stranger, had been slashed or shot. I wasn't sure, but one moment they were next to me, pushing to keep my pace. The next they were gone and their last action resulted in a spray of blood across the back of my body. For all the times that my dad used to joke that the only way to survive a bear attack was to run faster than the slowest person, the crude reality didn't sink in until I survived by running faster than that man.

When we had decided to get fresh clothes, we all knew that they could easily be bloodied again. But we had to push forward, there was no way to go back, we had to stay on the run. And in some way, new clothes helped us to mentally block off then from now. And now I was wearing tight, skin-hugging maroon corduroys and a plain black t-shirt. There was no room in my pockets for anything, but I figured that if I could get out of this room that some of the supplies in the cabinet would eventually be useful. I began to scavenge.

First, I took the pile of cloths that felt papery and began to assemble a make-shift satchel. I filled it with bandages, gauze, the liquid stitches. I worked my way through the other cabinets and began to fill it with cotton swabs, tongue depressors, plastic gloves and surgical masks. I couldn't anticipate a use for many of these items, but each day of the past twenty-one had been a new experience that I could have never expected in my wildest dreams.

I had a good store built up when I found plastic, slippery and easily opened, plastic bags. I grabbed one of the bags with the hazardous waste triangle printed on them and put the entire paper satchel into it. I grabbed the additional bags and tied them together with a double knot, leaving room for my hand to grip the knot as a handle. I had kept the Ace bandage out of the bag and began to wrap my left knee tightly. The swelling had already allowed my knee to balloon to the size of a navel orange. The pressure of the bandage felt great, and I knew I would be able to make do with this for the time being.

I had my supplies. But now, I needed an exit. I wanted to think quickly, act quickly and get away. But I had no idea about what could happen if I went out the door that I was thrown through. I set out along the length of the room, following the cabinets. I searched the dark corner and proceeded along the next wall to feel for a door or a break or a void that might lead me out of the room. As I passed within the darkness of the room my eyes began to adjust to the lack of light and I could start to see the remainder of the room. I had made my way back to the door that had been my point of entry when I heard the deep and menacing voices on the other side. I backed away from the door just in time. The door flung open with force, and I jumped back.

It took a second for it to ascertain that I was only a few feet away, ambulatory, and potentially a threat. Before I could move, or guard myself, a cold and metallic glove was clutched around my throat and my feet were off the ground. My eyes burned right away. Quickly, and without any taunts or threats, I was placed in the center of the light and dropped. I hit the ground on my feet but, quickly lost my balance. I dropped my bag of supplies on the ground and shoved them quickly out of the light.

The metallic table was wheeled next to me and I was again picked up and this time dropped onto the table. The wheels slid as the weight of my body flopped down on the thin sheet of metal. One harsh and menacing sound was made: "Krazetha" it sounded like. One hand was held out. I had no way to understand their language given that this was the second time I had ever been this close to one, but I was fairly sure that it meant "Stay." I laid still.

I saw it pass back out of the light and plod across the room, its heavy legs pounding against the floor with each step. I had no time for panic; I tried to memorize the features I had finally been able to see. Through a thin veil of tears pooling in my eyes, I made out their size and shape. A dark black metallic suit covered the entire body, or maybe that was their body. The design of the metal led me to believe it was a suit, with mesh on the shoulders and solid lines across the facemask; it appeared to be a suit of both form and function. There were small tubes connecting the body of the suit to the helmet. My first assumption was *their* need to breathe and the potential compatibility with our atmosphere. I was so curious about these evil creatures and why they had decided to inflict their will upon us.

My human need for answers, for justice, for an explanation had kept my mind whirring for weeks. I had yet to give up hope of understanding *them* and ultimately defeating *them*. But, with my back on the cold and unforgiving metal, I began to worry that I might never leave that room alive.

The door opened again and two of *them* entered the room, this time with a human man. The man was short, five foot, three inches at most. He wore glasses and his hair was a mess. But then again, all of us humans looked frazzled now. His overall appearance was squirrely and anxious. With the two brutes, each six foot four inches robotically leading him into the room, I didn't find fault in his human worry.

The alien on the left pointed to me and began to speak. The words this time were too quick for me. The human must have understood because he held up his hands and said "No!" He looked over at the other alien and repeated, "No, I won't do it. No." This man must have understood what the intended purpose of this room was.

The first alien repeated the request again, this time much slower. "Hirothia lethumina." Two words, slow and clear. I had no reference, but the more words I could gather the more I would be able to understand what was coming.

"No! No lethumina!" The man had his hands up, covering his face. His mouth was refusing but his body language conveyed a beaten and defeated attitude.

The second alien very quickly, and without patience, hit the man on the crown of his head. The man fell to the ground like a deflating balloon. I couldn't be sure if he was dead or incapacitated. It didn't seem to matter to the aliens because they both focused on me now.

The first pointed to the second and gave the same instruction. The second hesitated; apparently, he did not like the order either. *What horrible task was being asked of this creature?*

The second started to speak quickly, shooting off a retort. A short exchange ensued, of which I understood nothing. I did hear the words "hirothia lethumina" several times, and I could almost be sure that the responses included a variation of the verb. *Were they conjugating their verbs?*

As they continued to argue I tried to formulate a plan. I couldn't take on one of them, let alone two. I had no idea what their weaknesses would be. Humans I could easily take on, aim for the eyes, the nose or the throat. But these metal covered mysteries were daunting, and I had no information about them beyond the small observations I had made in the past thirty minutes.

Finally, they stopped arguing and the second alien approached me. It began to move my limbs and I did not resist. My arms were placed above my head and my legs were straightened and spread on the table, each ankle at one corner.

Then it walked into the darkness toward the cabinets.

This memory is the most clear to me. In the months that have followed, this exact moment is what I rewind and replay over and over in my mind. Though my eyes were watering and my eyelids felt like sandpaper each time I blinked, I remember this series of small events vividly.

The alien reappeared from the shadows. I inhaled, but couldn't bring myself to expel the air from my lungs. *It* was positioned at my midsection. The mental image of that gruesome suburban bathroom with discarded organs flashed in my mind, panic took over. I could feel my blood as it slid through my veins. Adrenaline was coursing easily and each small detail stood in stark contrast to the preceding moments.

With *its* right hand raised above me, I could see a thin metal object in the alien's grasp, it was a scalpel. I could have predicted that its next move would be to push my shirt up and expose my stomach before it cut in. But I would have been wrong. Instead, *it* lifted *its* left hand, a small oblong metal coin glimmered and distracted me. What a curious item it was. I didn't recognize it as a medical instrument, and I had no idea what it could ever be used for.

The alien moved in its thick, black suit with grace and deftly picked up my left arm, pulling it up by the wrist. I knew whatever mutilation was about to ensue was imminent. This was when I saw the man, the one that had been hit on the head, rising silently behind the other alien in the room. Both of them, the man and the alien, were in the dark corner by the door. The man's eyes were wild, and though there was no red light in the room, I could have sworn I saw his eyes burning with red fire. He lifted his hands toward the neck of the alien and in a quick motion pulled at something. The alien collapsed almost instantly. The creature standing over me turned and dropped my hand.

The remaining alien charged the man, but the short man was able to duck and dodge quickly. I sat up to watch the scene unfold. If I could grab my bag of supplies and get to the door, or just get to the door in this commotion, I might be able to escape. But I couldn't run, and I didn't know what was on the other side of the door.

This was when the alarm began to ring. The loud and pulsing whine of the alarm spread through the entire building. I could hear running in the hallways, whether human or alien I couldn't be sure. I jumped off the table and landed, luckily, on my right leg. I hopped to the location of my bag, it was still there, and grabbed it. The man was now on the back of the alien, digging his hands into the dark metal suit, looking for something with intensity.

He must have found it because the second alien fell, the scalpel and metal object slipping out of the creature's hands. The scalpel landed near the feet of this man, and the metal coin landed near me. Without thinking, I picked it up and pocketed it.

The man reached his hand out towards me and I gladly accepted.

This was the exact memory that I recall most. I replay it in my mind often. At first, it would be an occasional curious review, but recently it has become a scientific fascination. These few minutes have been the most significant in the past months, and while I will detail everything that follows, I must never forget this moment. I feel that it is the key to the final portion of my quest.

This was their mistake. The small detail that *they* dropped. It could have been any would-be victim on that table that *they* forgot to perform a basic procedure on, or what we have now come to understand as the most basic part of *their* systematic tagging of the remaining human population. This was the error, this was the mess-up, and this was the flaw.

The man was sweaty, his face was wet and his receding hairline was clinging to his moist scalp. His hands were sweaty too. He pulled me close to him and I hobbled along to the doorway. The alarm was still crying out like a child with no mother. He became very still and listened closely to the door.

"You should have screamed out by now; the others may get suspicious soon. We can use this alarm to our advantage." He was extremely technical in my narrow avoidance of such pain. He spoke in an even tone, not shouting to be heard over the alarm, but somehow whispering with force. His voice was almost feminine in its high pitch, but still distinctly male. He pushed the glasses that were sliding down his hooked nose back up and lifted his free hand up to his mouth. He cupped his hand over his mouth and looked at me intently for understanding. It wasn't the standard universal symbol for silence, which would have been a single finger pressed to his lips, instead he completely covered his mouth. The emphasis was effective, and I tried to slow my breathing to make absolutely no sound. It seems odd that he made such a request when an alarm was blaring and drowning out most other sounds, but he seemed to know a great deal about these *things*. I trusted him based on these small context clues. This was my mistake.

He opened the door ever so slightly to peer into the hallway. He quickly pulled the door the rest of the way open and yanked me through it. I hopped along to keep pace with him, each step was agonizing, but I had a chance to escape, and I could not stumble or falter. The bag of goods was in my left hand, and it slapped against my leg in a painful rhythm, but I heeded the warning I had been given and didn't make a sound.

We headed down the stark white hallway. I could see the exit in front of us, but very quickly he guided me to the right, down a separate passage. My mind told me that this was the wrong way, but I had no other choice but to accept this path. He brought me through two more passage-ways until we came to an alternate exit. The hospital was a maze of identical hallways, only distinguished by the rancid smells emanating from the rooms and safety posters that would not be of use anymore. The bland interior and the poorly powered lighting were eerie in how normal they looked. It was as though the last three weeks hadn't happened. With the exception of the odor of rotting corpses and limbs, this hospital was quite in order.

Finally, we emerged from the building and into the sunlight. I was tired, in pain, and on the precipice of collapse. My fight or flight response was dampening. The neurotransmitters were equalizing and the fatigue in my muscles was causing them to stiffen quickly. It was unlikely that I would catch another break to aid in my survival. I should have remembered this when the truck arrived. Surely, I could not be so lucky, but I was eager to hope, and so I hopped in.

The truck was a mid-nineties two-tone Ford with wood built-up on the sides of the truck bed, making a fence and allowing weary, weak human travelers additional space to rest their heads. The man who had been dragged in by the aliens to take part in my torture, who had refused, and then ultimately led me away from the gruesome hospital was named Mitch. He shook my hand properly and I introduced myself, as though those social niceties still mattered. It felt safe and comfortable to still recognize these traditions, but he could have been lying and had I given it more thought, then maybe I would have lied too. *What do names matter when we are all only a few missteps from death?*

Mitch was a father and technology developer from Omaha who had fled the mid-west after the seizure of Sioux City, an event that took place on day three of the invasion. While he was miles and miles away from the imperiled city, he knew it wouldn't be long until they spread out, and he wanted to seek refuge in the desert. He assessed the odds of survival to be small for any living being in the desert and hoped his years as an Eagle Scout would help in his wilderness survival.

As he told me his story his sad eyes came alive, like he had a purpose, and it was to make sure his journey was known. He set out in the family van with his wife and two daughters, but along a lonely stretch of highway as he made his way into Utah, they were stopped on the side of the road. The next part sounded familiar. The family was removed forcibly from the vehicle. His wife lay unconscious, he hoped that it was just unconscious and not a more permanent state before they covered his head and loaded him into a van. Mitch said that he could hear his daughters calling for him from a distance; he realized that they were being led in another direction.

The van that Mitch had been placed in drove for days to arrive at the hospital. He had been held there almost two weeks. Once his torture was complete, he was free to roam the halls, albeit heavily monitored and guarded. He found food, just barely meeting the definition, in the vending machines throughout the building and distributed it to the other captives that he could find. After one week, the aliens began to include him in their mutilation. They would make him watch, and when he covered his face at first, they did not object, but soon they held his hands and head so that he was forced to stare directly at their hideous work. He wouldn't describe it any further to me, I was glad for that.

Apparently, I was to be the first captive they expected him to perform their sadistic mutilation on. Mitch had become a caregiver for the other captives and had settled into the role easily in spite of his personal loss. "I just kept thinking that if I proved useful, they would open a door and my girls would be sitting there, unharmed and that we could go home." He smiled weakly as he said this, revealing his own disappointment at how foolish the thought had been.

"I have no idea where they are, I have no idea where to begin looking for them. But they're smart girls. And hopefully, their mother is with them, if she is still ok. It's too much uncertainty to think on, so I've been telling myself that the best possible outcome must be true."

One of the other passengers on the truck, a haggard-looking woman with leathery tan skin and dry, broken bleached hair, scoffed at Mitch's optimism. "You think your women are still okay?"

Mitch nodded, his naiveté was endearing, but I found it inspiring. If he could be optimistic, then so would I. "I don't feel like they're gone. I think my soul would have somehow notified me if they were gone forever. I'm a spiritual man-"

The glass-half-empty woman, whose name I would later find out was Barbie, not kidding, had an easy retort, "Well what does your Spirit say about *these things*?" She was making a reference to the aliens, the beings that after just a few hours in their captivity, I was certain I never wanted to be near again. *Had I been overly lucky to have escaped their captivity so soon? Was it just too easy? Had I been given a healthy dose of false hope?*

Mitch kept quiet. His emotional intelligence was off the charts, he read the situation and knew to keep his mouth shut. Barbie was looking for a fight, she seemed like the kind who was always mad and stubborn, uneducated but somehow always had to be right and prove herself to be in the right.

"Thank you," I said to Mitch. "For saving me and for not-"

"It was nothing" Mitch was quick to cut me off, the look on his face told me not to say another word. I offered a questioning look in response. He shook his head once, very slowly, in a solemn manner that told me not to bring up this topic in front of others.

"How is your leg?" Mitch began to lean over and inspect my bulging knee cap beneath my tight pants. I didn't want to cut them off because I needed protection from the elements, but I didn't want to risk infection either.

"It hurts less in some ways, but more in others." I gently circled the area with my hands, extending my thumbs and forefingers around my left kneecap.

"Do you have any syringes in that magical bag of yours?" Mitch gestured at the red bag, which I had placed behind my back.

"Let me see," I was wary to display my goods in front of the others, for fear of attack or theft, but I knew it was better to share in the hopes that the favor would be returned. It was scary how quickly the thought of violence and theft sprung up in my mind, just a few weeks ago that never would have been the case. But now, I had started to see the things that humanity was capable of. At the time I thought it had been the worst possible, but I would soon see more depravity that would convince me otherwise.

The sun was high in the sky, but well past noon. It was bright enough to be able to see everything in the bag clearly, which was fortunate. I found a syringe and pulled it out. Still hermetically sealed in a plastic sheath, the sanitary, clean needle was a small victory.

"I might be able to drain the fluid to get the swelling down," Mitch began to explain what he intended to do. He seemed confident in his explanation, perhaps his Eagle Scout skills already at work. I hoped that this was more than a trained guess, but as long as the pain went away, I was okay with that for now.

"Doesn't the fluid help with the healing process?"

"Yes, but right now removing it will help with the pain." Again, he was very self-assured in his response.

"Really?" I couldn't help but sound incredulous.

"I'm gonna be sick if you stick that in her leg, man," grumbled the young man sitting to my right. He was no more than sixteen years old and spoke in a low and drawn out tone. He had been silent for most of the drive so far. His name was Gavin, and he had been at the hospital for two days. He gnawed at his thumb in silence, pulling the nail to shreds and chewing at the stray bits of his cuticle as well. A uniform signal I would soon learn to recognize.

"So, don't look," Barbie offered.

"Gavin, don't pick at your nails, it's unsanitary." Mitch began to roll up my left pant leg, and once he reached my knee my eyes began to water. "I know, it'll hurt a bit, but it's for the best." The fabric was so tight across my knee; it was a sweet pressure and a painful ecstasy for the seconds of tight constriction that the folded fabric offered. My hairy leg was exposed; I hadn't been able to shave regularly since the invasion started. Barbie looked at me in disgust. Where had this chick been hiding out, a spa?

Mitch held the needle in hand and was about to open the package. "Wait!" I stopped him and reached back into the bag, fumbling and hoping some sterile swabs were in there. In the dark operating room, I had grabbed all that I could get my hands on.

After it seemed that hope was lost, I felt the sharp tips of the sterile swab with my fingers and extracted it from the bag.

"Right, good call Dora." Mitch set down the sealed needle and opened the sterile swab. He was diligent as he prepared the area.

"How old are your daughters, Mitch?" I knew I might be pushing too far, but I had a curious desire to know.

"Uh, about your age actually. Laura was- is," he corrected himself, "nineteen, and Beth is twenty." I nodded, impressed that Mitch had accurately guessed my approximate age, and also that he didn't look more than forty-three and still had grown daughters.

"So, tell me about yourself, Dora, I know that you're from Florida and that you're a fitness instructor. But what brought you to this fine stretch of the heartland?" Mitch was unwrapping the syringe. I could tell that he was going along with the distracting small talk that I had initiated, helping me as he led up to the most painful moment.

"I was traveling with Don and Becca." I hadn't said either of their names out loud since the events of that morning. I had been so focused on my own survival that I had pushed the gruesome thoughts of my last moments with them from my mind. My voice was a little shaky as I continued. "We were headed further west, but we were stopped as well. Just this morning actually. Don didn't make it. I don't know where Becca went. I think *they* brought her to the same place as me, to that hospital, but I don't know." The syringe went in. I wanted to scream, but instead, I bit my lip and let out a dull squeak. I looked up at the sky and waited until Mitch told me it was ok to look.

"Well, you came in by yourself. I didn't see them unload anyone else from your truck, but they might have taken her to another site," Mitch explained as he continued to work on my knee. He seemed very knowledgeable on the aliens and their process. I wondered how much he could really know after a couple weeks of observation. Had they been that routine in their patterns, or did Mitch just think he knew their motives?

"See, fluid out, swelling down. All better, right?"

"Sure, it feels better. I just hope I didn't break anything."

"We'll find out when we get off this truck." He applied fresh gauze directly to the skin and helped to roll the fabric of my pants back over my leg.

"Do you know where we're going?" I finally asked the question. I should have asked immediately, but I was in no position to bargain when we left the hospital and my body had needed to rest so I had let the question go unasked.

"Yeah Mitch, this is your show," Barbie chimed in.

Mitch was leaning back against the truck and moved his right arm to tap lightly on the glass separating the cab from the bed. The man driving, an older man with sierra toned skin and wise eyes surrounded by rivers of wrinkles slid the glass partition open. I could barely hear them. Mitch was speaking in broken Spanglish and this man was responding in hurried, impatient Spanish. It appeared that Mitch's instructions had been disregarded because he continued to say Denver, at first in a normal tone, then slower and louder, but the man in the front continued to insist. "No, no, no Señor! No Denver!"

"Manuel," Mitch emphasized his name, "DEN-VER!"

"No Mitch," which he pronounced Meesch, "No! Tahoe!" At first, I thought he said trabajo, after my life in southwest Florida I had picked up on some marginal Spanish. My mind tried to make quick connections, maybe that Manuel knew of a place to work, to earn something in this upended economy, or perhaps that Denver would not work. But Mitch clarified for us.

After sliding back the glass partition, Mitch smiled at Barbie, Gavin and me in an insincere manner. He was clearly not happy with this news, but he delivered like a manager would deliver a severance check. "We're going to California!"

At this point, it would make sense to explain a bit more of what happened between laying in a quiet and peaceful field, and how I became injured and starving in the back of a truck with complete strangers.

The invasion was a gruesome attack. In case you somehow blocked this from your memory or if you were unfortunate enough to be born in a post-Porth world, that statement is universal. It was a global tragedy.

It was as though *they* never existed one minute, and the next there was an invasion. It happened at night. Or in the United States it happened at night. It seemed to have started all around the world at once. There had been no ominous spaceships looming in our atmosphere making their presence known, no threatening message saying "take me to your leader." *They* already knew when and where to hit. We only had thirty minutes of news coverage before everything went dark.

I woke up early on a Thursday for my run. I always got up at five am, which some people find unusual, but as a trainer, my work days started with my first appointment, which was at seven. My jog was quiet and calm, as though nothing out of the usual was happening. But about ten minutes in I realized that the streets leading to the interstate were jam-packed, I saw people on the sidewalks screaming. I made a decision to cut my routine short and sprinted home.

When I arrived to see everything the same as I had left it, a disarming comfort, I switched on the television. Everything was being destroyed. No earthly destruction could compare. We weren't at war; we weren't being over-taken. We were being eviscerated. I packed a bag and began to run. A week's worth of protein bars, a canteen of water, my hiking pack and climbing gear were all included. I may be pretty, but I'm not dumb, survival requires being prepared. I figured that my car wouldn't get me too far given the traffic I had already observed.

I wanted to head north. For some reason I had an instinct to flee to harsh frozen climates; I was halfway down my block when my vision began to blur, I heard a low rumbling coming from behind me. *Good timing, am I right?* It was an invasion. Somehow, *they* were everywhere at all times.

I ran as far as my feet could carry me and found brief refuge in a 7-11 where a family with a small child crouched behind the counter. A few teenagers were busy looting the back of the store and I told them to sit down and be quiet. My voice said it all, there was no potential criminal repercussion to fear, in this case, the only consequence of their continued activity would result in certain death. They sat quietly with their loot and I ducked into the walk-in beer cooler.

I was hoping to check that the back was locked, but before I heard the door latch behind me the front of the store exploded. I ran through the back exit. The next few hours followed a similar pattern. Run, find shelter, shelter is destroyed, keep running. I made it from Tampa to Jacksonville on a HART bus that was stolen by an elderly woman and operated by a large black man. They were happy to take every person they could find along the way. We made the entire trip without interruption. A false sense of security if there ever was one.

Once in Jacksonville, the bus headed for EverBank Field. I was highly skeptical of a plan that would lead us into a population center. After a few minutes of trying to reason with the man behind the oversized wheel, I asked to be let off, and sure enough, I was on the streets of Jacksonville by myself. The smoke and gray rubble that we had passed in Tampa was present in Jacksonville as well. It was the new and ever-present sign of the defeated. Nothing was clean anymore, no one was whole, nothing was left undisturbed. I could go on and on about the children I saw orphaned, the animals limping in the street. Do you want me to paint a picture so vivid that it causes you to have flashbacks? I didn't think so, we all lived through that day, and what came after. For some reason I find this day the most difficult to detail, it is at the core of my psyche, constantly making me doubt myself and the means by which I have survived. So, excuse me for not ripping out my soul just yet, not just yet.

I was alone in Jacksonville, sticking out like a sore thumb, and asking for annihilation. But not for long. I had lived in Jacksonville as a small child before I was moved to St. Petersburg. I was in a familiar part of town and made my way over to my old house. I saw it, beautiful with its white siding, green shutters, and gabled roof. I went to the house next door and by cosmic happenstance, my old friend Becca, whom I had not spoken to or thought of in years was there with her boyfriend, Don.

This was a critical mistake, but I was scared and alone and dog-tired. It took me a few moments to realize what had become of Becca, a strung-out junkie with her dealer boyfriend held-up in her parents' old house. I still do not know what happened to her parents, but I have a suspicion that the invasion is going to hide the secret of their murder at the hands of Becca and Don.

I wanted to leave again, but it was easy to just go along with them. As a weak human, I wanted the comfort of other people, we as a species were all under attack and needed to stick together, right? And so, my following few weeks were torturous and pained.

This was why, in the back of the truck with Mitch, Barbie, and Gavin, I did not sleep. Though I was tired, and the pain in my knee had subsided enough that I could have easily slipped into a deep and restful slumber, I did not. My entire body was focused on surviving and that meant being aware of my surroundings at all times. I needed to live, though I was not happy with the options I had in my life now, my body would continue to push me to live. I also needed to cope with the massive changes happening, but I had no luxury of tears or catatonia. With all of this, I had no ability to stretch my willpower beyond surviving and fending off a psychotic episode. The amounts of mental and physical stress were more than enough to handle. Messy human problems like worrying about what happened to Becca, or getting to know the people around me were second to my most pressing needs.

I had an instinct to trust Mitch, the fact that he had preferred Denver to

Tahoe affirmed this for some nonsense reason. Colder climates tended to be less populated and may have been a smaller priority for the aliens to monitor or control. Arctic climates were nearly void of all human life, so that I assumed was my safest bet. Denver was more of a close shot to Canada from where we were than Tahoe. At least that was how I reasoned this. Although Mitch had said his initial plan was the desert, why change course now? I pushed that thought aside.

Mitch was asleep across from me. Holding his glasses in his hands and with his knees pulled in close to his chest, he slept easily it appeared. He trusted that the people in this truck would help him continue to survive. I decided that once he awoke, I would sleep. I did not know or trust Barbie, Gavin or Manuel. I barely trusted Mitch, but if he would trust me, I could at least try to trust him.

So, we rode on, further west, the sun was still high in the sky and with each passing minute and each passing mile our exposed skin began to burn, our dehydrated bodies began to cry out for water, and Barbie and Gavin continued to express their anxiety and fears by silently and ferociously chewing at their fingernails and scratching at the tips of their index fingers.

At dusk, Mitch awoke with a start. I recognized the scared look on his face. It was the same look that all of us that were still alive had, we were still adjusting, each new morning brought on the same question, "where am I?" and the same ungodly answers waited for us.

You may wonder how I can know that all remaining humans had this same experience, couldn't there be pockets of humanity that were battling and winning against the aliens? Couldn't there be communities that were persisting and comforting each other? There very well could have been. There still could be. But from what I've seen so far, I doubt it. No one has come to save-the-day; no one is leading an insurrection against our occupiers. The rest of my story will only help to confirm this.

Mitch offered me a small smile, and he quickly appraised Barbie and Gavin. He looked as though he was at a loss. He had sustained himself by providing guidance and leadership for those trapped in the hospital. Now he was a passenger, and the control he had over his own situation was with a man who insisted on taking us through Nevada, rather than Mitch's expressed plan of traveling to Denver.

Barbie jumped at the chance to question Mitch. "When we gonna eat?" she grumbled, barely looking up from her closed hand. She had the slouched speech of a lifelong loser. Likely born to an illiterate family that earned menial wages and never once encouraged her in school, she seemed to be the type of woman who had planned on getting through life on her looks and social status only to find that her looks faded as did her reputation. My evaluation may seem harsh, but it was necessary. She was scrappy, the kind of girl who didn't shy away from fights; she could easily be the next greatest threat to my survival. And she was hungry. Like a dog backed into a corner, her next move could not be anticipated.

Mitch answered without any acknowledgement of her hostility. "I'll see what Manuel can do," he tapped lightly on the glass again and had a much easier conversation with Manuel this time. A final destination may be up for debate, but hunger is universal.

Forty minutes later Manual pulled over to a small gas station. While he worked on siphoning gas from the stores beneath the cement, Gavin and Barbie hopped off the back of the truck. Gavin ran in to relieve himself in the bathroom. Why he even bothered was beyond me, the plumbing systems weren't being maintained so his shit could sit in the commode until it rotted away, but at least he went in the toilet.

I had to go as well, and even though I found it foolish for Gavin to use the no-longer-functioning facilities, I used the ladies' room myself. The human comfort of the familiar cannot be understated. Mitch helped me hobble to the side of the convenience store and kindly waited for me so that I could use him as a crutch again as we entered the store.

Barbie had already begun to scour for her favorite creature comforts. She grabbed packaged cakes and cookies and shoved them in the front pouch of her oversized sweatshirt. She looked like a scrawny pregnant kangaroo; her pouch engorged but her limbs thin as sticks.

Gavin emerged from the restroom and headed for the beer cooler. His under-aged brain was frantic with the new freedom of being able to imbibe without many consequences.

I pointed to the front corner of the store and Mitch obliged by carrying me to my desired stand. I grabbed the thin metal wires at the top of the stand and began to survey the available items.

"Hey Mitch, grab some bags from behind the register." He accepted my request and grabbed a large stack. He handed a few to Barbie and Gavin who looked somewhat ashamed to have not thought of that themselves, but accepted the offer nonetheless and continued to pile the sugary goods into their store.

Mitch returned to where I was and began to open the top bag. "Ok, so what do we need?"

I was glad to accept that I was the expert in this area. "We need to keep our bodies strong. Sugars will burn out quickly and ultimately leave us weaker." I saw Barbie mutter under her breath as though she was imitating me in an ungrateful tone. I tried to ignore her uncouth, childish manners. The people who could most benefit from strong leadership are often quick to deny it, smashing it back in the face of those who offer it.

I pointed Mitch to the cereal bars and protein bars that still filled the shelf. "We will need all of these." He set to work quickly and pulled the snack boxes into the bags. "We may want to check the back as well for more before we leave." We were lucky that this stop hadn't already been picked over. Had no humans made it along this route without being abducted before hitting this station?

Mitch began to stack up the bags while I swiveled on my right leg and turned to the refrigerated doors behind me.

Water.

Gallons upon gallons of water.

"Gavin!" I called out. He looked up, his eyes darting with guilt and after a few seconds of internal debate, decided to answer.

"Yeah?"

"You can have all the beer and cola that you want, but first, I need your help getting this water into the truck." He ambled over, one plastic bag in his left hand filled with 16oz. beer cans and energy drinks. The thin plastic looked as though it might rip at any second. He placed the bag down carefully and began to pull the water jugs out of the cooler. The bottom row had twenty-gallon sized jugs. Above that was a row of one-liter bottles, followed by two rows of twelve oz bottles.

"Why does he have to take orders from you?" Barbie asked. She was the poster child for oppositional-defiance disorder if there ever was one to be found.

"I'm not giving orders. I'm explaining options. Hydrate or die." I was firm in my resolve. I had dealt with insufferable clients, who after paying me hundreds of dollars had refused to change their eating habits and complained about their results. I knew when to break down the basics for people to understand.

"Well aren't you a little know it all," she said with her face pinched, the wrinkles forming around her mouth emphasized, making her look at least two decades older than she was.

"Hey, we all have our talents and skills Barbie. Dora made her living by helping people reach their fitness goals, which means she knows how the body reacts under stress. Right now, our goal is to survive. We should listen to her." Mitch had popped his head up from the shelves, now half empty, as he began to grab bags to haul out to the truck. I was emboldened by his recommendation.

"I'm going to start carrying this out and see if Manuel can come in and help. I don't want to stay here much longer." Mitch was nervous and he had that squirrel-like look on his face that he wore when I first saw him on the metal gurney in an alien occupied hospital. I nodded in agreement and began to fill some bags myself. Protein bars, not the best to live off of but better than sugar-loaded crap.

"Well, I'm gonna check behind the counter for some cigs," Barbie announced. "Gavin, you want any?" she called out as she carried her one bag over to the far side of the store.

"Eh, yeah, sure," he called back as he finished emptying the refrigerated case and began to push a group of gallon jugs along the floor to the entrance.

"Can you see if there are any hot dogs or pizza rolls back there, Barbie?" I could hear her sneering from behind me but I continued to gather as much as I could.

Mitch came back in with Manuel and grabbed the gallons of water that Gavin had been moving towards the door. Manuel stopped and looked at the load of water, then saw that I was still stuffing bags full of high-protein snacks.

"This is too much!" he said in a heavily affected accent which made it sound like "doo much."

"We need water in the desert Manuel," Mitch was trying to explain the need.

"It will weigh on the axel" he gestured to the truck, a midsize truck when compared to the massive store of water.

"We need it, I'll sit up front with you Manuel, to make room in the back." Mitch smiled and nodded. Manuel still looked concerned but nodded and picked up two jugs.

"I'm almost done here Mitch, when we have the water moved, let's check the back," I called out without looking up from my task.

"I'm not sure Dora, we're gonna be full up with the water." Mitch shook his head.

"It's not good to be hydrated if we starve. Besides we may not find any other food for days." I tried to implore him with my logic that had barely scratched the surface.

"We'll see what we can do, I want to get out of here ASAP!" Mitch seemed panicked, and while we were all certainly on edge, his anxiety seemed to have reached a new level. I looked over quizzically and tried to read the worry on his face. He was breathing slowly and a fresh layer of sweat was brimming on his forehead. Again, I had decided to trust Mitch, so I read this as a sign that I too should be worried. I moved my fingers quickly over the remaining boxes.

I hopped up to the pile of waters and dropped the last bags, then I bounced back and grabbed a bag full of Gatorade and for fun, a twenty oz. bottle of Diet Coke and a package of Reese's Stix. I carried this last bag as I tested my left leg with some weight. It hurt, but I moved much faster when applying weight to it, can't deny basic human biomechanics. We would be back on the road in a few moments so I endured the radiating pain knowing I would soon be stuck in a seated position for a while.

"We're almost good to go, Gavin and Barbie, be sure you have everything you need." Gavin smiled up at me and hurried back to his bag of booze. He looked back as if asking for permission to grab more. I gave a reluctant nod and he went back to get some more, I hoped he had some additional food in his bag otherwise, that kid was going to be hung-over.

Barbie emerged from behind the cash register with three full bags, one with her cakes and cookies, one full of cigarettes and another full of candy. "Did you see any hot dogs?" I asked as she walked past without looking over at me.

She didn't stop or bother to answer. I rolled my eyes and half walked/half jumped back to the counter. I saw two bags of hot dog buns and a metal shelf below the rotisserie, which had- BINGO- two packs of uncooked hot dogs. I filled another plastic bag and saw Gavin head for the door. I looked down as I tied the top of the bag shut and saw an outline in the dust of the shelf hidden beneath the register. A gun had been there and had very recently been removed.

Signs of life. That was my first thought. Whoever had been working here three weeks ago caught wind of the invasion, grabbed their piece and ran for it. But then I looked around and saw that the only disturbance had been us. Two revelations occurred to me in this instant.

The first, this place had been untouched. This meant that the nearby human population had been decimated before any looting or panic could spread. No one had the chance to run, no one was able to grab provisions. This meant that they could be close by. But there was a chance that if this was an easy conquest, that they moved on. I blinked rapidly, testing my eyes for any trace of an itch. Nothing. At least not yet. I became very aware of my hair as it lay across my shoulders, my back felt incredibly exposed, even though I was still wearing the same clothes as I had been earlier.

The second revelation, the much more pressing one, was that there was a very real possibility that the gun had still been sitting there when we arrived, and Barbie was now carrying it.

I hopped quickly out of the store, Gavin and Manuel were still loading up the back of the truck, filling in the water towards the back of the truck bed. Barbie was sitting on the wheel well, rummaging through her store of goodies. I hopped towards the truck and Mitch started toward me to relieve me of the last bag of hot dogs. I picked up two of the small water bottles. I handed one to Manual, "For you to have now," I said with a smile. He accepted it and took a long sip. After returning the cap to the bottle he walked towards the front of the truck and put it in his cup holder.

I handed the second to Barbie. "Why don't you sit up front with Manuel for this next bit?" She looked at me as though I spoke a foreign language.

"Music and AC, I figured we would all take turns sitting up front. Enjoy a nice cushioned seat for a bit." My explanation was reasonable, and she eyed me suspiciously for a moment but took the bottle of water and scooted off the truck bed on her rear-end. She hopped down and reached over the side for her three bags. She grabbed her haul and walked quickly to the passenger side and got in. I could see her settling in with her load, rearranging her goodies. She popped open a Monster Energy drink, I didn't see what she did with the water, but she was not concerned with it. Mitch looked at me like I had just slapped him in the face, "*Hello, I wanted AC and music!*" He didn't have to say it out loud, he wasn't happy that I'd taken that decision from him, but I lowered my head and my right hand slowly as if to say "*Hold on, there's a good reason for it.*"

I helped Gavin with the last of the water and Mitch headed back to the store. "One last check," he called out. He looked at the front entrance and around the corner a bit. He closed the door and headed to the far side of the building, likely to make use of the facilities. I watched Gavin climb up into the bed of the truck. We had blocked off the first two feet of the truck bed with a barricade of water and protein bars. We would still fit very tightly into the back even with only three of us. Gavin squeezed into the corner where I had sat for the last several hundred miles. He used the wheel well as an armrest and quickly began to open a package of Twizzlers.

I saw Mitch starting to make his way back towards the truck. I started toward him, not wanting Gavin to hear what I was about to say. I smiled and started with something easy, "Fuel for the truck and fuel for us, I think we're in good shape, Mitch!" He smiled as he got closer to where I stood, some 10 feet from the truck. He reached his arm under my left shoulder and took up his position as my human crutch.

"Barbie's got a gun," I whispered as his head was close to mine. I smiled as I said it so that no one would be able to suspect from my face that I had just delivered this news. Mitch looked directly at me and saw the smile on my face, I tried not to concentrate too hard on smiling because I was afraid it would look fake.

"How certain are you?" he mumbled under his breath, he looked down at our feet. Not an unnatural thing, since he had done this before when he had helped me into the building.

"Seventy-five percent. Saw an outline in the dust below the cash register." I said it quickly, as we were approaching the back of the truck. Mitch didn't respond but continued to help me across.

I used my right knee to get back into the truck bed. With Mitch handling the weight of the left side of my body, I pulled my right foot up into the tailgate and pulled the rest of my body up. I stood uneasily on the tailgate before hopping forward slightly and letting my right knee bend down to sit on the far side, diagonal from Gavin. Mitch ambled up quickly and folded his legs in across from me. He pulled up the tailgate and gave the side of the truck two loud thwacks. The sound of his open palm slapping the metal side of the truck reverberated and I could feel the impact on my own back and the metal that supported me. Manuel started the truck on Mitch's signal and we were back on the road, heading west.

We spent the next twenty minutes or so in silence. Everyone was snacking on a few goodies. Barbie was blowing smoke out of the passenger side window, her elbow resting on the window frame, her head slightly turned out, and the wind whipping her damaged and dry hair. I finished the candy bar that I had nabbed and enjoyed some of the cola as well. I offered it to Mitch, but he declined, content to snack on the beef jerky he had selected for himself. Gavin had finished his first beer and let out a loud belch, which led to a moment of laughter.

"You'll need this," I tossed him a small water bottle. "Trust me."

Gavin took it and rinsed his mouth a bit.

"Man, if you keep pounding those back, you're gonna mess your pants." Mitch looked over at Gavin with a knowing smile. "We're not gonna stop again for a while."

Gavin let out another small burp and laughed at himself. "Alright, I'll have some of these bars, but I'm gonna savor this first beer."

"That was your first ever beer?" I asked. I couldn't believe that a kid who went straight for the alcohol at his first opportunity hadn't already been testing those waters.

"Yep," Gavin nodded. I could tell there was more on his mind; he looked off at the dusty horizon after he answered. This reminded me that we all had a good reason to drown our current reality.

"Well, cheers. To Gavin!" I said as I lifted up the cola in my hand.

Mitch joined in, lifting his water in the air.

This was the first time in three weeks that I felt like Dora. I had been running on autopilot and hadn't stopped to savor any moments. I had been in a constant panic, and in that moment, I had let my guard down a little. I was just Dora, now a friend to both Mitch and Gavin, disliked by Barbie and still trying to make a good impression on Manuel. I was the young woman who tried to help others when she could, and celebrated the little moments in life. I belonged to this group now; we had bonded over manual labor and shared starvation. I belonged to them and we belonged to this vehicle.

The excessive sweetness of the cola made my mouth sticky, and I had consumed two water bottles by the time the sun began to set. The sky was orange and purple and the patches of green on the land had become less frequent. I stared out at the lines on the road that were running behind us, as though they were trying to catch up, but could never reach us.

Gavin fell asleep and had snored once or twice, fidgeting and readjusting with each noise. I noticed that Mitch was rubbing his eyes and that there was a very real potential that he might drift off to sleep soon. I looked quickly to see that the glass partition was closed and leaned over to confirm that Barbie did not have her window open.

"Mitch," I whispered.

He looked over and returned his glasses to his face. "Yes, Dora?" I could hear the exhaustion in his voice. I didn't want to bother him for much longer, but I had some things I had to ask him, and I wasn't sure when my next opportunity might be.

"Thank you, for not doing whatever it was they wanted you to do." I couldn't look at him when I said it.

"Of course." He smiled weakly, briefly.

"What-?" I began to ask as I reached into the depths of my back pocket and grabbed the small metal disc.

"Put that away!" he said quickly, in a hushed voice. It was as though I was carrying the visual representation of every human sin. Whatever it was, it was not meant to be seen. It was dangerous. I put it in my front right pocket, pushing it way down to the lowest corner.

"I'm sorry." I wanted to know, but it was clear that this was a dangerous topic.

"That should be *in* you," the emphasis he placed on that word sent a cold chill down my spine. "That's how they're tracking us." His eyes shifted, checking that no one had heard. He had leaned forward, closer to me. His voice was so low and he whispered so forcefully that each word sounded like the hiss of a serpent. "I don't know how they do it, but that is how *they* keep us all in line." He leaned back and rested against his side of the truck.

I nodded, showing my understanding. "OK," I said. I vowed to not bring this topic up with Mitch, ever again. I looked down at his hands and saw that he had his index finger pressed tightly against his thumb. This was Mitch's tell, that was where his was, embedded in the tip of his thumb. Like a poor poker player, he called attention directly to the one thing he didn't want me to notice. I had so many questions in my mind, *were they tracking us all, right now? Couldn't they find us? Could they use this to kill us all right now? What is the purpose beyond just tracking us? Does it light up? Does it spew blue light that looks to be far too advanced and high-tech for any human to ever fathom?*

I returned my focus to the lines on the road, starting to count them, and Mitch leaned his head back and closed his eyes. As the count grew to over 500 my brain shifted focus. While my eyes stayed on the road, my thoughts went to the small round piece of metal pressed tightly in my pocket, wearing an indent into the skin of my thigh.

When the sun had mostly set and the road was dark, I took a deep breath and finished my water bottle. In the past three weeks of traveling with Don and Becca, I had learned that no street lights would turn on. Nights were consumed by darkness. In the invasion, the public utilities had been cut, locally and nationally, perhaps globally.

Internet. Water. Plumbing. Lights. Electricity. All gone. The hospital from earlier in the morning had lighting, but surely, they were able to control the emergency generators for their own evil purposes. As the color in the sky morphed from light purple and turned into a deep royal color, the stars began to poke through. I expected Manuel to turn on the headlights, but he kept them off. At first, I was worried, because of the potential road safety issues. Don had at least turned on the headlights when he drove, but he did usually pull off the road not too long after dark.

From what I could see Manuel had no intention of stopping soon. I could see that Barbie was sleeping in the front; all was quiet in the back. I thought of reaching forward to tap the glass and remind Manuel to turn on the lights. But then another thought struck me, and it seemed so obvious I was surprised I hadn't realized it sooner. If all of the lights are out, except ones that the aliens are controlling, then by turning on our lights, we could give ourselves away. *Jeez, Don could have gotten us caught last week.*

I thought of the large beings, with their thick black suits, hiding on the side of the road, waiting for some stragglers to reveal themselves. *They* could be hiding nearby, protected by the shadow of night. I suddenly felt very afraid. Now I would not be able to sleep all night. That would put me at another eight hours without sleep if I was able to fall asleep at all in the morning. My exhaustion amplified at the thought. I tried not to let myself get scared, I busied myself by trying to find something to eat.

I had accepted that I would likely starve earlier that week when Don and Becca had finished our store of food (yes, they finished it without me). Today's find was a pot of gold, and the rational part of my brain knew that the food and water should be rationed, but the hungry part of me wanted to eat. I remembered the hot dogs and found a solution to the two issues that had recently crossed my mind. We would need to cook them and that would require us to stop. Honoring Mitch's position as our de facto leader, I nudged him awake.

"Mitch," I whispered as I tapped his knee. He roused slowly.

"It's dark, shouldn't we be stopping to make camp for the night?" From his response, I could tell that he hadn't considered this as an option. Then I thought back to how he had started out, and he likely didn't have any nights of camping, since he had spent most of the past few weeks in the hospital.

"Right, right." I could still see the shape of his head across from me, but I couldn't see his face very well. "Let's ask Manuel." He climbed over Gavin and the store of water to tap on the glass partition. He spoke to Manuel quickly, I could see Barbie's hair, tied up in a high bun, move. The conversation must have woken her.

I saw Manuel nod and Mitch leaned back and closed the partition. "We'll pull over soon." Mitch was quiet; he had the tone of an exhausted parent.

"OK." I was tired and somewhat ashamed that I had allowed my fear to be so transparent. I wanted to sleep, but I would know no peace in my rest. I wanted to feel safe, an emotion that eluded me since the first day of the invasion, a feeling that I have not felt for a long time now. We pulled further into the night for another mile or so and then stopped. I didn't know what arbitrary landmarks Manual used to determine when to stop; I could see no difference in the land in front of us, behind us and around us. Beyond ten feet I could see nothing, the universe had shrunk to a small circle and the enormity of the world was forgotten.

That first night was calm, although mentally tumultuous. It was nothing like the evenings I'd experienced with Becca and Don. We pulled over and made a camp quickly. Mitch, Gavin, and Manuel scoured for rocks in the dark, groping at soft sand and tufts of tumbleweeds, occasionally palming something substantial. We built a perimeter of rock around the fire, which I started while Barbie looked on. She was proving to be utterly useless, but suspecting her to be armed and unintelligent I didn't bother to remind her that everyone else was helping out. I made a silent promise that if we ran out of food, we would "Donner-party" her first. The small joke in my mind released a little tension, but then I realized that could be a real situation and chided myself for even thinking it.

Once the stone circle around the fire was complete, the men-folk set out to find larger rocks, boulders, or branches to build a circle around us. (Yes, believe it or not, the Patriarchy is alive and well and the presence of our interplanetary invaders has only exacerbated the subjugation of women on this planet, but more on that later).

We all went to work establishing our rudimentary shelter. Mitch and Manuel walked heel to toe for fifty paces and began to dig a small hole by hand, for our latrine. Then dropped pebbles on the way back, as a guide.

I set to roasting the hotdogs, and fortunately found one stick long enough, thin enough, and strong enough to roast them on, one at a time. Barbie was unhelpful, and in her eyes, I saw a learned helplessness. I couldn't be sure if it settled there before the invasion or after, but she had lost the thing inside of her, that is within all humans, to push herself forward. I was spiteful and short; my lack of energy had contributed to an aching lack of empathy. My capacity for compassion was waning as my hunger increased.

We ate the hotdogs and shared some of Gavin's beers. It was a good ole fashioned campfire. Manuel told the story of how he had evaded capture, stolen his brother's truck, and lived in the hill country of Texas for one whole week by himself. He had once had to cross that land on foot and was familiar with the terrain. At the end of the third week, he was unable to find any more game to hunt, he said that it was as though they had all vanished. He gestured with his hands as though something precious was clenched inside his fist and with a soft pop, it had evaporated. Manuel was a magnificent story-teller.

He drove and drove until he saw the large vehicles moving across the land. They were large black boxes on round wheels, oddly shaped and foreign to him, rushing across the land. He said that they were quiet, eerily quiet but he could see the sand kicking up behind them. He followed, he was afraid the whole time that they would catch him, but no one did. And then he saw them heading to the hospital and carting people off in blindfolds. When he got to this part of the story I shivered and thought back to the painful walk and the firm hand gripping my arm and that unknown, unforgettable smell that was so neutral it terrified me. Had the aliens smelled of rotting flesh or garbage or sulfur I could have accepted them. Bad smell, bad aliens – that made sense to me. But they were so sweet-scented, like *they* bathed in car fresheners, their scent so very off-putting.

I wrapped my arms around myself tightly and tried to focus on Manuel's story. He had gotten to the part where he found Mitch scrounging for food in the dumpster behind the hospital and offered to take as many people as he could far away. Mitch grabbed Gavin and Barbie, the two humans who were the most ambulatory in the hospital and told them to wait in the truck, then Mitch returned and went further into the hospital. He had intended to save someone else. Mitch didn't admit this part, but I knew it, why else did he continue further back into the halls? I took someone else's place, someone else who should be living on the land and breathing in the fresh air of night. I took their place and maybe took their life. A crime I didn't even know I was committing until that very moment.

Mitch said that was when he was called over by one of the alien guards, taking over the story for Manuel. Mitch explained that he understood the alien words well enough to know he needed to come with them. He didn't elaborate on the next part of the story, he merely glossed over the details of how I was the one who he saved, excluding any side notes about not saving another captive. The details he obscured kept my secret, secret. That he was brought into the surgical theatre, that was when he refused to torture me, and that he was knocked out cold, that he stopped the procedure and now I was untracked, untagged and untortured. I was very aware of the metal disc in my pocket.

The story ended and we sat in silence for some time. This was the origin story of our motley band. It wasn't nearly as beautiful as the Aboriginal Dreamtime, but for our pack, it would do.

In our silence, I could hear the fire crackle. I could hear the blunt sounds of Gavin's teeth wearing at his fingernails and his saliva washing the fragments back into his throat. We were all still, except for Gavin, but he seemed to be unaware of his repeated motion. The fire kept my face warm, but I could feel the cool wind at my back, and with just a t-shirt I would surely be shivering through the night.

I wanted to break the silence because I hated how silent the world had become. But it didn't make sense to tell jolly stories from our past lives. Everything that we had known and almost everyone that we had known was gone. We could eulogize them by retelling our memories, for someone else to hear how they lived. I almost started to tell my favorite story of making s'mores with my mother. Her smile as she showed me how to place the marshmallow close to the flame, but not in it. The hot wet chocolate that smeared on my face; the enticing smell swam into my memory. I could see the warm light that shone off of her kind face and amber hair. But then I realized, if I had told them all about her, these strangers, then why not talk about my father and my cousins, and my neighbors. The list of people that I had to mourn, the burden of honoring all of their lives weighed heavy upon me and sealed my lips. Like I said, this night was mentally tumultuous.

The fire began to die down and Mitch offered to stay awake for a few hours and let everyone else sleep. Reluctantly I agreed to close my eyes and rest my neck against a well-worn log. In the past few days, the only humans who I had made any contact with and been forced to continue with were dead or lost to me. I met a complete group of strangers, and against the odds, found a way to trust them enough to allow them to take me across many miles and sleep near them. I may have been teetering on the edge of a mental breakdown, but I found it easier to trust than to stand guard and make it known that no one could come near me.

I even slept with Barbie ten feet away, knowing there was a gun in her pocket and trusting, beyond all odds, that she would not wake up in the middle of the night, kill us all and make off with the food. I understood her need for protection, she was frail and tiny. I was strong and had been stronger when the attacks first happened. My body had been my shield in this world. In an orderly society, I felt safe, but I had my endurance and muscles to help me if anyone tried to get out of line with me. But that defense system proved ineffective in the chaos that was now scourging the planet.

Don's torture had limited my capacity to engage in normal human behaviors with others. I was glad that he was dead and I felt no remorse. I have struggled to be able to admit that because it sounds so callous, but I am glad that he is gone. The fears I battled, worried that he might somehow return to this world, and be reanimated on the deserted strip of highway, have since subsided. My release from his grasp with the swift thrash of an alien's arm had freed me to find another small group. Like early hominids on the open range, we had formed a small tribe. And that night I let the tribe protect me from coyotes, roaming cannibals and the ever-present fear of alien capture.

I insisted that we each sleep with a water bottle near us. I didn't have a clear idea in my head what might cause us all to separate and be without water, but it eased my anxiety to know that no matter what, we would all have something to drink in the morning.

I didn't dream, and I finally woke up with a panicked, exasperated breath, but my body did not feel any more rested. My left leg was throbbing and my muscles ached. Manuel was up, looking off towards the east, the sunrise sparkling in his eyes. He had his fingers in his mouth, biting at his nails. I felt as if I had walked in on him during a sacred morning ritual, he looked so at peace. He didn't look nervous or stressed, his face was plain and calm. I smiled at him and he waved for me to go back to sleep, but I was awake and wanted to make myself busy.

I marveled at Manuel for a moment, a man who could have continued on his own way, but he stopped and offered help. He offered to help as many people as he could. And he was taking us to Tahoe, which based on the little that Manuel had revealed about himself, was not his home. I half expected him to suggest that we cross the border into Mexico and that he would take us to where he came from. Wouldn't it make sense to yearn for a home in these terrifying times? But, then again, no one had a place to call home anymore. Nowhere was safe, nowhere was warm. Not even our global home, Earth, was a home anymore.

I slowly and carefully stood and hopped back to the bed of the truck. I downed a protein bar and a cereal bar quickly and finished a water bottle. We had already amassed a small collection of empties. We would need to find a water source soon so that we could replenish. I tried to stretch my arms above my head but the pain in my knee superseded all of these feelings. I rummaged inside the red bag I had taken from the hospital. I found some heavy dose painkillers and debated taking them, but I wanted to be alert and that meant no dope, even for the busted knee.

Mitch and Gavin started to move and had their breakfast as well. I took care to collect our litter. Not that I expected to deposit the wrappers in a trash bin with the expectation that a truck would be along shortly to pick it up. That idea would have been laughable, but still, I couldn't bring myself to not care about leaving litter behind. I am still surprised by how many habits, ingrained from childhood still remain with me in this new reality. *Aliens are trashing our planet, why shouldn't I?* But I just can't bring myself to do it.

Mitch offered to drive for the morning; I quickly jumped at the chance to sit up front with him. I needed a fatherly figure to give me safety, protection, and guidance. Had it been any other man to pull me from that surgery room, I would not have been as trusting. But surely this father of two young women wouldn't treat me in such cruel and inhumane ways as Don had. Mitch needed his daughters, or as a proxy, someone to rely on him. It was easy to fall into these roles.

We set out, headed northwest and the road lay out before us, open and quiet. I imagined that it might have looked this way when the settlers first came across the land, their ambitions and dreams packed up in their buggies. I wondered how long the aliens had been traveling to find our planet, maybe they had set out into space before those pioneers ever hitched a wagon to their horses. I found myself lost in these thoughts, much more curious and peaceful without the background noises I had been growing accustomed to, Don and Becca fighting, Becca crying, Don yelling. It was so nice to be rid of them. *Gosh, what a horrible thing to think about the dead.*

With the exception of the long narrow road, there were no structures or signs that humans had touched this place. I hoped that maybe these aliens; might leave one corner of this planet untouched and pristine. For the small amount of the planet I have seen in my life, I do know that it is beautiful. If the clear waters of Florida have been marred with blood and bones, then maybe the secluded inlands would be safe.

Mitch stayed quiet. He initially kept both hands on the steering wheel and his spine erect, but after an hour he slouched and used his left hand to support his head, leaning towards the window. The boredom and fatigue were drawn on his face. We had eaten a breakfast, but we were all hungry. We had slept but we were still exhausted. We had some protection in numbers, but we were alone and scared. I marveled at how Mitch had been so generous in saving us, in spite of his losses. Surely a lesser man would have cowered in fear and grief, but Mitch was a do-er.

I thought back to a short story that had been assigned in middle school, it talked about be-ers and do-ers. Be-ers, they just are and they let things be, but do-ers can't let things be and they have to take action to make them better. Mitch was a do-er. Barbie was a be-er. I was a do-er by habit. It had been a boring story and I didn't fully grasp the interaction between the characters, but the phrases stuck with me. How unimportant reading comprehension turned out to be; unless I would somehow be pardoned from any alien violence by explicating a poem or summarizing a book with exact grammar. Perhaps these supremely intelligent beings would grant me clemency based on my report card, perhaps not.

I hate myself for thinking it, but after three weeks of running and no sign of organized rebellion or human triumph, I was at the edge of embracing fatalism, nihilism and every black and dark thought in my body. If you asked me today, I would say that reading comprehension and the ability to share and communicate concepts that connect us across time and culture is extremely important, and it is a human trait that needs to be protected. But that day, on that road, on that long and silent drive from our first campsite to the next, I was ready to disavow my education and the human desire for self-improvement if it would buy me one moment's peace. I slid into a light sleep and pictured myself back on that patch of cool grass.

I could feel the hum of the vehicle below me; I kept my eyes closed in the vain effort of falling back asleep, but I was awake. I felt the hum of the engine and the tires flat against the road. The consistent rhythmic sound almost pushed me over the edge of sleeping when a loud sound like a thwarp, startled me and I sat upright in my seat.

Mitch was struggling with the steering wheel and we were headed over to the side of the road quickly. His face was steady and his expression strained. "We blew a tire" he muttered as the truck came to a stop.

I opened the passenger door and stepped onto the pavement as Barbie and Gavin peered over the end of the truck bed. Manuel was maneuvering his way down from the tailgate. The front passenger tire was flat and pathetic. Gavin began to ask agitated and desperate questions.

"What are we gonna do? We have to keep going, man! How are we gonna hide?!" The words blurted out so quickly, he mustn't have expected an answer. Gavin was aggressively running his hands through his hair, uncomfortable and anxious. "What are we gonna do?"

Manuel knelt down beside the tire and in his quiet enigmatic way began to tinker with it. Gavin was pacing in a small circle, nails to mouth, moaning and panicked. Gavin was the poster-child for PASD- post-alien stress disorder. And the worst was yet to come. I had seen Don and Becca freak out when the food ran low or when the roads seemed polluted with abandoned cars and eerie silence. But we had evaded capture together for weeks. This was the first time I had been among captured and now escaped humans. I hadn't expected there to be a difference, oh but there was.

As Gavin continued his hysterics Barbie found a boulder twenty feet from the side of the road and sat down in the small shade offered by it. Mitch was kneeling beside Manuel discussing the damage to the tire. I wanted to calm Gavin down because he was likely to give himself a heart attack, but I didn't know how to console him. The same fears that he was verbalizing were hammering into my mind. We were sitting ducks, and with the recent arrival of the aliens, it was open season on all living beings on the surface of the Earth.

I stared down the road where we had just driven; looking for something that might have caused the tire to burst. I left Barbie to her rock and Gavin to his circle, he was treading a well-worn path with all of his worry. I strode slowly along the shoulder, trying to keep my pace level so that my limp might not be noticeable.

I saw no debris in the road, and after about a hundred feet, I turned back towards the truck. Looking at the group from this distance I felt alone. I felt scared and outside the invisible circle of protection that the group-dynamic offered. I walked much faster to get back to the place where we had stopped. Just as I was back by the side of the truck, Gavin began to wail.

I tried not to blame him; he was still a child. But he had clearly reached his breaking point. Gavin fell to his knees and tried to pull at his own hair. Mitch pounced on top of him, trying to calm him.

"You know what will happen, Gavin. You need to calm down!" Mitch said firmly, but in a quiet tone. Mitch reached for Gavin's wrists and held them out, away from his body, pushing them to the ground. Mitch was trying to keep Gavin still. The boy was writhing beneath him, still scared and without comfort.

"Shhh," Mitch whispered. "Shhh," he offered the calm command for silence into Gavin's ear. With a nod of his head, Mitch beckoned Barbie over, she had been intently watching the whole ordeal. She scuttled over on her hands and knees, too lazy or too tired to fully stand up and walk over, and set herself down by Gavin's head. She cradled his neck on her knees and rubbed his head.

"It's okay, Gav," she croaked in her hoarse voice, the product of decades of smoking and lung damage. She ran her hands over his forehead and gently massaged his temples. I was taken aback by the whole scene unfolding before me. *Why had Gavin, who had been so silent, suddenly snapped, and what was going to happen if he didn't gain control of himself?*

I didn't know what to do, how to help or how to stay out of the way, so I did nothing. And after a few moments of Barbie's (surprisingly) soothing hands, Gavin started to take fewer large deep breaths and more paced, calm sips of air. Mitch let out a deep sigh of relief and wiped the sweat off of his brow with his forearm. Manuel observed that this crisis within a flat-tire crisis had passed and cleared his throat. With his hands on his hips, he told us the plan.

"We need to get another tire. I don't have a spare or a jack, but I did see one at the gas station."

"The one from yesterday?" Barbie sounded girlish and her tone had reached the highest pitch I had observed yet.

"Yes," Manuel offered his answer with no acknowledgement of the insurmountable problems that this plan involved.

"It's too far to walk Manuel," Mitch tried to reason with Manuel, he had sat down near the rock that Barbie had vacated.

"Then we stay here or continue to Tahoe on foot." His resolve was unflappable. I could feel the panic beginning to build up in me. If we stayed, we might survive for a few days, but when rations ran low, we would need to migrate on foot, which would cause problems of finding resources and potentially prolonging our journey when the need to find safety was immediate. If we all left on foot now, we would have to leave most of the water and might not make it out of the desert before we collapsed from thirst and became a feast for a murder of crows. Solving for the flat tire gave us all the best chance of survival, but it would still be difficult.

"Odds are, this is our best chance," I offered my opinion into the tense silence.

"But we're a seven-hour *drive* from that station; it would be more than a full day's walk there, and longer on the way back with the tire and jack," Mitch said out loud what we all knew. But the additional part that he left out was that it was likely that within two days' time we would be found and recaptured by the aliens. The ultimate trump card in the "how to not survive" game.

"Have we deviated from this highway, Manuel?" I asked, ignoring the challenge presented by Mitch.

"No, same road as yesterday." He gestured with his arm down the stretch of roadway that we had come down that morning.

"Have we passed any other gas stations?"

"No, but if we passed any in the darkness I wouldn't have seen," Manuel explained, he gestured towards the empty road with his hand. However, I had asked him to pull off the road quickly after the sunset, so the chances were small that we had missed another station.

"Most cars can't drive more than eight hours without needing to refuel. There could be another gas station closer to us that is further ahead." I pointed towards the receding horizon, which curved sharply behind a twenty-story rock formation three-hundred meters ahead.

"That's a big risk, Dora," Mitch began, as though he was about to tell me that another one of our limited options was less impossible.

"So is doing nothing," I snapped back quickly. For all the gratitude within me for the daring acts that saved my life, I was frustrated with his defeatist attitude. It was like a rotten egg passed between the five of us, each one taking our turn in wanting to give up. I saw the confidence drained from his face, the exhaustion in his weak knees. He was wearing that defeat.

"Could be a better option," Manuel scratched his head. "I could walk until noon, if I don't see anything I could double back."

"That would waste five hours, Manuel," Mitch had a reply for each option presented.

"We've already wasted thirty minutes," I muttered, not wanting to be overly defiant, and not wanting to threaten Mitch's authority past the point that his pride would allow. I needed to belong to this group; I couldn't risk a dispute that would divide the tribe. Mitch must have heard me though because he looked directly at me when he offered another solution to Manuel.

"We could wait out a day, another band of humans on the run could pass by."

I had no response; this was the same as staying and doing nothing in my mind. Barbie finally joined the conversation after staring blankly at the dirt surrounding us.

"If we wait, the next thing that comes down that road could be *them*," emphasizing the word, displaying the terror in her trembling voice. This was our impasse. Gavin was silent, scared and while he was starting to resemble a man, he was still a child that needed protection. Mitch was the de facto leader, but Manuel was the one executing the plan. Barbie was dead weight, and I was the only one with endurance, however, my injury nullified any value I could provide to the group. We would either need to compromise and come to an agreement or part ways.

"So, we vote," Mitch must have read my mind. In the most democratic fashion, much like the enlightened civilizations that we had once modeled our society upon, we silently raised our hands to indicate what we wanted for our group. Staying and waiting for another group of humans, one vote- Mitch. Walking ahead to see if there was another gas station closer but further up the road- everyone else.

With that, Manuel began to grab some provisions, a 1-liter bottle of water and a handful of Barbie's packaged cookies. She opened her mouth as if she was going to object, but stopped herself. Manuel took off quickly, within ten minutes we could barely see his silhouette disappearing, the ripples of heat rising from the asphalt blurring our last view of his sauntering journey to find our salvation.

And we waited. The sun heated the sand quickly, and I tried to guard my arms against being burned with one of the now empty plastic bags from the gas station. The slick plastic stuck to my sweaty arms and insulated me, making me hotter and hotter until I couldn't stand it any longer and got up to sit in the truck.

Barbie sat, drawing patterns in the dirt with her right index finger, twirling the hair that fell out of her bun with her left hand. Gavin rested for a while but eventually got up and sat in the bed of the truck. Mitch paced idly for several minutes but then began to wander further from the side of the road.

"I'm going to try to find some wood, just in case we need to make camp tonight." We all heard him but were all too distracted in our boredom to comment. Mitch wiped the dust from his pants and clapped his hands firmly.

"Gavin, come with me, it will be good for you to get up and moving." Gavin looked at Barbie and then to me. I had no objection to him going or staying, Gavin must have realized that there was no value in his inaction and moved off the truck to travel with Mitch.

As they started out, Barbie turned violently. "You're just going to leave us here without any protection?" She gestured to me. I was dumbfounded by her comment until I realized what she meant. We would be two women alone, stranded on the side of the road, in a potentially vulnerable situation should some lascivious men come upon us and try to steal our honor. Again, the Patriarchy prevails.

"Dora will protect you," Mitch said plainly. I smiled at his confidence in my abilities. For all of the strides that feminism had made, in that moment I saw the possibility of true gender equality among the people of our society. But I also saw the ignorance of our current situation. Don had traded me and Becca like currency and in return, we had survived the first three weeks of the invasion. Judging by the look on Barbie's face, she had seen some form of this same evil. So, when society was calm and life was easy, the differences between women and men were being washed away. But when all rules were eliminated in the violent marching of our invaders, we reverted back to the deeply-rooted habits of our genetic ancestors. Barbie was right, we were two women on a planet with no government, no laws, and a dwindling sense of human responsibility. I could try to protect us, but Barbie was right. For once in her life, she was right.

Mitch and Gavin continued on their way without another word. I opened the passenger door to the truck and slid over into the driver's seat, inviting Barbie to join me. The waiting continued. Stretching into infinite seconds where we prayed for some motion on the horizon to signal our ability to move, to leave, to run, while simultaneously on edge, because any movement detected aside from the men in our tribe, Manuel, Mitch, and Gavin, would surely be a sign of something bad to come.

My eyes longed for sleep, as they often do when unchallenged and unstimulated for extended periods of time. I found myself wishing I had a book, something to distract and entertain myself with. I could have struck up a conversation with Barbie, but I didn't care to, and I was hoping that she would soon fall asleep so I would be spared the inconvenience of idle small talk. Social niceties could be ignored now that society ceased to exist. If I had known that these would be the last few quiet and calm minutes for months on end, I might have savored them and appreciated their tender delicacy more. In this moment, if given the option I would gladly return to that abandoned stretch of highway in an immobilized truck with a vapid co-survivor if it meant I could erase the past months from my memory. I doubt anyone would make me that offer, switching one oblivion for another. But still, it can be my wish.

I tried to play some mental games. Naming the presidents in reverse chronological order (again), listing prime numbers, and working through the few words of the alien language that I had been able to discern. Each had their own limitations. Prime numbers became frustrating past one hundred. The language of the aliens that I had heard was rushed, only a few of the words had been slow and enunciated. I would need to hear more to better understand it, and I certainly did not want to be near those *things* ever again, so I convinced myself that it would be a fruitless effort. Thinking about the presidents that had once ruled over this land, I wondered at how insignificant, how thin their power had been. I had heard no news of our current President; however, I could only guess that he and most other world leaders were deceased. Most people were, deceased, that is.

After some time, I noticed movement in my peripheral vision. Mitch and Gavin were walking back with a large load of sticks and branches. I slid out of the truck and worked my way over to help them. My left knee was stiff and sore, but it had been starting to feel better. After walking several yards out and back, the pain returned.

Barbie remained in the truck as we began to make piles of the wood. Mitch was eager to get a fire started, but I pointed out that it wasn't even noon yet, so we would have time to set one up before nightfall without worry. "Besides we don't want a large smoke signal broadcasting our location, do we?" Mitch nodded in agreement and continued with his pile of wood.

We each had a quick lunch of processed and refined sugars, washed down with noisy gulches of water. Once we had settled back into our isolated silence, Gavin and Barbie picking at their fingernails, and me staring off at the horizon where Manuel had disappeared, Mitch began to speak.

"I think we should all rest now, during the day. That way we can all stay up tonight with no problem and stand guard." Mitch was directing his comments towards me, although he left it open-ended enough that Gavin and Barbie could have felt included.

"Okay," I agreed, not seeing any reason to refuse. "If we are going to take turns sleeping, I think we should use the truck since it's cooler." Mitch nodded in agreement. "And I'm going to take something for my knee."

I gave Mitch a look, hoping he would understand the strength of the pills I was referring to without tipping off Barbie. I had no evidence to suggest that she shouldn't be trusted, but I had a weighted feeling that she should not be. She likely had a weapon and I wasn't about to reveal the heavy dose of painkillers in my bag. That would have been a mistake. Mitch gave a silent nod and I moved over to the truck, I walked around to the far side, standing on the road as I reached over and grabbed the pills from the red plastic bag. I popped open the cap and took out one oblong white chalky pill. For a moment I debated whether I should take it or not, if we were ambushed in the next three to four hours, I would be useless. But if I didn't take the pill, I would be in pain and unable to rest, leaving me useless for the rest of the day. I bit into the pill as close to the halfway mark as possible and swallowed the half that was in my mouth. I put the other half back in the bottle. A half dose was a compromise I was willing to make. It was also the last time I used reason and logic as it related to substances that altered my perception of reality, but I was on the light end of a mental fulcrum that was about to swing down, down, down.

I kept the red bag with me as I crawled into the front seat of the truck and folded my body up, lying on my right side. And for the first time in three weeks, I slept. I was completely unconscious and unaware for three and a half wonderful hours. My body was greedy for sleep and it accepted the darkness of my closed eyelids.

I woke up just as the painkiller was wearing off, the left knee somewhat numb but also creating a pressure beneath my dirty and worn pants. I had rolled onto my back at some point during my nap and remained there, with my eyes closed, letting the world filter back into my mind. It took twenty seconds. I recognized the warm air around me and smiled at the pleasant ambient temperature. I noted that my neck was stiff, likely from sleeping without a pillow. And then it all came crashing back into my mind. The worst side-effect of sleep was waking up in the same reality.

I sat up in an odd jerky motion; I saw Mitch, Gavin, and Barbie, all sitting around a small pile of rocks, each methodically tending to their digits. I looked out the windshield, searching for some sign of Manuel. The road was clear and the day was silent. I slid out of the truck on the passenger side and heaved the red plastic bag back into the truck bed. Mitch acknowledged that I was now awake and made a quick gesture to Barbie. She jumped up, hurried over and slammed the door to the truck, eagerly taking her turn to sleep.

The loud sound of the slamming door jolted me, but I was still feeling the effects of the painkiller, my response was dulled. I raised both of my hands in the air and stretched. The familiar feeling was so comfortable I began to fall into my usual morning routine, a fifteen-minute series of calisthenics that had been ingrained into my mind. I didn't even realize I was moving, until I started my ground exercises, and strained my left knee. I pushed through and even though it hurt, the comfort of moving my body again felt glorious.

Mitch and Gavin were ignoring me, which was nice since I didn't want to have to explain myself. When I finished the stretches, the series of movements that my muscles had memorized, I felt the urge to run, to jump, to work my long-developed and deteriorating muscles. Since my knee would whimper under the strain of a walk, let alone a jog, I settled for some push-ups.

I had hit twenty and was moving at a fair speed when Mitch called out. "Hey, cut that out," he had briefly looked up from the pile of rocks that had been fascinating him.

"Sorry?" I offered as my only response and began to work my way back to my feet. I joined Mitch and Gavin in the circle that identified our campsite. "I know it must seem callous to make time to work out in this situation, but it relaxes me."

"It's not that. Your trigger, if you elevate your endorphins, you could set off a reaction." Mitch explained, as though I should already know this.

"Oh," I responded. Gavin was staring at me. I was starting to understand that the episode that had happened earlier was somehow related to my basic push-ups. "Right, of course," I added, trying to sound as though I had somehow simply forgotten this very important fact.

"Effective, huh" Gavin muttered and placed his right thumb in his mouth, biting at the last phalanges. I was disturbed by the devotion of his teeth, the white blanching of his thumb and the red and irritated skin on his hand. I looked over at Mitch, I wanted an explanation. I was without information, and while it seemed fortunate that I was not marred and marked by the aliens, I knew that not having this common language with the rest of the group could quickly label me as an outsider and thereby leave my motives in question.

"It's disgusting, Gavin." Mitch retorted, his hatred for the aliens evident in his words. "And take your fingers out of your mouth. You haven't been able to wash them in clean water for weeks." Gavin quickly folded his hands in his lap, I could see through the small motions in his forearm that he was still kneading at his thumb. I had so many questions that I wanted to ask, but I didn't dare expose myself. I was not like them, my metal disk was still in my pocket, not implanted in my fingers.

"Maybe that's what they want, they want us to get infected." I offered as an explanation.

"I think that would just be a happy side effect for them. But if they had wanted any of us to die, they would have done so, instead of spending time and energy forcing us to be tracked." Mitch explained without directly addressing either of us. "From what I've observed so far they want us to stay calm, and if we panic," he nodded at Gavin, "or get agitated or get brave, they can simply knock us out."

"That's so sophisticated," I wondered at the many years of testing that would have gone into such a solution. A docile and enslaved population, unable to keep themselves strong or solid. What a devious little plan.

"The metal secretes some kind of toxin, I don't understand the science, but I know it works." I could see the memories of his weeks at the hospital playing before his eyes. How many people had he seen writhe in pain, or pass out mid-sentence? I could only guess what a gruesome scene it might have been if Gavin had somehow reached the point where his 'trigger' as Mitch had called it, had been set off.

"Will it kill us?" I looked down at my hand, to insinuate that I was afraid of the impact it might have on me. Implying with my pantomime that this metal disc was inside of me. I could get away with being a new initiate to the captured and tagged club.

"I don't know. Maybe? I would think they would be able to. I think they can track us with it as well."

"That's why I had to keep my cool," Gavin added, the shame and guilt on his face were easy to read. Mitch nodded and reached his right hand over, patting Gavin on the shoulder. It was a father-son moment, regardless of their lack of blood relation.

I looked down at my hand. I had to convince myself that I too had this piece of metal inserted inside my skin. I had to believe it so well that I could feel the edges when I pressed into my skin, that when I used my hands to grip something I might strain under the added pressure. The metal in my pocket felt hot and called my attention, I wondered if the toxin would secrete even if it wasn't implanted. Would it be just as impactful if it made contact with the top layer of my skin, instead of being implanted between layers of the fascia?

I didn't ask any more questions. There was so much more that I wanted to know, but I had learned that not all questions would be answered. My first questions had been why and how. When I sat on the crowded, hot bus headed north on I-75 I had so many questions running through my mind. I listened in on the conversations around me. Some people thought it was a military take-over. Maybe the Russians or North Koreans. Maybe our own government turned against the people. But then someone said they had seen what was marching, and it wasn't of Earth. That helped with the why. It must be to harvest our resources, why else would another life-form come to our planet and forcibly take control of the population? The rhetorical question was easily answered based on the science fiction that our population has been exposed to for decades.

The how was still troubling. So maybe they were a highly militarized alien species, but how could they have so many of them invading so quickly? I reasoned that they had to be everywhere, a synchronous attack. If they had just attacked one city then the National Guard could have been called in to stop the attacks. If they had only chosen to attack our country or continent, surely aid from our allies would have been evident by now. That only left the possibility of a global effort.

How many of them did it take to gain control of each massive population center? How many people died? How many escaped and were on the run like us? How many of us would be allowed to survive? What would happen next? I had mulled over these questions in every brief silence and every loud and panicked turn of events. And now, knowing that they had captured humans and outfitted them with a tracking device, it seemed that a catch and release program was in play. Similar to how sharks are tracked and monitored off the Atlantic and Gulf coasts of Florida. Their movements are monitored and studied using tracking devices implanted just beneath the skin. However, those devices don't have the ability to secrete any mysterious fluids, at least none that I was aware of. *So, they expected to eventually release Mitch and Gavin and Barbie, why else would they have taken the time to implant a trigger?* My memory immediately flashed back to the gruesome suburban home, the entrails, and organs piled up. *Maybe they had been experimenting and perfecting their techniques. Or maybe some of them were more savage than others.*

I paused and listened to the distant wind, battering the high cliffs that were far off in the distance. I looked at the incomprehensible patterns that our footprints had left in the red-orange dirt. I tried to focus on the land and the miracle that had pushed this patch of ground up from the depths of the ocean after Pangaea had started to drift apart. How many thousands of years had this spot been at the bottom of a forceful river, carving beautiful designs into the rock and leaving the now endangered humans a wonder to marvel at? I let my thoughts drift to the magnificence of nature and time and wondered how quickly our species would be forgotten. Just a several thousand-year blip on the geological scale.

Barbie fussed in the truck and tossed herself over with a whining grunt. Mitch was drawing a figure in the dirt with the end of a stick, planning for something no doubt. I listened and tried to set my mind at peace. And Gavin, he picked and gnashed at his fingernails, until they started to bleed. The blood from his cuticles was sliding across his teeth, the plaque and saliva mixing with the red liquid, and a single thin line of blood sliding down his chin.

After her turn sleeping, Barbie emerged from the truck and sauntered off without a word to the defined latrine area. There was no darkness to hide her, so we instinctively kept our eyes focused in the opposite direction. I could hear the force of her streaming urine, no doubt eroding the ground and hoped that it would quickly evaporate before it had the chance to slide its way toward camp.

Gavin was next. He walked like a lost teenager, like the kid in high school whose locker was stuffed with trash one too many times, like the kid who was equally likely to lash out or cry at the earliest provocation. He took off the dark sweatshirt, that was no doubt unbearably hot, but a necessary precaution against sun poisoning and rolled it into a ball. His lanky arms were thin and lean, and his loose gray t-shirt revealed his hip bones. He looked as though he was in the early stages of starvation, but I reminded myself that many of the boys in high school looked this way, their bodies burning more calories than they could ever consume and their figures becoming leaner and leaner by the day. He took his balled-up sweater, no doubt his make-shift pillow, and silently took his turn to nap.

Barbie walked about for a bit, never far enough that we couldn't see her, but sometimes she would wander to the point where I couldn't hear her lazy soles shuffling against the ground.

It was easily three in the afternoon and the sun was unforgiving. I attempted to cover myself with the plastic bags again, but lasted no more than a few minutes before it was unbearable. The bored silence was almost too much to handle. I thought I might start to hallucinate and see a mirage on the horizon, that I might go a little crazy with heat stroke just for some form of entertainment. But the more time that we had for silence, meant that there was no threat on our heels in the moment. It also meant that Manuel had been gone longer and longer.

After Barbie made her way into the circle and dumped her heavy bones down, Mitch began to tend to the pile of wood for the fire.

"It's still too soon," Barbie snapped.

"I know, I'm just trying to make it easier for later," Mitch explained with a smile on his face. I was surprised how anyone could be patient in this heat.

"Well don't. It'll just make me anxious." Barbie was sullen and clearly the rotten, sour mandarin of our group. Every gathering of people had one, the negative Nancy, the problem finder, the gossiper, the unhelpful. Barbie was ours.

"I'm sorry, I don't mean to make you anxious. Just need to do something with my hands to pass the time." Mitch placated her and sat down with his hands folded. Silence.

"Well, then go and hunt for a real supper then," Barbie's retort was a minute too late to sound clever. Mitch had no weapons, and there had been no signs of game, no lost animals on the horizon. Manuel was the most likely of us to have wilderness experience; he had told us that he had survived for a while in some abandoned caves, and his hands looked rough. A man's hands can say a lot about him. Mitch's were smooth, soapy, and clearly suffering under the strain of this new existence.

"What will we hunt for you? Iguana?" I asked, too sardonic to be able to pretend that I was just trying to be funny. I was biting back at her verbal attacks. But I knew she would balk at the idea of a lizard dinner and realize how silly her suggestion was. Barbie's face pinched and mustered a "well, whatever," before falling back into silence. I shook my head wondering how a woman who was so clearly bent on doing nothing to save herself or anyone else had survived for three weeks.

The sun began to dive towards the ridge that was still ahead of us, the same ridge that Manuel had run off towards. The bright colors in the sky were like a watercolor, too beautiful to be happening in the same time and place where aliens were hunting down and killing humans en masse. The sunset was miraculous. When Mitch wasn't fiddling with the fire and Barbie wasn't complaining that there was a limited variety of granola bars left, I could focus on the maroon and blood red sky that faded into orange and then gold, it was breathtaking. The horizon stretched so far and blended so perfectly with the firmament that I almost forgot that the sky I was staring into had betrayed us all. The beauty of the sun and the mysteries of the stars had captivated us as a species for the entirety of our written history and unfortunately, had cloaked the beings now seeking to capture or kill us.

I considered offering my help to Mitch, but he seemed happy to make himself busy. For the first time in days, my mind found itself absolutely unoccupied. My attempts to keep myself thinking of anything else had worked, but my well of errant thoughts was running dry. And now the memories of darkness and the fear caught up with me, as though they had been trailing behind me on an invisible line of wire. As I heard Mitch scratch at the flint he had piled together, I was overly aware of the thin layer of safety that had helped to calm and protect me for the past twenty-eight hours. A paper-thin layer, but a feeling of safety and belonging nonetheless.

Before I had been rescued by Mitch and my swollen knee drained, before the blaring sound of the alarm, the fumble and lost trigger in the surgical room, before I was hauled to the hospital that was being used as a torture chamber, before I was thrown from the vehicle, I had been slowly sinking into the grimy darkness that very few humans have ever ventured down. And what disturbs me most is that I almost let it swallow me whole, I almost allowed that scary and bottomless pit of existence to cloud out the hope and potential in my soul. Now I can see that what I once thought was the worst fortnight of my existence was just the beginning.

Before, when I had found Don and Becca, I noted their anxious twitching, I saw the gun in Don's hand and noticed Becca's eyes ominously floating, fixated on the ceiling or perhaps whatever was on the second floor of her parent's house. Becca, was short, as though she hadn't grown more than two feet since I had left Jacksonville as a child, but her hair was much longer and her face thinner. Her pale skin was dewy with a cold sweat and her mousy brown hair was frizzed and unkempt. Don was tall and moderately thin, although he had an oddly round gut that was visible through his t-shirt like he was five months pregnant with a small bowling ball or a developing beer gut. He told me that the blood on his shirt was from his sister, that the attack in Jacksonville had started before dawn and that he had started out trying to save his family, but continued to run until he made it to Becca's house. Don continued to tell the story as Becca stood by quietly. He said that she was alone when he found her and that her parents had abandoned her. She nodded along as though she was being told the truth, not hearing the truth being repeated back to her. My suspicions were heightened, but then again, we were mid-invasion, perhaps my sense of intuition was thrown off by that event. (No, I should have listened to my instincts, oh well. Hindsight is twenty-twenty).

Don welcomed me easily and Becca, who was in a state of shock, gave me a silent and weak hug. I had taken their unusual behavior as a reaction to the ongoing invasion. However, I remember now that when Don handed Becca the gun, she pulled back her hand, the heat from the barrel causing her skin to blanch. If I had been more aware, I would have realized that a hot gun meant that it had been used very recently. But I didn't make that connection at the moment, I was happy to find people that I knew, or used to know, and tried to convince myself that the gun would be useful for our safety.

Becca and Don were eager to leave and head north, towards his relatives in the mountains of Tennessee. I was happy that they invited me along and even happier to leave sprawling and wide-set Jacksonville behind. If the invasion of Tampa was any indicator, there would be a significant loss of life in Jacksonville as well, if there hadn't been already. We piled into the car, I sat in the back, my hastily packed duffel bag at my side. Becca was directed by Don to load some items into the trunk. She slammed the heavy objects into the compartment directly behind me. The two were moving quickly, frantically. I suppose I looked frantic when I arrived at the front door, but to a harried person, they looked even more out of sorts.

Don took "the back roads" out of town and avoided the major highways. Becca agreed that they would be busy and crowded, but as we passed under several overpasses, I could see no cars utilizing the interstates. I didn't want to interrupt the plan, so I stayed silent and potentially cost us another thirty minutes of road-time. The streets were partially empty; there were people, lost and staggering in the streets. Some men were in front of their houses, nailing plywood to their windows as if a hurricane was preparing to make-land. I stared out and observed the pandemonium, it was slightly comforting to see other people in a panic. It allowed me to keep my fear inside and calmed my growing need to scream.

The beat-up car that Don was driving was, in fact, his own, which is a surprising fact to think on now, given his penchant for taking things that weren't his. We crossed into Georgia at Valdosta and continued heading northwest, up through the Peach State and into Tennessee. As we left Florida the land became more varied, the tread more graduated and finally we saw a series of rolling hills.

The many fields and farms that we passed looked calm, they looked as they always had when passing them on the highway. Lush and green, vibrant in the fruitful bounty that was scheduled to be harvested in a few months' time. But there would be no harvest of food, not for a long time. There were a few other cars on the road at first, but then, after an hour or so of driving there weren't any other vehicles. No one in front of us, and no one behind us. Don had scanned the radio for noise and found three options. The first was a bluegrass band, the song sounded old like it was a recording from the early 1900s. The song played over and over like the DJ had left the record on and had fled the station before thinking to change it. The second option was the harsh honking of the emergency communication system that continually announced that the system had been activated, but offered no news about where to go and what to do. The third option, which was the most ominous, was silence.

I pulled my cell phone out from my back pocket. It was thin and rounded at the edges, and had been the greatest of creature comforts. I saw that the time on the screen was stuck at 9:23am, but it was well past 1:00 pm. I tried to pull up CNN or NBC or FOX or any one of the many networks in the alphabet soup of news for information on what was happening. No new pages would load on my browser. I thumbed through my Facebook app, but nothing had updated past midnight the previous night. I could still see information that was on my NewsFeed then, but there was nothing new.

Becca started to cry and at first, we all said nothing, I reached my hand forward from the backseat and set it on her shoulder. Don kept his jaw tight and stared ahead at the road. I positioned myself in the middle seat so that I could see the windshield clearly. I wanted to ask Don and Becca what they knew, and what the plan was, and what to do next, but there was a silent tension building in that small cramped car. The pressure from all that tension would cause each of us to snap. Becca continued to cry, she would wane and wax between heavy choking sobs and quiet soft sniffles. Don kept his eyes on the road, the mechanics within his mind working on his next plan. I sat and observed and tried to process each piece of information I could absorb from my surroundings.

Within another hour, I gave up on my futile attempts to find information on my smartphone and put it away. I stared up at the bright blue sky, a perfectly cloudless day. It was eerily deceiving. And then, out of the silence that had enveloped us, breaking the pattern of the tires thumping against the road and the wind whipping past the windows, a pop punctured the air. It sounded as though it came from behind us. Becca turned quickly to see it, I looked through the window and saw nothing at first. I turned completely and gazed out the rear window and saw a white smudge in the sky. That faint pop was now a growing subtle rush of sound. The white speck in the sky was growing, and quickly. I hoped for a moment that it was our military, sending fighter jets to do what they needed to in order to gain control. As the speck grew to a dot and then expanded into a stream across the sky it changed from pure white to a smoking gun metal object, speeding through the atmosphere, trailing fire and smoke along the way. As it grew closer, the sound intensified until finally, it passed overhead.

The clear sight of a metal cylinder with glass wings on fire, crashing to the ground at a speed that didn't match the size and mass was truly awesome. I held my mouth agape, unable to find the words to explain the wonder and horror of the flaming satellite hurdling past. The sound finally caught up with the object a few seconds later, the impact of the energy and the boom both jolted the car and distracted us all for a moment. Don lost control of the steering wheel and we spun for several seconds until we stopped in the middle of the road.

"Everyone's alright," Don announced. He didn't ask, he didn't state it in a manner that displayed his concern and worry; he demanded it with this statement, regardless of any physical or emotional whiplash. I tried to hold my breath, I didn't want to give the impression that I wasn't alright, although my shoulders were sore and my mind was reeling. I spent a significant amount of effort trying to convince myself that everything was a dream, but I could feel the faux suede of the seats on my hands, I felt the sharp tug of the seatbelt across my chest, and I could smell the harsh and pungent burned tires from our spin-out. This was real.

Becca was still trembling, her mind crumbling under the pressure. "Wh-wh-wh-what was that?" Her voice was shivering, starved of the familiar warmth and familiarity of routine, it trembled as though she was in an ice box.

"You saw them, Becca," Don hissed at her. "It's aliens!" Don enumerated the word slowly. This was the first time I heard the word out loud. Yes, there was speculation on that hot bus ride, but no one said the word out loud. For all the times that I had heard of people who had conspiracy theories or supposed evidence of extraterrestrial life, this was the moment when reality set in. The materials falling from the sky, on fire and evidence of violence at a larger scale, were all the proof I needed. *They* were here, we were on the run, and this was the new way of things.

Becca continued to shake and let out her whimpers of worry, I couldn't decipher any clear words. Don leaned over and tried to comfort her for a moment before announcing, "We'll keep going, we can't just sit here. They could be coming after that thing." It was apparent to me that Don was unable to identify it as a satellite. They were taking out our means of communication, without satellites there could be no wireless phone calls, no internet connection, and no way to coordinate a resistance. These were very smart aliens. I confirmed this on my phone, still reading the same time as it had several minutes earlier, and a blinking "No Signal" message in the top right corner where I would usually see bars of service.

As we continued, slow at first, then finally reaching road-speed we saw large chunks of scrap metal, burning in the fields where they landed. Pastures with cattle and horses fleeing from the fire and rows upon rows of magnificent crops marred by hot metal alloys were our view now. At first, it was only every few fields, but soon we cleared another hill and saw laid out before us, that every farm in sight was ablaze. Some of the metal landed on the road and Don had to swerve to get out of the way. One piece of metal set a silo ablaze, and the smell of burning grain filled my lungs with a hunger and with an unsettling fear.

The severity of the situation was starting to sink into the air pockets in the spongy bones that made up my arms and spine and legs. I could feel a new level of adrenaline begin to spill into my nervous system. And I had been running off that high level of stress ever since.

I sat in the dark, my eyes focusing on a horizon that was no longer visible. I had been shaking, shivering in the cold desert evening, and hadn't noticed. The chattering of my teeth must have given it away to Mitch, who had found the sterile paper blankets that I had pilfered from the hospital. He passed one to me, Gavin and Barbie. I was hoping to save these items for potential medical uses, knowing that the state of our society had degraded beyond the point of prompt medical care. But I accepted the offer and without thinking wrapped it around my partially clothed arms. The action brought me out of the fog of memory and into the reality of the moment.

Each moment felt so intense and severe, but that night was particularly raw. Manuel had left, and if there had been a service station around the bend, he likely would have been back by now. So, he either continued much further down the road or he met some danger that we would never know. And with the black of night covering the sky and the land, sweeping around us, we would never see that danger coming. We might have all been thinking this, but no one was saying it.

Mitch had created a roaring fire, providing warmth, but also a signal that could have been seen for miles. Perhaps he thought other disparate humans, struggling to survive, would crawl out from behind the brush-weed and desert rock formations, and that we could help them. I worried about what else might slither across the barren land toward us that evening. Gavin helped Mitch distribute new bottles of water and protein bars to Barbie and me. Barbie demanded additional snacks for her meal, I could hear the frustration in Mitch's voice as he tried, again, to explain the concept of conserving resources, but he relented quickly and provided additional bags of chips to each of us.

"Stop biting your nails, Gavin," I heard Mitch utter in the darkness.

"Sorry," the teenager mumbled, but I was already lost. Lost in the echoes of my mind. *Stop biting your nails, Pandora.* This raw exposure to the elements, excessive heat and near-constant fear of death was messing with my head.

We sat quietly, the long day having spent any potential conversation between us, and ate, facing the fire. Our circle was small, and no one said what was surely on everyone's mind. We were stranded, and if Manuel would never return, then we would either die in this desert from starvation, dehydration or, the newest threat to human life, by alien capture.

I ate what was handed to me in small bites, nibbling and trying to convince my stomach that it was full. I was not nourished, I was not satisfied, but the food that was given without anticipation of a physical payment was enough to allow me to relax, if ever so slightly.

After we ate, Mitch spoke, "Manuel could return tonight, although I would expect that he's already made camp somewhere. We each need to watch out for one another. We each have to protect our side of the camp." I could see Gavin nod ever so slightly as he stared directly into the fire. Barbie smirked, shrugged and lit another cigarette. And that is how we stood guard that night, we each turned away from the fire, our backs overly warm and our face squinting into the night. We were like Aesop's Oxen, standing guard to protect each other, but just as in the Fable, the protection was only as good as the trust between us.

Now, this is the part where I will recount the most significant of the endless errors made by me that have yielded my current circumstances. One of them was assuming that if Barbie had a gun, it was a bad thing. Because of this concern, I had told Mitch, and this is something that he had somehow relayed to Manuel. Another mistake was that I saw Manuel as a calm and quiet man, nibbling at his well-worn and harden fingers, and did not see this action for what it really was. I had again, assumed, that this was his bad habit, his morning smoke or weekend gamble. I failed to recognize this as the now ubiquitous sign of a captured and tracked human; he was biting at the constant irritation caused by the trigger that had been implanted in his thumb. This made the story that he had shared on the first night that we were all together a fabrication. He had told us that he been hiding in the caves and had yet to be captured, this story was no longer culpable. He had been captured. And he was somehow convinced to run captured humans from Texas to California, but the flat tire had created a snag in the plan. I had also let Mitch know that I had maximum strength painkillers in my possession.

The full consequences of my errors would come to bear in short order.

I'm not sure how many hours it took, the sun had set, we ate, and then I stared into the void, keeping watch of my part of that which could not be seen. I could feel my eyes starting to grow dry and heavy. There was a bright yellow dot that was on the furthest edge of my peripheral vision for a while before I really noticed it; before I consciously saw it. It was static and, then it seemed that once I turned my head to face it, that it began to accelerate, moving toward us.

I scrambled up to my feet, the thin paper cloth falling to the ground. Barbie would have been directly facing this spec, this bright yellow unknown, when I turned to see her, she was slumped over, her head resting on her knees, fully asleep.

"Mitch!" I tried to yell, but instead, it was a hoarse whisper. The terror that was trapped in my throat constrained by vocal cords, only allowing so much air to pass, and thus impacting my intended volume. I could hear him stir almost immediately, he was on and active and ready for my call. Gavin shuffled to his feet as well. I could make out their feet most clearly, their torsos were shadowed and partially visible in the firelight and their faces were barely lit by the fire, a deep red hue covering the lower half of their faces, their eyes and hairlines were shrouded in darkness. Mitch's glasses were bright yellow and orange, the only part of his face that I could see, his eyes mimicking the doorway to hell. I should have known. The fire had provided the comfort of vision, but the ominous shading on the faces looking at me was spooky and unnerving. I couldn't see if they were scared, or shocked or perhaps offering a more sinister glance my way.

"There's something coming," I pointed emphatically toward the bright yellow spot moving toward us. I realized that they might not be able to see my gesture if the same firelight only partially revealed the top half of my body, but they saw and they understood. Gavin moved quickly towards the truck, and in the blackness that hid almost everything from sight, I heard him stub his foot and gasp in pain. Mitch threw the remaining water in his bottle over the fire, trying to dowse it.

"If the fire is out, then they can't see us," Mitch explained. All I could think was that the fire had already called whatever it was towards us, the advantage of a few dark moments wouldn't save us from what was coming. I also began to wonder if we would also put ourselves at a disadvantage without any light to be able to see what each other was doing. This was Mitch's actual plan; I am sure of it now. I am certain.

At this point, I could see some vague shadows in the minimal light provided by the distant stars in the sky. I saw what I assumed was Mitch head over to Barbie and try to rouse her, she had somehow managed to sleep through all of this. Gavin had returned from the truck with four additional water bottles, he put one in my hand and passed the rest to Mitch and Barbie.

"This is where we run," Mitch whispered and I began to realize that our only option to survive would be to spread out and thereby confuse and force our soon-to-be attackers apart. There was no discussion that what was coming might be friendly. There was no hesitation. We took off, I decided that my best bet would be to cross the road and head off in the direction that I had been staring all day.

"What? That's all you've got Mitch. We just run away. They'll catch us in no time," Barbie pleaded. "D'you know what will happen to me if I am alone out here?"

"Gavin, you're coming with me, alright," Mitch didn't bother to answer Barbie's complaints.

"Wait, you'll protect the kid, but you'll leave me an' Dory to the wolves?" I wanted to defend myself, I couldn't stand that she was implying that we would have anything in common. I also didn't like her trashy slurred speech and calling me 'Dory' instead of 'Dora,' but that is neither here nor there.

"Barbie, this is what we all need to do to improve everyone's chances of survival." Mitch snapped at her.

"Never mind that the females are most likely to be slow and starve," Barbie shouted back. I couldn't stand it another minute.

"Speak for yourself, Barbie, but every second we stand here that thing gets closer and closer to us. And if you hadn't fallen asleep while the rest of us were staying awake trying to protect you, we could all have another ten-minute head start." I didn't need to see her face to know that she likely gave me a glare that could kill.

I picked up the cloth that had fallen from the shoulders and hastily folded it and tucked it under my shirt. I started towards the truck and grabbed three bars, I couldn't read if they were protein bars or granola bars and shoved them in my back pockets. Then, without another word, I took off. I crossed the hard asphalt and once I felt the loose sifting dirt beneath my feet again, I began my uneven hobble-run that would not get me very far very fast. I could hear Barbie and Gavin snapping at each other and tried to focus on making the voices grow silent by putting more distance between us. Again, one of the countless errors made by my limited human brain.

I had made it maybe twenty yards when the yellow dot had reached the truck. It was the bright singular headlight on a clunky and oddly shaped vehicle. It looked just like the alien vehicle that Manuel had described in his campfire story. It was *them.*

I longed to hide behind something, anything before any lights could be waved in my direction. And then I realized *they* would be looking for humans, standing tall, erect, perhaps on the run. That's exactly what I was, standing, limping, galumphing along trying to hold my pained gasps inside my mouth, my left knee trying and failing with each foot that I crossed. I stopped and very slowly, and while trying to not whimper, bent my knees and crouched on the ground. If I was still and small and low to the ground, maybe they would only look on the other side of the road. And while being alone in this desert was a death sentence, at least it would be a death on my own terms, at least I would live a bit longer and figure out how to survive after this crisis passed. I swallowed that feeling that was creeping up into my throat that I was a bad person for hoping that the others would be caught, that anyone would be taken, so long as it wasn't me. My Catholic guilt chided my actions inside my head, a one-way conversation about all the ways I wasn't a good person. It occupied my mind and kept my hands still. I pulled my knees closer to my stomach, feeling the thin and folded cloth push into my belly.

The wind continued to whip around me and the brief bit of warmth that my racing blood had provided when I was running was wearing off quickly. Soon I would shiver, soon my teeth would chatter. Without thinking I moved my hand up to my mouth and bit on the joint that connected my thumb to my hand, taking a preventative measure to keep my front teeth and incisors from clicking away as though they knew Morse code and sending out my location to all living things in the vicinity.

Those few panicked minutes where I was focusing on my own survival were full of activity. The aliens climbed down slowly from the vehicle and searched the truck quickly. There were four of them, I briefly counted eight legs as they stood in front of the headlight. One stayed with the vehicle. Two took off towards the unseen paths that Mitch, Gavin, and Barbie must have taken. One started towards me, it was as though they could see me or smell me or use some of their inhumane senses to find me in the dead of night. My eyes were starting to itch, my sinuses flooding with excess fluid and filling the rim of my nostrils with a circle of moisture that I wanted so badly to wipe away. But I needed to be quiet so I fought my instinctual urge to tend to my discomforting congestion.

Then my ears were on fire with a series of sounds. The gun was the loudest of these noises and occupied most of my immediate brain power. *Who was shot? Who fired the gun? Would this be good or bad?* And my brain also started to process the words at the same time, they had been whispered, but they were jettisoned across the wind as though the voice had originated not two feet to my left.

"No Barbie, it's me!" that was the recognizable voice of Gavin, his adult voice unsure of itself, breaking as he began to panic. The gun had gone off after he said this, but my ears heard everything at once. I wondered why he hadn't been knocked out by his fear, his adrenaline, his panic yet. How had we all been able to run without stopping? My answer was easy enough, the aliens had messed up and didn't stick that metal disc in my finger. But Barbie, Mitch, and Gavin were all under a high amount of stress, they would surely be working against a short timer before they were incapacitated. Famous last words, kid. "No Barbie, it's me!"

There was a quick movement of heavy boots, all four ran towards the sound of the gun, and I heard Barbie cry out in terror. I wanted to run far away, but at the same time, I wanted to help save her. That's the human instinct, right, to want to help others? The isolation and helplessness were too wretched to feel so I bit down on my hand even harder. I let silent tears find a path down my face and convinced myself that it was an involuntary reaction to the pain in my hand, nothing more.

Where was Mitch? Was he shot too? Wasn't he supposed to be with Gavin? I wonder if they can find me by the tracker that's in my back pocket?

I heard the doors of the vehicle open and one hard thud on the metallic base of the space-van. I heard Barbie continue to scream and struggle. I pictured her arms jerking against the grip of the aliens. I recalled the feeling on my own arm not even forty-eight hours earlier. Hard pressure, unfeeling and without a pulse, tight and unwavering. It was not a good feeling.

And then I heard the most betraying sound of all. "No, there were four of us, you only have two. One more is out there, she's injured."

Mitch.

He was communicating with them. I didn't hear when or if he had been nabbed. Maybe he went quietly. Maybe he easily surrendered and figured that his life would be spared if he cooperated. Or maybe this had been the plan all along. I didn't want to reason it out, I wanted to escape. The irony of being on the free open land, yet feeling imprisoned while the open airs blew grains of red sand into my eyes was not lost on me. Thousands of open miles on each side and nowhere to run to.

I heard footsteps coming closer to me, closer and closer.

"RUN DORA!" I heard Mitch bellow. This was confusing and terrifying and yet, even though I knew that making noise would give away my position, and I knew that I would not be able to run flat out in a sprint, I sprung up and started. I pumped my arms and willed my legs to move at the same speed. I felt the dull pain that had been living in my left knee spring to life and begin to grip my entire leg, but I ran.

I thought of the old joke again, the one that my dad had told me. It seemed ubiquitous and commonly understood. What's the best method to survive if a bear attacks? Be faster than at least one person in the camp.

I could feel my body starting to carry me away, and in the dark of night I had convinced myself that I must be half a mile away, but that could have been the ache in my ankles talking. My feet were pounding on the ground beneath me, inefficient and bad for my joints, but I put every last molecule of energy into that run. Perhaps that is what Mitch had counted on, a loud and flat-footed thumping to give me away. That mother-fucker.

A hard and massive hand landed on my shoulder. I squealed; a horrible whiny high-pitched sound came from my mouth. The same sound made by a fat hog as it is led to slaughter. Their hands were all over me, subduing me and handling me. I didn't pay attention to their movement, but it seemed to be too quick that I was suddenly in the vehicle, hands tied behind my back and seated next to a bawling Barbie.

"I didn't mean to kill him, I thought he was one of them," she mumbled over and over. I could barely see her face as my irritated eyes began to swell shut, but I tried to look at her, to make eye contact to show her that she wasn't alone. She didn't look up from the floor, there was a small aisle formed by the two rows of facing seats. In that aisle lay the long and lifeless body of Gavin. Curly hair, youth, and no one to look out for him; that is what he died with.

They had rounded us up like border jumpers; like we had no right to be out on the open land at all. I found a dark humor in the fact that aliens had captured us in the Mojave, and that for all the time and effort spent keeping "illegal aliens" out of the country, we had missed the looming and now pervasive danger of actual aliens.

I could hear garbling voices outside of the van, and it sounded like they had all come to some agreement. I saw two climb into the front of the van, one on the driver's side, the other in the passenger seat. I looked to my left, to the open back doors and saw two more of them standing guard, weapons in both hands, suits as black as the night around us. In between these two things stood Mitch. He looked small and cowardly and weak. A big hand pulled my hair and yanked my head back. And then another hand was inside my mouth prying it open and putting a pill inside my mouth. I began to fight, kicking my legs and trying to move my arms, but I was bound too tightly. I ended up kicking the metal seat across from me and Gavin's leg. Sorry, Gavin. Then a rush of water was dumped into my mouth, the full liter of water forcing the pill down my throat. These were the same pills that I had informed Mitch of, those heavy and sedative painkillers.

Most of the water ended up all over me. I recall thinking quickly that I hoped that it wasn't cyanide, but then wishing that it was because then this would all be over. My head was released and the same alien that had forced me to swallow the pill; climbed in and did the same to Barbie. She made much more noise; it was not pleasant to listen to. I thought that she was going to drown. But then she was released and she had swallowed her pill as well.

"I'm so sorry," Mitch shook his head. His trembling voice feigned an apology, but I couldn't believe it. I wanted to spit in his face and remind him that people just like him could be selling out his own daughters at this very moment. I wanted to call him every name in the book. I wanted to murder him. For the first time in my human existence, I wanted to be a murderer. I was so scared at the thought that I stopped myself, held my breath, and wondered who I was turning into.

But before I could pull off this hot and pointed remark, telling Mitch how small and weak and evil he was, promising my revenge, a dark bag was placed over my head and a hard, flat, heavy item pressed down on my skull with amazing force. There was a black void, *hello good friend.*

We were moving. My limp body was swaying with the motion of the vehicle. Barbie's left shoulder was rubbing against my right arm, her lazy leg hitting my one good knee. My feet were touching the dead legs of Gavin. I started to struggle against the restraints binding me. My leg felt fine, and I knew then that the pill I had been forced to swallow was a painkiller, and that my senses would be compromised, but I still tried to resist. The hard item slammed me again.

When the second darkness ended, I was sure my brain could not sustain more injury without the risk of permanent damage, so I remained still. *My brain must not have been that badly bruised to have that mental function, right?* I tried to focus on my breathing. I let my mind slip into sleep and visions of deeply wooded mountains and ransacked motels flooded my mind. The twisted and carnal world of my weeks with Don and Becca that had once been my worst nightmare, would, in time, be only a vaguely more miserable memory.

Becca's nerves were fried. Her years of drug use had made her weak and dependent. Don had given her a healthy dose during our first day, the first day for any of us survivors, and had given her a bigger dose to get her to sleep. He was her lover, her dealer, and that night he was her enabling angel, helping to calm her nerves and allow her to rest. Or at least that was how Becca saw him. Her doe-eyes always looking up to him in wonder, searching for guidance and love. He had proved to be helpful thus far, taking us up into Georgia, in the mountains and found an empty motel, popped the necessary locks and let us all in.

What I soon realized was that Don wanted Becca to be so passed out that she wouldn't hear him as he groaned and humped on top of me. I tried to resist him at first, his sleazy words and vodka laced breath repulsed me, but the reality of the situation was that all humans were under attack and that I had no resources, no food, and absolutely no clue where we were. My odds of survival with Don and Becca were dismal, but they were nearly impossible without them. The night was cold and I might freeze or starve on my own before any aliens bothered to hunt me down. So, I told myself that it was what I wanted too. I lied to myself so that way I could stand to live inside my own skin, I agreed so that way it wasn't rape, even though it was. I tricked my brain and my body so that way I would be permitted to stay until the next morning.

The whole time I was thinking of how to best escape. Wait for dawn, steal the car, and drive as far and as fast as I could. When he finished, inside me, without a condom, I sprang up and ran the shower until the hot water had run out. (I was fortunate that the water was still running then. It hadn't occurred to me that it would shut off, until 5 days later, when it did.) I tried to clean everything out of me, hoping that he had no diseases, but realizing that the life expectancy for even the healthiest of Americans had now been cut by a factor of ten or more. I scrubbed and scrubbed until my skin was raw. The faded yellow wallpaper and beige tub were constant reminders that nothing was clean or white or pure in this room. I wrapped each of the towels around me, one for my hair, one for my waist and one for my shoulders, building a cocoon of well used and thin brown towels. They were heavily starched and uncomfortable, but they covered my skin and enveloped me.

I waited in the bathroom, the door was closed and the steam had been trapped at the ceiling and had completely covered the mirror. In my life before the invasion, I might have wiped the mirror and looked at myself, primped and poked at my face before brushing and drying my hair. But that night I refused to look at myself, I didn't want to look myself in the eyes because then I would have to admit to myself all that had happened already. I slid to the ground, feeling the warm wetness in the towels press against my skin, and then slowly it felt cold, and then it felt dry. I looked up and saw that the steam had dissipated from the mirror and decided that it had been long enough and that surely Don was asleep by now.

I put my clothes back on and opened the door. Becca was sprawled out on one of the double beds and Don was on the other. We had found a motel that was completely empty and could have easily taken the keys to a larger room or two rooms even, but Don had insisted on the room closest to the front office. It was small and cramped, and it smelled old and musty. The décor screamed nineteen-seventies, but at least the mini-fridge was full of booze, which was what mattered to Don and Becca at least. I grabbed one of the extra blankets from the tiny closet. There were a mini-ironing board and a safe for valuables. Don hadn't placed the gun there; it was under his pillow. His charm and paranoia never ceased to annoy me.

I pulled the soft blanket from the boxy plastic casing and tip-toed to the armchair by the window. The air conditioning was on full blast, so I swiveled the chair so that I was facing the door.

Don sat up quickly, gun in hand, and pointed it directly at me. I wanted to scream that it wasn't fair, that he couldn't do that to me and then just kill me. But I didn't, all I did was blink and contain my panic and fears. After a moment he put his hand down and went back to sleep. I let out a deep breath of relief. This was far worse than any of the nights I had spent in the care of the great state of Florida. But it felt much the same in some ways. I had no home, had no one looking out for me, and there was something sinister on the periphery of my life that was lurking and trying to kill the light inside of me. *Alien invasions are just like moving between foster homes.* I smirked at my ill-framed metaphor and stared out the window at the stars. They had changed, between the night before when I was staring up at them in the grass and now. The stars, every last one of the billion stars that littered the sky, had changed. I had once gazed upon them in wonder, and now the one peaceful constant in my life had betrayed me. I cried silently and with great shame and fear. I let the thick tears pool on my lower eyelids and spill over. Eventually, I fell asleep without realizing it, curled up in the armchair in the fetal position.

I didn't run away; I was too weak and scared to do it. I continued to convince myself that I couldn't survive alone and that the next night I would be comforting Becca or I would be unwanted by Don. But none of those things ever happened. As I thought about my forced but consensual capture by Don, I realized that I would have been far better on my own for a few days. I might have ended up dead in a ditch, but it would have been better than continuing with Don, trusting Mitch, or in that van, moving towards an unknown, but surely menacing and brief future.

Finally, the vehicle stopped. It seemed appropriate for me to be awake, so I turned my head slightly towards the door, not visible beneath the shroud, but I was hoping to catch a glimpse of some movement through the porous fibers. I wondered if this was the same exact van, the same exact shroud, the same exact aliens from the other day. In fact, I wondered how long we had been driving and whether it was a new day or not. Would I be hauled back to the same Texan hospital, brought back to the same room and forced to undergo some painful procedure to have a metal disc inserted into my fingers? *Would I soon itch like the others?* Would I soon be biting away at my fingers, gnawing at the skin until it was ground like hamburger meat, trying to alleviate the irritation just below the surface?

The doors to the back of the vehicle opened. I heard one of *them*, breathing loud and raspy through their mask, fumbling for something on the ground. I heard something sliding nearby, and then I realized it was Gavin, his exposed body being pulled feet-first from the van. I gagged silently, not wanting to vomit into the material, knowing that it would pool near my face and cause another round of nausea. The more I thought about it, the more likely it seemed it would happen. I could feel the bile start to crawl and reach its acidic hand up my throat when I was grabbed by the arm and pulled from the truck.

I don't know why the black cloth was placed over my head because the moment that my feet touched the ground the bag was removed. It was quick and rough on my face, a few of my stray hairs yanked out by the brut who had taken me from the truck. The colossus of an alien, a clear foot and a half taller than my five-foot eight-inch stature stood behind me, casting a shadow that seemed to swallow me; I was completely hidden from the sun. The idea that no one looking down could see me at that moment, not even God himself, was humbling and terrifying.

I looked down at the ground, the color of it cooled by the shade provided by the Goliath alien. It was sandy, it looked gray in the shadow, but a bright reddish yellow in the sunlight. We were still in the Mojave region, so clearly not back in Texas. I let my eyes adjust. At first, my head instinctively ducked at the thought of light after so much darkness. The first light of morning was rising over the crested mountains in the far distance to my left, I wasn't familiar with the geography of the region so I can't say which mountains they were. I moved my head subtly as Barbie was pulled from the truck.

The mountains in the east were miles and miles away, a barren land in between their foothills and the place where I stood. And not but twenty feet from me, off to my left was a large pit. The alien that had grabbed Gavin was walking his limp body towards that ominous hole. It threw Gavin in and walked away. Like he was just cleaning up after a picnic and tossing a wrapper away, the unfeeling beast strode back with no worry on his conscience. Of course, how could an alien have a feeling of grief or remorse? Those were human emotions, and soon to be extinct, along with the rest of us.

As he walked toward us, I stared at him. This alien was tall as well, but no more than six and a half feet tall. His suit was more faded than the ones that had tried to slice open my thumb in Texas, but maybe it was the way the desert sand was clinging to him that gave it that appearance. The labored breathing that came from the mask was ferocious, like the sound a dog makes when it is provoked and snarling. I pictured the alien's lips curled up and grimacing. Behind that mask any face could be lurking, one with blue skin or no skin at all, only raw and oozing muscles. Then it gestured at me, hurling some words my way, the alien behind me punched me hard in the back, and I fell to my knees. My healthy knee went willingly, the semi-injured/semi-healed left knee let out a rebounding pain, as though it was intensifying and getting worse for every second that I was on the ground. I get the feeling I just heard the alien equivalent of, "What are you looking at?" I tried to commit the words and sounds to memory. "Hoshakanothia urgunta blut" *It's all foreign to me.*

From my knees I looked up and saw Barbie's defeated face, her tears leaving tracks on her dirty skin. Maybe those were tears of sadness or perhaps her eyes were irritated too, trying to relieve the allergens that were taking hold of her inner lids. Next to her was Mitch. The sight of him made my skin began to crawl with anger. But I was conflicted with the feeling of defeat. I knew my rage towards him could do nothing to save us now, so what was the point of spending my last few moments alive mad at him? What was the point of all the running, when I should have been focused on how I could die on my own terms, in a place that would be comforting to me, rather than as a prisoner to sadistic space creatures, as of yet unidentified?

Beyond where we stood, beyond the alien van with oddly shaped armor, uneven and clunky, was a town. While I had spent weeks running into isolation, away from people, away from aliens, away from anything familiar and large, the aliens had been rounding up whatever humans they hadn't killed. Maybe these were all of the humans left in America, maybe all of the humans left on the continent, or in the World. Or maybe these were all of the humans left in the state. This was clearly a town that was being repurposed for whatever these aliens wanted with the planet. But I didn't know what that purpose was, and I still don't know entirely what that purpose is even now. The usual signs of life, a bank, a grocery, a hardware store were all still there, but the goods within the stores had been thrown out onto the street, now just more litter clogging the road.

I stared at the other humans that were milling around; they looked dazed and drugged. Maybe not drugged with narcotics, but maybe they were zonked out from whatever was implanted in them. I could see why the aliens wanted us calm, all of these rowdy and boisterous humans in one place, we could have coordinated, we could have schemed. Instead, we were forced to keep our cool or risk being knocked out.

There were maybe forty or fifty people that I could see in the immediate area. This was our prison camp perhaps, or yet another routing station maybe. Maybe there was another step to their sadistic process. I thought of the disc in my pocket and hoped that Mitch, in all of his betrayal, hadn't told them that I was still not being tracked. Although why I still counted on that fact as something positive, I don't know, but it stuck with me.

The faces of most of the humans were slack and they seemed completely unphased by our capture and Gavin's body being casually thrown into a hole. Had they been forced to be obedient and submissive since the very first day? How could people so easily forget how to feel? I didn't have much time to linger on these questions. The doors of the van slammed shut behind me, and I was brought back up to my feet and marched forward. The aliens were pointing us in the direction of a long and well-populated building. If I had to guess, I would say that it had been an elementary or middle school before the invasion. Now it was ground zero for experiments in human torture and malice. As they marched us forward, a firm grip on each elbow that was being held behind my back, I saw many of the other aliens dragging humans towards the pit. Some were clearly dead; others were flailing and kicking as they were being pulled behind their alien hauler. These humans, still alive but, being taken to the place where the dead were being stacked up in piles, were clearly in the bargaining and denial phases of death. The dead humans being dragged were silent. Another incredibly tall and large alien, perhaps the same size as the giant that was leading me towards a certain death, was dragging one dead human in each hand, trailing two behind him at once. The carnage was massive, the empathy was non-existent, and the mortal terror was real.

There were other buildings with many people standing in long lines to enter, alien guards were posted all over to ensure that the crowds stayed orderly. I found this to be somewhat silly. *If everyone had a trigger implanted in their thumbs and the aliens could set off a reaction to knock us out at any time, then why have guards watching us?* I tried to think of all of the logical reasons, perhaps they realized that as social animals we humans would stay in line so long as there was an authority figure telling us to do so, or maybe they wanted us to be conscious and awake so that we could remain productive and profitable. Perhaps these aliens just liked being able to assert their dominance. My mind was whirring, protecting itself from worrying about the reality of the situation.

As we drew closer and closer to the building, the assumed school building, I began to focus on what was happening, snapping out of my inquisitive thoughts and I began to panic. If Mitch was being marched there as well, then he had not purchased freedom by selling us out, and his motives for doing so were completely lost on me. Just as we walked up the small path that led to the front double-doors of the school building, I could have sworn that I heard a loud scream come out of a second-floor window. It was loud and piercing and made my spine tingle. This building; the one that I was about to enter, was one of death.

The fluorescent lights were on, they were consistent, as though they had only recently been changed and there was a steady power source fueling them, smooth and very steady. As we walked towards that building, I pictured that the interior would have flickering lights with panels swinging from the ceiling. I pictured hundreds of loose papers strewn across the floor and dried human blood on the walls. And when the doors opened, I saw a calm entryway, the trophy case of past championships was still intact, the golden statutes gleaming and staring up vacantly towards an aspirational imaginary sky. Everything seemed to be in order, with the exception of the prison-like conditions of the building, and the alien army patrolling and commanding us.

We didn't have to walk very far in the building before Barbie and I were each told to sit down, the words were foreign but the hard shove downward on our shoulders was easy enough to understand. Barbie and I were seated on the right side of the main hallway, our back to the colorful lockers and our bottoms on the cool and unforgiving linoleum floor. Mitch was not told to sit, his alien guard brought him further down the hallways and behind a closed set of doors. I let my legs sit out straight in front of me, giving my knee the opportunity to lay flat and continue to heal.

Barbie sat to my left and she either fell asleep or passed out in the unidentified and immutable time that kept slipping by. I wondered if the disc in her thumb had operated as designed, this was a high-stress situation. *Why then wasn't everyone else lined up along the wall passed out?* I was endlessly curious about the device that the aliens had failed to install within me. What was the purpose? What was their grand plan? My need for understanding was still alive within me, for a little while at least.

On the opposite side of the hall sat a line of men, in all different shapes, sizes, and colors. They sat cross-legged or with their knees pulled up in front of them. I looked down to my right and saw a similar line. The line that I sat on was for women only. The division between these two lines was patrolled by aliens, and more surprisingly by another human. This was the first time I had seen other humans taking part in this invasion, he was holding a gun and strutting down the hallways and his purpose was clear: keep everyone quiet.

I sneered at the first human patrolman to walk past me. He had a toned and exact look about him. He looked like he had done this forever as he walked up and down this exact stretch of tile and kept a firm hold of his control. He was composed as though he might have been in the military at one point, but I couldn't bring myself to accept that assumption. He was wearing camouflage cargo pants, thick steel-toed boots, and a black zip-up fleece. He looked the part, but I knew that the military had too many men of integrity for this scum to have been one of them. If the military had been involved with this, it would explain why no help ever came. Maybe it was just a few rotten apples that helped the aliens overthrow every earthly power, but then how could they have coordinated in advance? The third, and perhaps most disturbing idea, was that these men, that this specific patrolman, like Mitch, had been desperate to live, and because of their fear they had sold out their species and were now working against us. He was a smear on humanity. He was the evil that the world should have never known, but evil had slithered out of the Garden of Eden and now several millennia later this traitor had formed out of the primordial ooze. There is no need to muffle my disdain in this account, and for whatever you may read further, know that I held the same contempt for all who made this deal, no matter how subservient I had to be to them in order to survive.

The stiff jaw that popped up and down on a white piece of gum was lined with stubble, and I had a feeling that this man was so tightly wound that he probably had ground his molars into smooth stumps every night. I hated that man; I didn't need to know his name or his reasons. I hated him. It was one thing that in the wake of the alien invasion that some humans had taken advantage of each other, like Don, and exploited the opportunities created by the invasion and the power vacuum that followed. But to work with the aliens in their efforts to capture and kill us was despicable. After this less-than-a-man passed by me, his eyes focusing just above the heads over everyone in the line, I spat at him. It was a cowardly move to wait until he couldn't see me do it, but I had to spit at him. It may have been un-ladylike, but it was the least I could do to start to act out.

This was when true hatred took hold in my heart. Hate all man, trust no bitch. I felt the first grumblings of my animal tendencies scratching up from the ancestral part of my intuition that had long been repressed.

Barbie saw me spit and joined in. It was a lone moment of solidarity. She continued her silent tears and I saw her lips shaking, she needed a cigarette bad and they wouldn't be giving one to her anytime soon. I recognized the defeated look on her face, I'm sure if someone had seen me that first night in the motel room, a prisoner as I stared out the window, I would have had the same expression on my face.

The mercenary finished his patrol of our hallway and headed down the next. I stared at my feet, wondering at all the possible next options. Potentially we could be kept there indefinitely with no food, water or bathroom facilities and starve, dehydrate and catch a severe illness from pooling refuse. Or, the aliens could come in and fire away at the line of us, killing several dozen humans at once. They could even try to –

"Hey, did you just get in?" I heard a timid male voice speaking. I looked up to see who it was, there had been no order to stay silent, but I was fairly sure that we were not supposed to be speaking. And even if I had been commanded to be quiet, I wouldn't have understood it anyway. I saw several faces on the opposing wall looking around, but no one immediately stood out as the source of the voice.

"Yeah you, did you just get in?" I saw now that it was a man not two feet down from where Barbie and I sat who was directing his questions in our direction. I couldn't help but furrow my brow and look puzzled.

"Scared mute?" he challenged, making a slight sneer in my direction.

"No, I just know when it's in my best interest to keep my mouth shut," I snapped back. I was in no mood for a smart-mouthed stranger to taunt me for what remained of the rest of my human existence.

"Sorry, I was just curious to see if they brought you directly here or if you had been somewhere else first." His arms were tied behind his back, but I could tell that he was so used to gesticulating with each sentence that he couldn't stop himself from at least trying to move his shoulders up and down with each word.

"Straight here," I said. The man nodded, his black hair sticking out on its ends and his pale skin looked oily and marked with new pimples, but he was cleanly shaven. His overall appearance made him look a little mad, but I was willing to give every human in the present situation a pass on their looks, after all, we'd all been through hell to survive for this long. He had whole-rimmed glasses on his face, the lens on the right eye had a thin crack along the bottom. It was probably not enough of an issue to impair his eyesight, but not small enough to go completely unnoticed when trying to look through them.

"This is Barbie, I'm Dora," I offered, rolling my head towards Barbie as I mentioned her name.

"Nice to meet you both," he nodded at each of us. I could see his arms struggling behind him. "I would offer to shake your hands and formally make your acquaintance, but I'm detained at the moment." He laughed at his own joke. I usually couldn't stand smart know-it-all guys who laughed at their own jokes, but the situational irony was wearing on my nerves so I let out a small giggle as well. "I'm Simon," he said offering a kind and easy smile.

He reminded me of the people who would strike up a conversation while in line at the grocery store, or the bank, or the airport. He was one of the gregarious types who constantly reached out for human connection. And even in a place where aliens were about to do some unknown horrible acts of torture to us, he still wanted to strike up a conversation to pass the time.

"Hi Simon," I said. "Any idea what they're going to do to us next?" I heard a sharp "shh" from several feet away. Someone else was uncomfortable with our open conversation. I gave a quick look down the row, but didn't see anyone staring at me, willing a warning of absolute silence through their eyes.

"No, but I haven't seen anyone come back yet," Simon gave his opinion, "Although I've only been here for roughly an hour or so."

I accepted his explanation and returned my focus to staring at the floor and thinking through all of the possible ways that the aliens might handle us. Nobody came back yet, that was a foreboding concept and the lines of humans along the hallway suddenly seemed much shorter. "I didn't mean to say anything alarming," Simon whispered.

"It's okay," and I truly meant it. There was nothing that Simon could have said to make me feel worse, nor could he offer any comfort. An impression was the best that could be mustered because in this confusion and pain the truth was as elusive as a phoenix. There was no avoiding the harsh reality of where we were. The depths of an empty depression was starting to take hold, oblivion was near. I was starting to learn the ways of the world that we now lived in. I was deteriorating.

The huge Goliath of an alien started down the hallway, he came from the same direction that the human mercenary had just turned down. Likely they were both working the same circuitous route, monitoring their prisoners, keeping us all docile and in line, letting us all know who was in charge. The width of his shoulders, again assuming that it was a male and not seeing any differentiating factors to indicate gender I defaulted them all to male, took up most of the narrow lane between the two rows of prisoners. His feet made impactful and sonorous thuds with each step. His hands gripped a large rifle-like object, likely an original product from their home planet. I had never seen one of these rifles up close, although the four of *them* that had captured Barbie and me from our campsite were armed, presumably, with the same weapons. I wondered what a shot from this rifle might do to a human body, I was curious, but not in any rush to find out for sure.

As the large alien continued down the hallway, he did not move his head from side to side to inspect each prisoner. He was walking too quickly to really take stock of the condition of any one human captive. Maybe they didn't have eyes; maybe their sense of sight was based on sound waves. My imagination was limited to the scope of human and Earth biology that I had absorbed in twenty years. I couldn't think beyond what was familiar to try to make these beings make sense in my mind. I had yet to see any slits for eyeholes on the few masked aliens I had encountered yet. Finally, the behemoth stopped a few feet away. And what I heard next was unexpected and haunting.

"Scientist!" the word was ejaculated like a fluid bark from a mongrel, foaming at the mouth. Though heavily accented and muffled by the thick mask, the alien spoke a word of English. Had *they* been observing us for that long to be able to learn our language, or were *they* all quick studies? Perhaps the decades of errant radio waves being transmitted into space were our undoing because that alien spoke in English.

That word, that clear and decipherable English word from the alien made my heart stutter on the subsequent beat. *They* had the upper hand, there would be no language barrier that could shield us and provide cover for a plan to be hatched. Perhaps the humans who had surrendered also agreed to provide some coaching in proper accent and inflection as payment for their lives to be spared.

The alien had directed this word, this accusation at the man who had just been speaking to me.

Simon was staring intently at his hands, which were folded in front of him. "Scientist," the alien snarled again, this time turning more directly towards the man. Simon looked up at the creature; his mouth pressed into a hard line, and offered no response.

The alien kicked him quickly, a stream of alien words hurdling out now, aimed at Simon. Simon the Scientist.

The fluency with the native tongue was apparent and the meaning, while I could not translate, was easy enough to discern. Simon's silent defiance was not going to be tolerated. With each vicious kick, Simon was pulling into himself, closer and closer to the ground. And while I had paid attention to the detail-muting face masks, the broad suits and most recently the space-rifles, I have not yet observed the alien boots clearly. They had a dual-pronged tip, the purpose of which was now apparent. It was for beating and kicking, function over form. After a dozen or so direct hits of Simon's abdomen, the alien stopped and let Simon breathe. His catching and raspy exhalations were abrupt and his shirt was bloody.

Several of the other prisoners near us were captivated by the spectacle. I was silent through the entire ordeal, if my hands had been free, I would have tried to bury my face in my legs and cover my ears. But my hands were bound, so I was stuck in my current position, watching helplessly. This is a vantage point that I would soon learn to grow accustomed to, which is the worst learned trait that any human can acquire.

Simon finally spoke after a few tense seconds when none of us that were watching could tell if the beating would continue or not. "Yes, scientist," he assented, although I sensed that he did not appreciate the catch-all title. The large alien bent down and with one hand of his rifle and one hand on Simon, he pulled the man's battered body up until Simon was on both of his feet. Goliath pointed Simon in the direction that Barbie and I had just come from and prodded him to move forward with the rifle on his back.

Are they taking him outside to kill him? My mental reflex was still strong, but I didn't want to think that just a few words exchanged in a hallway could sign a death warrant, especially since I was the other half of the conversation. Had our brief discussion killed him? *I will never speak again*, I weakly promised myself. It was a half-promise, one that I made at the moment to appease my guilt, but it was not genuine.

I couldn't see him as he walked away, the enormous alien obscured any final view and with that, Simon disappeared out of the building. He might have turned to look back, and I'm glad I couldn't see his eyes pleading for help, because I was too weak, physically but also mentally, and I wouldn't have been able to move. My assumption had been that he would soon join

Gavin in the body pit. But as the old adage always says, it is not wise to assume.

The hallway was silent after the episode between Simon and Goliath. There were other guards that patrolled on a regular basis and every so often one or two more additional people were brought into the hallway and seated by their escorts. I leaned my head against the lockers, still cool when my skin initially touched the metal, but quickly my body heat neutralized the imbalance until it was just another hard surface. One surface to rest my head against, one surface that my legs were sitting on, and the ever-oppressive hard force of alien occupation bearing down on my flimsy grasp of reality and sanity.

Soon, another faceless, nameless alien guard came down the hallway. The heads of a few of the other imprisoned humans glanced up, but most had lost interest, sanity or track of time and thus remained fixated on the ground in front of them. A second alien followed quickly. They stopped in front of me and Barbie and we were pulled up and marched down the hallway, past the rest of the humans who were relieved that it was not their time to be called. Barbie and her guard were in front of me. I could barely see Barbie's feet as my swollen eyes began to water again. Her alien guard was directly in front of me. I saw the tube leading from the nape of the neck down into a power-pack on the belt of the exo-suit. I wanted to pull that textured and shiny tube, to just yank it and let the alien breath in our polluted air, but with my hands restrained and an alien so close behind me that I could feel the suit rub against my back, I didn't dare to make a move.

As we continued down the hall, we were escorted through the same doors that Mitch had been. In front of us was more of the same hallway, but this one was completely empty. The same pattern of colored lockers continued, with the entrance to a classroom at every few meters. The alien in front of me veered off and opened a door to a classroom halfway down this corridor. He shoved Barbie into the room and closed the door behind him. I didn't know what that thing would do to Barbie, maybe just watch and guard, maybe murder, or potentially something in between.

The alien behind me continued to force me forward. I turned my head, straining to look back at the door that Barbie had vanished behind. I felt no connection to her other than that she was also a human and potentially the last I would ever see. I didn't know what had happened to Becca, I had heard Gavin's last words clear across the desert night, and now I might die with no one who would mourn or miss me. I wanted to be brave. I was always telling my clients to face every challenge with bravery and that the body can accomplish anything if the mind is willing, although that was in the context of self-improvement in a safe environment. My mind was pushed to the precipice of resilience. I looked forward at the approaching wooden double-doors.

Across the front read in large block letters: "GYMNASIUM." I could sense that this was where we were headed, the alien guard and I. And I could sense that I would surely die in this converted school/prison.

As we drew closer the alien cried out in a screaming wail, it sounded like an animal with raspy vocal cords calling out to this pack, signaling his approach. The violent sound was distinct and unlike anything I had ever heard before. The left door swung open, beyond it was darkness.

As we stepped through the doorway, I felt a change in temperature, the gymnasium, as it was labeled, was hot and sticky, where the hallway had been cool and calm. I heard the door slam shut behind us and the back of my arms were released and then grabbed again. An alien changing of the guard.

The large space was almost completely black. I looked up to see the scant light peering in front of the high ceiling. The gym itself was wide and open, taking up two stories. I could see slivers of daylight peeking through at the top of the wall, at first, I thought that was by design and that the lights had been shut off, but I noticed a spotlight on the far end of the room, to my right. I was being steered towards that light. I continued to whirl my head around trying to understand the uneven and oddly shaped light coming into the room. And then I saw one of them move. The entire room was lined with rows upon rows of *them*, the aliens. They were standing shoulder to shoulder on rafters and those standing at the very top were blocking the sunlight from coming in, their black-as-night suits blocking out the sunlight.

My mouth opened, slack and agape, as I was moved into position in the spotlight. I thought of the failed surgical procedure in Texas and wondered if this time the aliens would be successful. I was thinking hard and focused on the metal object in my pocket. The item that was pulsing, I felt that it was growing hotter and hotter until finally, I knew that it must have actually been changing temperature. I let out a yelp of pain and folded over in an attempt to compress and alleviate.

I heard a "hmm" of approval from the shadows. And then I heard Mitch.

"This was our deal, I had to bring as many people as I could to this station and my girls would be released." His voice was familiar, but his words were repugnant.

"That was the deal however the vehicle broke down, meaning that the Porths had to bring them the rest of the way, and-" the sharp and accented voice rebuked Mitch. *And what was that word he used? Porths?* "One of them arrived dead, not alive." I could see a man on the periphery of the light. He was tall and wearing an olive-green t-shirt, his long hair pulled back into a pony-tail holder behind his head. His voice sounded smooth, like a rich and decadent dessert from a European country, silky and with unfamiliar flavors. I was surprised that Mitch was speaking with a human, but perhaps this was a translator. English to God-knows-what language translations would potentially be in high demand.

"I brought two women, I get my two girls, Gael." Mitch was trying to drive a hard bargain. I could picture him jutting his chin forward, trying to invoke some primal dominance.

"Yes, and one of those two women is a murderer, which will need to be ferreted out."

Mitch was silent. I felt as though the people standing and watching me were a jury, judging me based on my appearance of guilt. Surely, they didn't think that I had shot Gavin. And given the rate of human death in the past few weeks, I would be surprised if these aliens now tried to hold us humble humans to a different standard.

"This one is strong, she survived uncaptured for weeks." Mitch was offering an analysis of, I assumed, my attributes.

"Uncaptured?" the sharp and accented voice that Mitch had identified as Gael snapped.

"Uncaptured until two days ago," I didn't like the implication in Mitch's voice. Why would that be a valuable piece of information?

The second voice was silent, although I heard footsteps, soft and close to me.

"Strong? How so?" I heard the voice from behind me.

"A physical trainer by profession. And I've seen her manage on a busted knee better than anyone else could have. She would be a great asset to the operation here." Mitch was a used car salesman, which made me the unwanted and used car. I winced with disgust.

"Hmm," I heard again from behind me. Gael's voice may have been handsome, but his tone was worrisome. He sounded like a man appraising cattle or a piece of meat to be purchased and consumed. I did not want to be his or anyone's meal. *Perhaps that is what these aliens wanted, humans as food?* If that was the case then they had wasted quite a bit already. "What is her name?" I heard his voice, again from behind me, but this time closer. I thought I could smell his breath and a shiver ran down my spine and then back up.

"Dora," Mitch called out, but I screamed over him,

"My name is Pandora!" I shouted at the faceless darkness ahead of me as I felt my last bit of patience and sanity wring from my body like moisture from a sponge. I would speak for myself and not let these men determine my worth with their quick words, or that was the emotion that drove my action at least.

"Well Pandora, thank you for speaking up," the soft, but menacing voice whispered as he passed on my right. After a few moments of silence, he spoke again.

"Alright Mitch, you have your deal. Release his daughters." I heard Mitch sigh and offered pleading thanks to the faceless Gael. I pictured him dropping to his knees and kissing the feet of this man and the surrounding aliens. Their hot alien stink was filling the room and making my salted perspiration feel like their slime was covering me.

"Place her in the first room on the left, I will collect her later," I heard the smooth European voice say in a cavalier manner. And then darkness.

PART TWO

The Fear of God

"Then Jesus went through the towns and villages, teaching as he made his way to Jerusalem. Someone asked him, "Lord, are only a few people going to be saved?" He said to them, "Make every effort to enter through the narrow door, because many, I tell you, will try to enter and will not be able to. Once the owner of the house gets up and closes the door, you will stand outside knocking and pleading, 'Sir, open the door for us.' But he will answer, 'I don't know you or where you come from.' Then you will say, 'We ate and drank with you, and you taught in our streets.' But he will reply, 'I don't know you or where you come from. Away from me, all you evildoers!' There will be weeping there, and gnashing of teeth, when you see Abraham, Isaac and Jacob and all the prophets in the kingdom of God, but you yourselves thrown out. People will come from east and west and north and south, and will take their places at the feast in the kingdom of God."

- Luke 13:22-29 (NIV)

It happened that quickly. It wasn't a slow motion, overly vivid sequence when I realized what was happening, but it was too late. It happened fast and with the heavy scent of chloroform, I was pushed into a hazy awakening.

I thought I was still dreaming, a distorted and blurry version of reality. But I was, in fact, awake and doped beyond coherence. The sandy gray images swirling around me were dirty human faces that could never quite take form. The moving sparkling boulders with arms and legs that gargled their words and spat them out at me were aliens, encased in their armor.

I woke up in the evening, the cool gray-blue omnipresence of the night sky filling each pane on the laddered windows. The schoolroom was eerie with dancing monkeys holding the letters of the alphabet circling the room. The desks were all pushed to the back of the room, piled and thrown on top of each other in a haphazard manner; each chair and desk dangling precariously on a mountain of metal and plastic. I had crawled over to the wooden cabinets on the side of the room, facing the outside windows and finally blinking away the last bits of disorientation as the last speckle of orange and purple disappeared from the sky.

I thought that I had just been knocked out for the rest of the day, but my stomach was howling, flopping and complaining for attention. I was hungry and the drugs leaving my system did not help with the heavy nausea and anemia I was feeling. I tried to pool enough courage to stand up and walk over to the door and try to open it. I was afraid to just stand up, sure that a sniper would be ready to shoot me at the first sign of movement. I had no rational explanation for this specific fear, but I'm sure that the fluid that was injected into my left arm, evident by the swelling and dry blood in the crook of my elbow, was a bad mixture of drugs whose side effects included impaired vision and paranoia. I hardly needed any help to be panicked, but perhaps the aliens wanted me to be afraid of everything that wasn't there so that the horrible atrocities they were committing would seem more tangible and less frightening. My mind was constantly turning over each new thought and morphing it into many new ones, I couldn't keep up with one idea long enough to really ruminate on it.

I did not and would not ever know the fate of Mitch and his daughters, of Manuel and his errand to find a new tire, and potentially flag down the aliens. I would never know what happened to the other people in the hallway or what cocktail of drugs had been pushed into my system, and whether they were injected by a sterile or dirty syringe or by some similar alien mechanism. I didn't know what day it was or how long it had been since I had lost a credible accounting of days. I would never know what injuries I had sustained; I had an idea that my brain was bruised from the rifles jammed into my head in the van and that my kneecap was likely not dislocated, but just sprained as my leg was becoming more and more pliable. But I would never know for sure.

The unending and dizzying inner monologue made me exhausted and at some point, I passed out from hunger, exhaustion, and delirium. I slumped over and slept on the cool tile floor, my back and neck slowly aching for relief, and at some point, in my sleep, I rolled onto my back.

The fluorescent lights blinked on with the familiar buzz of the tubes sending electrons back and forth between the ballasts. The light began to bring me out of a slumber, but the loud bang as the door to the classroom flung open and slammed into the wall jolted me awake. Then I instinctively crawled backward on my elbows moving away from the door and towards the tower of school desks. The light in the classroom made the window panes look like black glass, reflecting the details of the classroom into the night.

A medium sized alien, wide in the middle and in the legs, stomped into the room with a harried and wild looking Barbie. He swung her thin and flimsy body and they were both facing me directly. Her bleached hair was sticking up straight out of her messy bun, the sweatshirt she was wearing hung off of her pointed shoulders and her sagging tanned skin. She looked ten pounds lighter than when I had last seen her, maybe I had been out for much longer than I had thought. The alien shoved her forward a few inches, indicating that she should speak, but still keeping her next to him, his grip on her skeletal arm tight and unyielding. She made a muffled noise, like a moose caught in a trap, desperately trying to escape.

"Dora?" she looked at me as though she was not sure if she recognized me. Perhaps I looked just as bad as she did, perhaps we would both only continue to recede into our bodies, becoming less and less of ourselves with each day.

"Barbie!" I answered, shocked to see her alive. Of all the people on my unconceivable journey from safe and warm Tampa to this unknown location in the desert, Barbie had been the most odious, but for some reason was the person that I was fated to continue this journey with. Or so I thought.

"Dora," she let out a sigh of relief. "Dora, you need to tell him where the gun is. The gun that shot Gavin. Where did you put it after you shot him?" A fresh set of tears began to spill from her already wet and puffy eyes. The dirt on her face had given the brief appearance of makeup, but her weeping had left her face ugly and aged.

Her words were nonsense to me. Perhaps I was still hallucinating all of this. My delayed senses were riddling through her words and I instinctively pushed my eyebrows closer together and felt the skin on my forehead fold onto itself.

It was an honest mistake and an easy betrayal. I didn't have to say a word to demonstrate that what Barbie had said was a lie. She had decided to lie to them, in the hopes of saving herself. Perhaps she had counted on my being dead, which would explain her surprise and confusion when she saw me alive. Even the most sophisticated and generous women can't help but compete with each other and hate each other because of the scarcity of male respect that can be allotted to each of them. So, when I was confused by the question, my brain still working out that she had implicated me as the gun wielder in the desert, the alien that was gripping her arms tightly made a snap judgment. It realized that she had lied and that she was willing to blame me and see me punished for her crime. (That any of them were interested in sentencing crimes was the root of the meaning of irony given the global genocide that they inflicted upon us.)

Unlike the corporate world, this female on female attack ended with Barbie's brains on the floor. I drew in my breath and covered my mouth with my hands. Blind and raw panic surged through me instantly. The weapon had made a low whonking sound and for the second time in several days, I saw a body with most of its head removed. Her head was completely erased as though it had never been there, but the body still intact, like a mannequin that had once sweat and moved, but would now no longer be of use.

The alien dropped her arm, her body now limp, and what was left of her slumped to the floor with a thud. It looked at me and I didn't require any device in my thumb to force my body's next reaction. My elbows grew weak and betrayed me. I fell back to the ground, hitting my head on the cold tile. I was out for maybe thirty seconds at the most; based on the distance the alien had crossed towards me. The alien was getting closer to me, the same metallic prongs on its shoes as the Goliath that had beat Simon and marched him away towards an execution that couldn't be avoided. An image of the spikes punching into my eyes flashed in my mind and I jerked up into a seated position.

I would be docile and quiet no more. I was over the edge, I wasn't sure just when it had happened, but I was no longer a sane and predictable animal. I was not offended at the loss of my traveling companion, although perhaps I should have been. I was incensed at the near constant threat to my life at every moment. Seeing Barbie murdered reminded me that I could just as easily die with no warning, no time to plead, no option to beg for mercy or bravely stare death in the face. The pink splatter on the wall was the only proof that Barbie had once been alive in this room, even if only for a few seconds.

"You stay the fuck away from me you piece of cosmic shit!" I must have looked like a mad woman, my unwashed and greasy hair on its ends, hurling obscenities at a thing that likely couldn't understand me. It still drew closer. I put all of my weight on my left hip and wound my right leg around and kicked the shin of the average sized alien. I expected the exo-suit to be harder than steel. It looked like vulcanized rubber, but of course, it couldn't be and once my foot hit it, my leg recoiled back in pain. It felt like an impenetrable metal plate. My futile attempt to fight back was pathetic and a waste of energy, and for that I was embarrassed. The alien grunted at me and strutted away. That was not a grunt of annoyance or dismissal, but one of "if that's how you want to play it."

I screamed blindly into the room and when the alien left the room, he shut out the light and slammed the door. I heard it lock. I screamed. Short high-pitched spasms of sounds propelled from my throat and out to nothing and no one. But I had to scream. I had gone over the edge. I skittered like a bug, crawling madly for the door, panting and whimpering on my hands and knees, as I worked across the room in less than a minute. I must have looked like a possessed woman in need of an exorcism.

I pounded on the door, screaming and grabbing at the air, hoping to reach the doorknob instead. I thought back to the shootings at Sandy Hook and wondered how I could be locked in from the outside, hadn't all schools changed their doors to lock from the inside? The change was made to let teachers lock out the madmen and keep the children safe, but now I was locked in. I longed for a simpler time when it was insane men without medical attention that caused harm to us humans. I could understand the lack of funding and social stigmas associated with mental illness and together as a human race we could have worked together to remedy such wide-reaching social issues in an effort to ensure that a similar massacre or school shooting would never happen again. But now there were real monsters, aliens, creatures that only a few had dared to dream up and they had reduced our numbers and tracked us to the point that we could never again work together as a human race to best their efforts.

I scratched at the lock for a few moments, feeling my now brittle nails, thin and peeling from poor nutrition, pull up a few splinters from where the aliens had pried out the locks and reversed them. I kept screaming, bruising my arms and hands along the way. When I slid back into a lucid state several hours later those bruises were my only reminder that my outburst had been real and that I had somehow made it back from the darkest and loneliest places in my mind.

After ten or fifteen or forty minutes beating at the door, I slumped back, sitting on the floor with my knees outstretched in front of me, my eyes unfocused, my hair ragged, looking like a well-used doll that had been left out in the rain one too many times. And without even realizing it, without even making the conscious decision I moved my right hand to my mouth and began to bite my nails.

It had been my most pronounced and worst bad habit when I was younger. I was a nervous child, and I would always bite and pick worse when my father was drunk and my mother was weak to his attacks. She would always tell me not to bite my nails, not to pick at my cuticles. She would chide me for getting blood on my clothes when I bit too far or pulled off too much of the skin on my fingertips. "Stop biting your nails Pandora!" she would hiss when we were at the grocery store, the library, a school recital, any place. But I couldn't help it, he would scream, she would cry, I would bite.

And the night, that night, the one that stands out like a bolded bullet point on a fine-printed list, I had a feast, biting every last of my fingernails down to the quick. My parents' story ended with two loud gun-shots, one into her and then a few moments later, after I heard a low moan of mourning from his animal and boorish throat, a second one, for him.

When the police came, they found me under the bed, fingers wet with saliva and blood. And then I became a ward of the state, a foster child. That was when I moved and the little girl Becca was no longer my neighbor and Jacksonville was no longer my home. Those memories flooded my mind as I sat in that classroom biting, freely and madly, in that dark room. My throat was raw from screaming, my back and my knees were sore, and my fingers were in my mouth. I moved methodically from one digit to the next, a process that would need to be completed once started. A habit so bad and buried within my psyche that I thought I would never do it again. Like an alcoholic for my own flesh and nails, *I'll never touch it again*. But I did.

And I fell hard. "Stop biting your nails, Pandora!" I corrected myself. I held both of my hands in my lap; the sting of the exposed skin now fresh and I pressed my hands into my legs to numb the pain. Now, even though I had no metal disc in my thumb, it was still in my pocket, I would look just like the rest of the enslaved humans: distant, in a psychotic daze and with red and puffy fingernails from excessive biting. The strain of the invasion and subsequent imprisonment had pushed what had been locked deep within me up and out of its cage. The darkness of the room enveloped me and I closed my eyes, my trip over the edge was at its end. I slept. With the headless body of the now deceased Barbie not five feet from me, I slept, but not for very long.

I had fallen asleep next to the door, so when the tumbler released in the lock with a loud metallic snap and thud, I heard it very clearly. It was a distinct sound and not one that could have been mimicked by my subconscious in a dream. The door really had been unlocked and next, it would swing open and the wooden edge of the door would slam into my skull if I didn't move. I leaned over hard on my right side and crawled on my right leg and arm to move a few feet out of striking distance of the door. These neuro-muscular reactions happened within seconds and I barely missed the door as it was alive, flying open with such force that it made a loud *clap* against the wall when the doorknob hit into the painted cement blocks that comprised the room.

The light was turned on, and fortunately, the fluorescent tubes whirred to life slowly, apparently just as asleep as I had been a moment earlier. The harsh light took a few minutes to fully generate and my eyes were grateful. The constant presence of them, the aliens, had made my eyes so itchy I was sure all of my eye-lashes must have fallen out from excessive rubbing. My poor swollen lids, my soft and itchy under-eye skin, my haunted face, how unfortunate it was to likely age early and sallow quickly in this environment.

The man, Gael, who had taken me from Mitch in exchange for his daughters' release, was standing in the doorway. I recognized the outfit that he had been wearing in the gymnasium and saw that his shoulder-length black hair was no longer pulled back, but now down and tucked behind his ears. His arms were crossed, and he wore a look of disgust on his face. His skin was pasty and a bland off-white color. He was pale, but had a dark look about his features, bushy black eyebrows, and deep brown eyes. His eyes looked so dark that he could have been the devil himself, inky black pools of greed and contempt. But he was not the devil, just a flawed and ruthless man who had only enough decency to be fair to others, so long as he benefited from the deal.

"Stand up!" he commanded as his stare bored into me like a hot poker. I stumbled to my feet as if I were in some kind of stupor, but my thin grasp on what was happening coupled with a fierce hunger and violently low blood sugar made the efforts of my limbs and joints uncoordinated. My obedience bought me no good will and he continued to snap orders at me, growing more frustrated and harsh with each word. "Face the windows," then "turn and face me," and "hold your arms out straight." These calisthenics were confusing and my head felt light, as though my brain was being tickled with over oxygenated cells, the gray haze in my peripheral vision was slightly entertaining, but not helping in my efforts.

"You struck an officer," he accused me. I hadn't recognized any officers, but then somewhere in the far reaches of my mind, as if it has happened decades ago, I did recall my kicking an alien before I began my screaming fit.

"I don't recognize my occupier as a valid authority," I half-mumbled. I hadn't realized I had actually spoken the words until he lunged forward, slamming the door behind him at the same time in one swift movement. Angry, frustrated, and in need of reasserting his dominance, Gael grabbed me. He moved too quickly to ever dream of fending him off. He crossed the small distance between us, and I could only slightly lift my left arm, an instinct that I had no voluntary control over. He batted it away and took hold of my neck with his right hand. His massive hand spread out and covered the area of my throat without any effort. He was the more powerful person in this equation, and I absolutely hated the defeated and powerless position I was in.

His upper lip curled; his handsome chiseled face released a low snarl at me. I had challenged his authority; I had spoken out. The reality of our existence had become a series of controls. The aliens controlled us all, but Gael and other human overlords had control as well. The aliens couldn't be bothered to manage us all, so men like Gael were put in place to keep us in line, and I had questioned his authority by implying that the aliens had no power over me whatsoever. The invaders had certainly found the right human for this task, Gael was vain and proud. Or perhaps the power they gave him evoked these emotions that otherwise would have laid dormant. But at that moment, I saw in his eyes that the hate and anger that accompanies egomaniacs was alive within him. He was drunk off of the power given to him, but, as I would find out, he was acutely aware of the limits of his authority and was looking for his next move to gain more.

"Don't you ever speak to me that way ever again," he commanded me in a brusque tone. He spat on the floor next to me, to demonstrate how lowly I was. I wanted to defy him, I wanted to spit in his face, I wanted to take him out. I was once a fierce competitor and trained others in MMA and kickboxing. I had once built a cherished temple with my body, but it was in ruins. My muscles had atrophied from hunger and thirst. I was breathing heavily; my heartbeat was fast and I could feel the veins in my temple pulsing as I tried to quell the rage I felt in that moment. His face was so close to mine I could smell his rotten breath, a combination of a day's worth of meals, and he wore the sweet-stink of the aliens on him. My eyes were starting to water from allergic concentrations on his skin, patches of alien atmosphere that were defeating me, making me look weak. My eyes may have been watering, but I was resolute in my need to not back down. Gael had tainted himself forever by associating with them. I stared directly back at him, not wanting to move my eyes down, to cast them lower and offer any action of submission.

And this was what gave me away.

Gael could see how frustrated I was in this position. He had his thumb on my artery and could feel the mad pumping just beneath my skin. I had the will to fight, but common sense to not push the boundaries and risk death, at his hands or those of our intergalactic visitors. He smirked, pleased with his ability to control me and reached for my wrist, he squeezed hard. It felt like he might snap the ulna and the radius of my arm with his bare hands.

I was so focused on my arm that I didn't see him draw back his free hand and punch me hard in the stomach. The air in my lungs burned and I fought to draw more oxygen back in. I bent over slightly, but pulled myself back up, forcing my spine to straighten, but had difficulty achieving this. With my wrist in his hand, Gael forced my attention with a quick jerk.

I didn't want to, but I let out a small whine of pain. It was quick and high pitched, the energy condensed so that it was over before I could even hate myself for showing weakness in front of this man, this human monster, Gael.

I was face to face with him again. I could see some of the long strands of his hair falling in front of his face. Through those strands, I could still see the malice in his eyes. And now he was squinting, examining me, pulling the skin under his eyes tight. He shook my arm forcefully. He lunged his face forward with a loud yell. My heart was racing, his behavior was completely unpredictable and I couldn't anticipate what was coming next. I was frantically trying to think of how to pull away and run, but I would need to appear contrite. I would have to cower in the corner like a beaten puppy, an act that would betray everything within me, but at that moment I needed to get away from him. That's right my brain was processing through my instinctual and evolved flight-or-fight response. And in all that quick thinking it forgot the one acquired reaction that should have also be triggered.

Gael growled at me, a wolf-like crawling growl, it lingered for longer than a breath and made my own throat sore. He bared his teeth and quickly jerked his head forward, then retreated. His face was suddenly calm. A terrifying smirk broke out across his face. I realized what he was doing, he was testing me, my response. His initial intent was to punish, but now he was intrigued by my reactions.

He smacked me across the face and I took in the impact of the blow and closed my eyes, and let the weight of my body pull me down. My trigger or tracker or whatever the official name is for that small piece of metal, had it been implanted, should have put me to sleep much earlier given the level of adrenaline coursing through my veins. The neurotransmitters would have picked up on the auditory, visual and sensory threats being posed by Gael and caused a reaction with the chemical secreted by the metal disc, causing me to lose consciousness. When I hadn't slipped into a sleep sooner Gael became suspicious. I had to play this one better than I ever had before if I didn't want to expose my secret. I started to pull towards the ground, the gravity of my body weight pulling me down, my body balancing precariously as he kept his grasp on my wrist.

I heard Gael moving, doing something with his other hand. I was so curious to know what it was, but I couldn't move. I had to stay still. I slowed my breathing; I tried not to move at all except for an even and metered inhalation and exhalation. It seemed as though the more I concentrated on it, the more uneven it became.

That was when I felt something cool and hard on my navel. "This is my knife, girly," Gael whispered, but it echoed in the concrete classroom, empty except for the stack of desks and chairs in the corner and the sweetly decorated signs dancing around the perimeter of the ceiling. I had to stay silent and still. My instincts told me to open my eyes and assess the truth, but I knew that exposing myself as not being tracked and tagged would be deadly. I didn't know exactly what would happen, but I knew this would be bad.

The sensation on my stomach abated, the knife was removed. I then felt it on my neck. "I could just pull, but I have a feeling you're much more valuable than I initially thought." His words sounded smooth and even, his English well practiced and seductive in this European accent. *How could I be more valuable?* Don and Mitch had already sold everything they could of my body, what else would Gael do now?

He moved the knife up towards my ear, I didn't feel any burning along the line where he dragged the knife, so I concluded that he must not have drawn any blood. I could feel his eyes focused on every detail of my face; I was focusing so completely on remaining impassive. Then, before I could sense anything, he flicked his wrist and cut off the lowest tip of my ear like he was slicing a pear.

I bit my lips to keep myself from screaming out, and I could feel tears build up in my eyes. People that are knocked out by their triggers don't cry, something I would later witness first-hand. I had no choice but to give myself away. I opened my eyes; the hurt and fury I was feeling were powerful. If looks could kill, I would have been able to escape captivity that night and Gael would have met his end much sooner.

Gael yanked me forward and waved his bloody knife at me, tossing the lowest part of my ear away. I would never be able to wear matching earrings again. Greater tragedies had already occurred, and more would surely follow.

He held my arm up, my hand was balled into a fist and he pried my thumb loose. He began to push into my thumb with his left hand, still clutching the handle of his knife. He didn't find what he was looking for so he moved to my index finger. I was so afraid that while he was maneuvering he would slice off one of my fingers. But he didn't.

"You have no trigger," Gael stated what was already known to us.

"I have one," I corrected him. His reaction gave no signs of curiosity, but rather frustration at my insisting that I did have one. "Am I really more valuable without it?"

"Potentially. But if you don't have one and you get caught then you will surely be taken into custody and either have one implanted or you will be murdered on the spot. So, I can't risk having you around them. You are a liability and I should kill you myself, but I could have a use for you." I was uneasy at the prospect of this human trafficker having the power of my life in his hands. I was all out of moves and had only one item left to play.

I took my free hand and moved for my pocket. He squeezed my wrist again, and I held up my hand, to show I meant no harm. He released me and I instinctively went to grab my left wrist to sooth it, but there was no relief. I refocused on why Gael had dropped my hand, to allow me to move at the non-verbal reassurance that I would take no violent actions, and focused on my front pocket. Still buried deep within the fabric, I nabbed the thin metal disc with my fingertips. I could feel blood dripping from my ear onto my shoulder. I wanted to clean my wound and wrap it. My thoughts had switched into recovery mode. My secret was all but lost now.

I lifted out the disc and presented it, still keeping a strong hold on it. "*They* were about to implant it in me when there was a commotion at the hospital. They had tried to get another man to do it, Mitch," I looked at him knowingly to make sure he was aware that I knew who had sold me, "when he refused, they knocked him out. Then two of *them*…"

"Porthana," Gael interrupted.

"P-what?" I asked.

"Porthana, that is what they call themselves. It is one of the easiest words in their language believe it or not," Gael was impressed with himself for having knowledge of their dialect. Now I knew the name of my enemy, but I found no comfort in this. Gael was standing too close; usually, when two people are talking they spread out to fill the space they are in. Perhaps it was his European background, but he stood so close that I could hear the slight hitch of the fabric in his shirt as he inhaled and exhaled.

"Right." I was frustrated by his interruption; I was frustrated by the cavalier manner in which he purchased me from a person who had no ownership over me. I continued my explanation. "The two Porthana in the room argued, one of them was about to do it," I made a slicing gesture at my thumb, "when an alarm went off. Mitch fought back and the trigger fell on the ground. I grabbed it and ran."

Gael reached for the trigger, but I pulled it away and put it back in my pocket. He reached his hand to his mouth and bit at his stubbed nails.

"I will make my decision by this evening." There was no emotion on his face. "If I choose to let you live, you will be permanently transferred to my residence. You are too filthy to enter in your current state. A guard will escort you to the showers. Go and clean up." He pointed to the door and I gladly took the opportunity. I was out of that horrible room and away from that man and I had some time to think and maybe put together a plan of escape, or maybe develop a mechanism to help me survive.

The human guard that had been patrolling the hallway earlier, with the tight jaw and gum, likely stale by now, nudged me forward towards the locker rooms at the end of the hallway. The room smelled dank and moldy. The entire room was covered in one-inch white tiles and the only lights on were by the shower stalls. The guard followed me in and sat down on the tile bench next to the shower stalls. I was fortified by the idea that I could be valuable to Gael, even if that in and of itself was another sentence of servitude. I crossed my arms and pointed to the exit. I would not allow this other man to sit there as I bathed. *I was valuable*, and I was still a person.

The traitorous guard looked at me harshly, I could see he was calculating the potential punishment for harming me in this situation and he either realized it wasn't worth it or burnt his brain cells trying to do the math, so he walked out and slammed the door behind him. I started the water, expecting that it would produce a thumping sound followed by the silence of a system with no running water. But to my surprise water did pour out, ice cold. It tickled my hands and I was grinning madly at the thought of actual running water. It had been two weeks since I had felt the rush of water on my skin. I turned the knob so that more hot water could pull in and waited a moment, expecting some toxin that the Porthana might have placed in the water supply to knock me out. But it didn't.

I took my clothes off slowly. Still uneasy, expecting some new threat to appear at any moment, I was cautious. I hunched over myself as I peeled my bloodstained and sand-encrusted shirt from my body. My pants, once skin tight were loose and fell to the floor easily. I folded them quickly as I stood naked and exposed on the cold tile floor of the locker room showers. I placed my only articles of clothing on the bench and turned to the waiting shower, steam just now visible over the curtain.

I thought the better of it and reached for my pants again and took out the trigger from my pocket. If it was something that could be valuable and might save my life, then I would never let it out of my sight, even if it was a symbol of alien oppression, it also became a symbol of my potential escape. I inserted it into my mouth.

I lingered in the hot shower, waiting for the flow of the water to run clean over my ear. When it finally did, the pain burned from the cut and the orange-red streak of diluted blood that flowed down my left side mixed with the dirt and grit of my body. I felt like a low human, I felt like an animal, a mongrel, a piece of waste. I started to scrub my body using my hands and the water alone to get the dirt off of me. I tried to get the water into my hair and began the painful process of pulling at each greasy knot and trying to make it smooth. But the water could not get rid of the buildup of oil by itself.

I took an inventory of my body. My left knee, though healing, was still swollen and visibly bigger than the right knee. My skin was completely covered with a thin layer of filmy sweat, dried and covered in ambient dust that had been collecting for weeks. I felt the velvety build up on my teeth with my tongue and after I had scrubbed my hands until they looked clean, I rubbed my teeth with my fingertips. I tried to push the plaque off so I could no longer taste or feel it. I could see my rib bones beneath my chest and my strong and lean muscles that had once defined me and my years of work were now dulled from lack of use, the tight and exact lines of my abdominal muscles now faded behind the skin. My legs looked the worst, the hard muscle that had once been there had withered and now my thighs appear to be much farther apart than they had been. My hip bones were starting to pop out as well.

I tried to think my way out of the situation. Mitch had made it clear that I shouldn't discuss the trigger with anyone, but he had turned out to be a liar. This was the one secret I had kept from everyone, even though I did have limited exposure to others, that I was untagged. I had never worried about leaving the trigger in my pocket, but now I had to be cautious. I felt it with my tongue. The taste was sour and I thought it had a trace of blood on it, the flavor was in my mouth.

Maybe, I could gain Gael's trust by discussing the trigger with him and convince him I could be a valuable asset. I hated Gael, he was a traitor to humanity, but I wanted to live. I hated all men at this point because since the invasion not one had told the truth or treated me like a person. All men are profoundly flawed and socially conditioned to subjugate women. I would hate all of them forever. I would also retain a weakness for wanting to trust others despite my instincts, but that is for later.

I turned off the water and dried my body with a towel. I was slow and methodical in my efforts, gingerly touching the towel to my skin, sensing that each touch brought me back to a reality that I so desperately wanted to escape. I found a first-aid kit affixed to one of the walls in the locker room and used the available bandages to patch up my ear. It was still bleeding and I knew that I had a high risk of infection. I looked at myself in the mirror as I dressed the wound, focusing on my ear. I caught a glimpse of the woman who was supposed to be me. But she looked nothing like me. She was weak and a victim and tired and looked as though she had aged from a healthy and nubile twenty-year-old to a hardened and haggard twenty-five-year-old in a manner of weeks. I tried to ignore my face, but there it was. After several layers of tape, I had a tightly packed, compact bandage on my left ear. I found a marker in the first aid kit and drew a diamond on the tip of the bandage, now I would have an earring on my left ear after all.

I dressed, again very careful to not be caught in a compromising position if someone, or something, barged through the door. I removed the trigger from my mouth and examined it, unchanged by my unsanitary human saliva. I stared at it for a few moments and marveled at the design and exacting nature of the device and the years of study and countless failed experiments that cost human lives in order to allow the aliens, the Porthana as they had been identified, to create such a device. I placed it back in my pocket and tried to not think of it anymore for the evening. But it felt hot against the fabric and I wondered if the same routine that had been run when I was on display in the gymnasium was being run now. But the metal didn't burn quite as hot as it had earlier so I relaxed, ever so slightly; I relaxed to a state of mere panic rather than full adrenaline blazing fight-or-flight.

I brushed my hair with my fingers, now clean, but still chaffed from my mindless gnawing. The process of cleaning myself for Gael's inspection was low of me, but the animal inside me longed to survive, even though my soul was already in the terminal stages of dying. I examined my clammy olive skin, now distorted, and the once vibrant green in my eyes, which was now a deep and cool forest green. I had the same overall look, but something was different, and it would never be the same again. I counted to ten inside my head and made myself promise that I would never look into another mirror again. Promises are broken all the time, but I did try in earnest to keep this one.

When I was finished with my clean-up I walked over to the door. It felt natural to be free to come and go as I pleased, but as I reached for the long handle on the door, I realized that I was not free at all. What would happen if I opened the door, but I wasn't supposed to? *Should I knock to signify that I am ready to leave? What would an act of submission like that cost me? What would it gain me?* In the moments I spent debating this decision I heard quick footsteps in the hallway, they were getting louder and coming my way. I stepped back from the door and, again, it flung open just seconds after I moved. Another close call.

Gael stood with his large and dominant hand holding the door open, his face was stern. At this point, I thought that this man must never have smiled in his life, and instead of finding that thought to be sad and pathetic, I was somewhat happy at his potential misery. He didn't deserve to smile, and I reasoned that it was likely that the things that would make him smile would be truly depraved.

"For now, you will live." His announcement was brief. I suppose I should have felt a wave of relief, but I accepted this fact plainly and without emotion. Now I was once again trading one prison for another. This bartering of my captivity would need to work to my advantage or else I would be stuck in this cycle for the rest of my time on Earth.

I nodded to let him know that I acknowledged his announcement. I didn't want to make eye contact so I continued to look over at the door.

"It is late, we are done here for the day. You will follow me now." Gael stepped aside and the door started to swing shut. I let the wooden door hit the frame and let the loud wh-bang fill the room. It was final then. I stood there for about thirty seconds and then willed myself to move. I opened the door and followed Gael, now ten or so feet down the hallway towards the exit on the other side of the Gymnasium. I would leave this place forever and never see the walls of this school that had been turned into a prison ever again.

I was surprised that I was allowed to follow him without a guard at my back. I sensed that everyone else had already left the school building, it seemed quiet and empty. My eyes were not burning, so the aliens had perhaps retreated to another venue or my allergies were building a tolerance. (What Gael eventually explained to me was that the aerosol poison that they used during their invasion caused the reaction, it was all over their exo-suits and eventually abated once they all cleaned themselves. It made me wonder how much human blood was still on their suits as well. Gael never responded to that question.)

Gael did not hold the door open for me, he breezed through it and by the time I caught up it was about to slam shut. I pushed my arms out to catch it. I was glad that he did not try to be sickly sweet or overly polite. I wouldn't have liked that fake kindness. I was glad that he showed his true self at all times. It helped me to clearly see him for who he was, I had no misgivings about the depths of his evil nature.

Once outside I saw that it was dark, deadly dark out. No stars were visible in the sky and no bright street lamps illuminated the parking lot that Gael was starting to cross into. I could barely see him as he moved across the fresh black asphalt. Had the alien invasion not occurred, it would have looked like any other school parking lot. But the invasion did happen, and there was a mangled and burnt school bus on the far end of the lot to show for it. The orange-yellow metal was barely visible under the charred and smoky ash covering the debris. Gael had reached a vehicle, just as black as the night surrounding us and opened the driver-side door.

I hurried from the building and across the parking lot. I could run, in any direction. I had been able to run a mile in six and a half minutes, which would set no records, but would have carried me far. But I was no longer in peak physical shape, and Gael had a car, which gave him a clear upper-hand. If I took off running, he would see me and run me down before I made it out of the lot and across the desert plain into the dark mountains. I knew that this would happen so I didn't even attempt to run. Maybe one day, when my body was back in shape, I would take off. My lofty dream began to take shape.

Gael was now seated in the car, but he hadn't started the engine. I headed toward the passenger side, and as I crossed in front of the vehicle, he flipped the headlights on. I stood for a moment in the light, staring directly at him, looking like a doe caught in front of a vehicle, too scared to move. I folded my arms across my body and slowly stepped over to the passenger side. I grabbed the handle and found that the door was still locked. I grabbed it again, and the door wouldn't budge.

Perhaps I should sit in the back? I thought and I shifted my weight, leaning over to the left and grabbed at the rear door handle. It was also locked.

The engine started and I began to panic. If I was left here, then I might starve or it might be a trap, and I could be recaptured by the Porthana. I wanted to escape this man, but I also wanted the security of knowing I would live until morning. My conflicting human desires for safety and freedom battled as I panicked. The motor under the window whirred as it descended, leaving a space of open air between myself, on the outside, and Gael, on the inside.

"Obedience and silence." His voice was crisp and clear over the hum of the engine. "These are my only two requirements, defy me and I will shoot you myself." I nodded and the door lock released. I grabbed the handle and quickly got into the car. I closed the door and I was now in a confined space, a motorized weapon, with Gael.

I sat quietly as he navigated the parking lot and surrounding streets. There was litter starting to build up by the curbs, but nothing excessively dirty. Most of the streetlights were out, but I was used to dark evenings growing up in Florida (the land of no sidewalks or streetlights). There were no other cars moving on the road, we passed a few that were pulled over on the side, one or more doors torn and laid on the ground. I felt a shiver run up my spine as I thought about how those doors became detached, making me think of that moment when I was thrown from the false-safety of Don and Becca's car.

As my eyes passed over what was visible in the dark, I could tell that this had once been more than just a town, it had been a community. And now it was a detention center, a wasteland for some of the remaining humans to be examined and enslaved. The past three weeks had revealed the worst of humanity and that life out there in the universe was not peaceful or welcoming, but that it was destructive and exacting.

Gael remained silent throughout the drive. I was left to stare out the passenger window in peace. The lights were not functioning, but I could still see a grocery store, with the front door shattered and food containers strewn across the ground. I saw bodies lying in the streets, mangled and bloodied and left for the scavengers. I had primarily been focused on the back-roads, the back-woods since the invasion, avoiding places with large concentrations of people. And now I saw what happened to most of those people. I saw wild animals, coyotes, and wolves hunting in packs across lawns and sidewalks, picking their way through the leftover human bodies and domesticated house animals. I saw the end of humanity and wished I had been taken quickly in one of the early explosions on that first day. I didn't want to see any of this, I didn't want to know how bad things were. I didn't want to see how bad they would become. I didn't want any part of it.

In the darkness of the evening, as my eyes glanced across the expanse of the sky with no hope for warmth or light, I felt truly alone. Even in the past few weeks, even when I was being attacked or when I was on the run, or when I was hiding, I was with another person. But now, sitting in this black car with a man whose soul was infinitely darker than black, I felt isolated and alone. It was the first time in over a decade that I considered praying to God. I quickly dismissed this option as the wreckage in front of me was evidence enough that a God did not exist, or that if he/she did exist, that they must not care about our suffering.

As the sedan glided along the streets and we headed further west, there were fewer and fewer signs of life. Gael kept his left hand on the steering wheel, directing the vehicle. His right hand was resting on the console between our seats. It was too close to me and I was dangerously aware of its presence. Finally, after fifteen minutes of driving in complete darkness, with only the headlights to provide a limited range of light in front of the vehicle, Gael turned and we passed by a sign that read "The ENCLAVE at Desert Point."

The front gate was terracotta and there had once been full statues to stand guard at the entrance, but they were now pulverized, only the bases remained as evidence that they had once existed. Past the entrance were a series of curved roads that passed by large lumps of blackened debris. It was only the site of red-hot embers atop a few of these lumps that revealed that the houses that once comprised this development, were now all reduced to rubble. We passed by smoldering piles for what seemed like a never-ending period of time, navigating deeper and deeper into a maze. Once a huge McMansion community, all but three houses were burnt to the ground. The saved edifices were on a cul-de-sac, an ashen kingdom spread out around them. The houses were massive, each with a three-car garage and grand front entrances. House lust had fueled the desire for these pre-formed homes that the upper middle class, and those desperate to enter it, so quickly gobbled up. The manicured lawns were starting to brown and whither, but those three houses were unscathed by the neighboring blazes. They were the last that remained of that Enclave, the only ones that were safe, or so it seemed.

The first house, I would later find out, was for the Porth commander. It was an enigmatic creature who I never saw out of the house, but whose dark shadow would often pass by the side window that faced the front room of Gael's house.

Gael's was in the middle of the other two and when walking up the long road to the houses, it would appear just over a shallow hill, ominous and massive. The two houses, one on either side of Gael's, stood as witness to the daily brow-beating I would receive from the top windows as we returned to his house. The shudders adorning those windows hid the horrors of my time in that house like eye-lids snapping shut at the thought of pain. The third house, stood empty. I would later realize it was only there as a reminder to Gael that he was replaceable. It was the threat that he too could find himself a pile of pulverized bones below a mound of ashes.

Gael pressed a button on the center console of the armrest and the garage door opened, loudly as though rust had filled every inch of the track. Once inside he closed the garage door from inside the car and I was entombed in the mansion. Gael got out of the car, again without a single word of instruction and entered the house through a side door off to the left. I was waiting, wondering if I was supposed to stay or not, and eventually, the motion-activated lights in the garage went out. I expected him to come back in and berate me for not moving quickly enough. I would not have been caught off guard if he came back with some sort of weapon to assault me with or some means of restraining me. But he did none of these things.

I've had a lot of free time recently, and what I realized was that with each action I took that evening: walking to the car, getting in the car, silently riding with no protest, and then eventually going into the house, I was bolstering a psycho-social relationship where Gael's actions were dominant to mine. I had taken each of these steps myself, though it was clear to me that I was not free, and therefore was accepting my place as a servant, as his property. Or some other Freudian bullshit like that.

When I did enter the house, I did so quietly, not sure if I should expect a shovel to the gut or yet another bag over my head. The first hallway was covered with a warm yellow light, and it was strongest at the end of the hall. I noticed how spotless the floors were and felt ashamed that my muddy shoes would clearly mark them up, but with my ever-dampening defiance, I strode with force down the hall, hoping to knock some dirt clods loose.

There was a powder room at the end of the hall, I caught my image as it passed the mirror from the side of my eye and almost gave myself a heart attack. Once I gathered myself, I took a few deep breathes and felt appreciative that there was no metal pin on my hand that would cause me to collapse, given how on-edge I was as I navigated the first ten feet of the house.

"Dora!" Gael's voice boomed, as though it was all around me at once. I heard three footsteps and his tall figure peered around the edge of the hallway. "Of course, it's just you," he said with a tone of disappointment. *Was he expecting someone else? Was he worried about an intruder?*

He leaned back to where we had been standing, now obscured from view and I hastily finished the few feet left between us and found him in the dining room. He was just sitting down at the end of the table. Candles were lit, the wine was poured, and the table was full of food. It was the mirage I had hoped to see in the desert, but it was real. All of that food was real. This man had food in ample quantities!

The first night he had a stately dinner prepared. Fresh meats that were still sizzling were served on fine dishes. It appeared that while the rest of humanity was running like cockroaches when the lights came on, Gael and the other traitors to our species were working with the Porths to build their fiefdoms, complete with slaves and formal dining rooms. I regret how greedily I stared and salivated at the food, but that regret has only come now. That evening I was glad to take in the sweet aromas and the tantalizing smells of fresh food.

I walked straight to the table, entranced by the spread. It was not until I was at the table, my hips knocked into the edges, that I questioned what was in front of me. *Will I be allowed to have any? Will it be poisoned? Will I be drugged? Will I be able to stop myself even if I find out that it will kill me?*

Gael seemed to be reading my mind. "You'll want to eat now." He was digging into the steak in front of him, possibly two inches thick and a bright red in the center. His knife was sawing into the flesh too comfortably for me and I thought of the dull pain in my ear and the cold hard plate of metal that he had held to my stomach only a few hours earlier.

I took a seat and tried to steady my shaking hands as I reached for what was in front of me. Bread. Rolls of delicious tan and yellow. I was content to eat only this bread for the rest of my small and insignificant life, but then there was a spiral ham close by as well. And potatoes. And broccoli. And spinach. And cakes! There were cakes!

A dark-skinned man emerged from the entry-way behind Gael. For a moment I briefly panicked, but simultaneously hoped that this was the intruder that Gael might have been worried about. Perhaps this unidentified man was about to smash the crystal goblet in his hand over Gael's head. Perhaps he would free me. But instead, he passed the goblet to Gael and nodded silently. Gael gave no words of thanks only a solemn jutting of his jaw forward and then back into place.

"Sundeep, this is Pandora." The man in the suit, dirty and wrinkled and possibly in need of dry-cleaning, grinned at me briefly, with a hint of surprise in his eyes, and walked away. Gael, focused on the goblet handed to him, paid no attention to Sundeep as he left the room, and continued to chew on the fatty meat rolling on his tongue. Gael took his wine glass and poured half of it into the goblet. Then he reached into his front pocket and pulled out a plastic bag with a white powder.

"That trigger that you keep in your pocket emits a neurotoxin when the levels of adrenaline and non-adrenaline reach a certain level within the bloodstream. Since your trigger has no means of measuring this, it is ineffective on you at the moment. This," he held the bag and shook it gently between his fingers, wagging it at me, "is the solid form of that neurotoxin. The Porths spent years perfecting it from their ships before they were ready to invade. They developed an aerosol for their initial invasion," at the mention of this I thought of the plumes of smoke along Bayshore Boulevard, the longest continuous sidewalk in North America with beautiful views of Tampa Bay, and on the day of the invasion, a death trap. "This should be enough," he took out a small portion with his tablespoon and dropped it into the goblet. He took the glass by the stem and swirled the wine and powder together. He placed the glass back on the table and slid it towards me.

"Why would I drink that?"

"Dora, I could have just given that to you without your knowledge, I mixed it in front of you for your benefit." Gael dismissed my question without bothering to answer it. I began to wonder if this had been a recent routine of his. How many others had been promised a life under his thumb only to be killed in privacy?

"Still, why should I drink that? I don't want their toxin in my system."

"Dora, you are going to have to accept that *they* are in control of this planet and in this house, *I* am in control. You are free to drink it or not drink it, but my guess is that you'd prefer to not have memories of this evening." This statement told me two things:

1) that something horrible would surely happen to me in a short amount of time and

2) that I would live to see the next morning where memories would potentially be played back in my mind.

He didn't have to speak for me to know what his next words would have been, they were all over his face, all over the table and spread out under my feet. The spoils of war. He felt entitled to all that was in front of him, but more so it was as though he was bored to have to take it all. He had soured on the glut of taking and taking and taking after so short a time, but he would continue to abide by the archaic standard. He thought of himself as being merciful for giving me an out, so to speak, but he was evil and only another evil man would excuse his behavior based on the premise that he was collecting on the spoils of a war that was being waged against his own species.

I glared at him as he ate the food on his plate, as calm and unattached as a man enjoying a good meal before returning to a long drive on the road. He was complacent and had quickly grown accustomed to his lavish lifestyle.

I took the glass reluctantly and drank it.

Why? Why did I comply with his request, why didn't I just pretend to drink it so that I could make my escape in the night and keep running? Why didn't I try to stab him with the butter knife, millimeters from my fingertips? I had run each scenario in my head. I could have tried to stab him. But he was tall, and I could tell that he was in moderately good shape. With one jab in his hand, I could hit tendons and not bone, it would only be enough to anger him, not stop him from lashing out at me. I could have pretended to sip on this drink and then make an unexpectedly lucid attempt at escape, but with my knee still recovering I likely would have hobbled less than a mile before being captured or just shot outright. And finally, I could have been defiant and brave and a strong woman who would face her punishment from this stranger with my faculties intact. I could have done this for the pride of my fellow females and the triumph of the human spirit. But I had already endured enough nightmares from the manipulation and molestation at the hands of Don. Gael was, regrettably, right. I didn't want to remember what would happen to me. So, I sipped the glass down, slowly and calmly until it was empty.

I gnawed at the bread that I had been so eager to devour until I felt a numbness coming over my face and hands. My nose felt like a rubber attached to my face, malleable and soft. The numbness was so omnipresent, yet elusive. I surrendered to the drugs and with it surrendered to my imprisonment with Gael.

For the time being the drugs were the only escape I could manage. In the morning when I did awake, I forgot what had happened for a moment. I was on a bed, with a sheet pulled up around me. There was a ceiling fan above cycling and whirring keeping the room cool. There was the smell of fresh eggs and bacon and a soft sizzle emanating from the kitchen. I could see soft light coming into the house through the open bedroom door. It was as though I had awoken from a nightmare and was now in a blissfully suburban reality.

But as I rolled onto my back and yawned, stretching my arms above me I was stopped. Chains that were cuffed to my arms stopped me from reaching further. My leg was softly in pain. My ear was sore. I was still in that reality. I wanted to sob and cry out each bit of disappointment that I felt. But instead, I closed my eyes and let all of the free-flowing emotion crunch and distort my face.

I heard movement on the stairs. I turned onto my side, my back to the door.

"Breakfast is prepared, I will find suitable clothing for you shortly. For now, you will dine here." Gael's brusque tone was the dreaded groan that I hated to hear. It was as though he was managing a pet, eat this, do that.

He was in the room now; I could hear him approaching the bed. I was suddenly very aware that I was naked under the covers and that I truly did have no recollection of the previous evening. I had been used, once again. I did a quick mental check to see what other pains I could feel. Yes, I felt sore on my thighs and I felt that skin of my labia crawl with disgust. I was a human pit, a dark void and there was no one who would care or bother to serve up justice. I would have to be the one to do it and I was losing my sanity.

I looked down at the foot of the bed through my half-opened eyes. Gael was right next to me. His hand touched my wrist. I flicked it away from him. I could see the anger in his eyes, but he waited to react. He took a key from his pocket and reached again for my wrist, this time I allowed him to hold it long enough to unlock me. I hated each second.

He left the room and I pounced on the plate that he left on the floor. The eggs burned my throat from being so hot, but I couldn't stop myself. After my sickeningly quick meal, I took an assessment of my leg by bending it, trying to stretch it, to see how it had healed and what still needed to be regenerated.

I sat naked looking at the four walls that surrounded me. The room was a soft beige with gold curtains. There were discolorations on the paint where the sun had faded the areas not covered by photos or posters, leaving bolder blocks of the wall where the sun had once been obscured. I was in someone else's house. The inhabitants were likely dead. Almost everyone now was dead. I was able to accept this thought much better now than in the first week of the invasion. The extreme violence was causing my perception to become calloused; my heart was hardening to human weakness. The inhumanity of the Porthana, and their human lackey, Gael, began to wear at my own humanity. It began to dry and flake, pulling away from me in small pieces with each minuscule movement I made to survive.

Gael did indeed find me clothing; he had raided some of the closets of the community before it had been incinerated. I realized that morning that he had planned to take a captive woman, he had planned to nab himself a female. His small Neanderthal mind had planned to find a club and drag someone back to the cave, that someone was me. He dressed me in sharp lines and solid colors. I was a docile and dolled up trophy to be his attendant. Gael had a very specific role, he monitored the humans being dragged in from the outskirts and sorted them as he saw fit, he appeased the Porthana, and was entrusted to keep the population calm and compliant with what the aliens had intended for us. As the human over-seer, he had a speech to make to the enslaved humans mining in the desert. I was to accompany him because with my un-triggered little fingers I was valuable and not to be let out of his sight.

I went along quietly. I was determined to observe, to take note, to try to get a grasp on what was going on so that I could one day evade and escape. We gathered at what was called Out-station Two. This station was mining for minerals. This appeared to be the main purpose of the invasion, to harvest finite resources. The cruelty to the human race was an ancillary effort to study us in order to advance the Porthana knowledge of our physiology, supposedly to aid in the invasion of other planets.

On the drive over I saw the dusty sidewalks of the town littered with dirty people. It seemed that those who were allowed to live were left to find shelter for themselves. The men and women were caked in desert sand and sweat, perhaps I should have been more grateful for a place to sleep and bathe and clean clothes. Perhaps the price I paid for them was too high. I saw men fighting over food, women cowering in the small patches of shadow by buildings that would soon be completely engulfed in the mid-day sun. The men starting to throw punches at each other, pushing and shouting. They both stopped and collapsed simultaneously, their anger and aggression triggering a reaction. I wondered if their heads hit the concrete too hard? *Would they wake up? Would they lay bleeding? Would they be mugged while they were unconscious?* I could only guess as Gael sped past, unaware and unruffled by the sadness around him.

Before the speech, I asked to use the restroom. Gael was hesitant, but I opened my mouth just enough to reveal the metal trigger that was sitting on my tongue. He had bought my silence, but I had bought his as well. Surely if I was to be killed for the "crime" of being captured and untagged, he would face some punishment for harboring me. We were mutually incarcerated to the same fate, and I began to think of a way to outsmart him.

Gael, the tall and handsome Spaniard, was our human overlord, answering to the aliens and serving as a middle-man to keep us in line. To me he was a mercenary, selling out his own species. I wanted to hide in that restroom stall indefinitely, but it reeked. One of the enslaved women had whispered about him in the lavatory. They sounded giddy, as though they might catch his eye and fall madly in love. In this place, in this epoch of human history, perhaps the last, there was no love. There was no light. The small pockets of human triumph that had worked hard to keep their candles lit were extinguished. The smoke had dissipated. There was no hope of warmth. And these women were hopeful that he might rescue them in some romantic fashion. Were they stupid enough to not understand? Surely, they had to be somewhat smart to have survived this long, but then again Barbie had survived for three weeks and she was fairly dull.

Among these frivolous females, forgetting the horrors done to their body, or threatened against their body daily, they swooned over Gael. I was sure he was gladly accepting of physical favors, I already hated him and I hated the naiveté of the women I overheard. One of the girls had whispered that he had given her extra helpings of watered-down potatoes and winked at her. The other said that she heard he used to race formula one cars. The rumor mill was churning, at least one of humanities best-honed practices had survived.

I knew that Gael had never been a racecar driver. Our brief one-sided conversation on the ride to this station had revealed that his occupation pre-invasion, did not differ much from his current line of work. Pushing drugs, providing discipline, keeping women in line, only the Porthana had elevated his set of skills so he was able to profit from his past life of crime and nefarious activities. But certainly not a racecar driver.

Even before the planet was threatened, I could never understand the hypocrisy of racing. Drivers would burn gallons and gallons of fuel and no one once suggested the sport should be abolished in favor of quelling the demand on the finite resource. Racers, pyramid scheme salesmen, and telemarketers all have a level together in hell, just above people who market cigarettes, but below people who create sham charities to rip people off. I made myself smile with my small joke, and then quickly realized that the majority of the population of the planet had met their maker and the lines leading into both heaven and hell were likely to be full.

I exited the stall and brushed past the shallow and vapid women. They appeared to have been spared what I had already been through. They hadn't seen how quickly a man can turn into a monster and how even the most sacred parts of our souls can be sold when water and food are scarce. I knew that if they survived it wouldn't be long. I felt sad that they would soon share my fate.

I didn't want to hear their idle prattling about the handsome Gael anymore. I would stand where I was told for this assigned gathering and listen and remain silent. But I would keep my eyes on the exits, and the ceilings.

I could tell that this had not been his first rousing speech. It was the first day of the fourth week of our alien occupation, but they already seemed to be well established with rules, lines, routines, and management. They had been unexpectedly efficient and thorough.

The assembly took place by a field, a barren space with golden and red clay below our feet and clear blue skies above us, save for the structure of corrugated metal where we had been instructed to enter. It looked like an airplane hangar, but it was too narrow, or perhaps a warehouse, but it was too short. We could have very well been on a Martian sand-dune for how unreal this moment was. But we were of Earth.

I didn't want to make polite conversation as we waited, I didn't care to get to know any them, those few remaining humans. I wanted to be alone, even though I was afraid of my solitude. I wanted to strike out on my own and head north into colder climates, perhaps on my own no one could betray me. Being stuck in the desert with so many people, and Porths, made me beyond nervous. I was anxious. Taking a cursory glance around, I could see that everyone else was nervous as well, all fidgeting with their hands, biting their nails and cuticles, and scratching their arms.

That's what we were reduced to, a band of stooping, shuffling, and huddling nailbiters. And that is what each human I observed was doing. They were picking and biting, chewing and peeling their fingernails raw. Some sat in ecstasy as they scratched away at their thumbs or their index fingers, releasing the itch and soothing the desire. It was such a profound need and want. It was clearly more important than food, people set down their forks to scratch and bite. The implanted metal was a foreign object and the body was constantly sending white blood cells, trying to destroy the device, but completely ineffective. I was relieved to be fortunate enough to not know the urge. But for the rest of humanity it was a "common unspoken", everyone sensed it, everyone felt it, everyone understood it. But no one ever talked about it, they just kept biting and scratching, defacing their digits until they bled.

Without the beguilement of media and guise of our social identities, we were all left with the option to truly look at one another, see each other and let others see ourselves. This was more than we could handle. Invasion, sure, terror, sure; we all saw that in our lives. We had lived through an unending war and attacks on native-soil. But having to be forced to peel away the layer of our own self-isolation? Never. We couldn't handle it; we were all going mad. We were all just about to snap.

There was a raised platform at the far back of the building, I made my way to the make-shift stage and took my place in the back corner, again under the watchful eye of Gael. While some distracted and idiotic women may have thought he was divine, I felt secure in the fact that he could not walk on air.

Gael began his speech, his voice moving with a soft cadence, his curled accent subtle, but noticeable. He paced slowly and deliberately across the platform and then to the other side. He explained our role and purpose in this compound. He was a viper, and he was surprisingly fooling them all.

"You are here to help with the last great effort of our species. Our visitors need our help. And while we may not be happy with the manner by which they have expressed their needs, we will help them. Because if we help them, then we can go about our time and do as we please.

"I am here to make this easier for you all. I will make sure that each of you has a bed and food to eat if you will make sure to follow through on what I ask." Gael was gesturing and emphasizing his words. It was clear from the way they looked that not all of these people had food or a place to sleep; would they revolt against Gael? *Oh right, that stupid trigger.* All I could spot were the lies and manipulation laced on each syllable. So well calculated, like he was the mathematician of our undoing. We were not free to leave, meaning we were imprisoned. There was no notion of helping towards a greater good anywhere, his words were so blatantly false.

"Each of you will be assigned a task. If you are not up to the task you may be reassigned or asked to leave." I wanted to roll my eyes, I looked at my shoes. I silently wished for another dose of whatever delirium had been administered the day before. *Asked to leave? Did he mean thrown in the long ditch?*

"In the past month, we have all had to question what it is to be human." He paused for effect and furrowed his eyebrows. "And ultimately what every man wants, what every woman wants, what every human wants is to be autonomous."

He said the word so delicately, as though it was the most beautiful and fragile thing in the universe. To be autonomous. I was almost inclined to believe him, after all, I had been focused solely on living, and protecting myself the best way I knew how. I had craved that independence and thirsted for freedom even more now that it had been snatched from me.

But he was wrong. I did not want to be autonomous; no human success ever came from autonomy. No inventions, leaps in science, or communities ever functioned with people working alone. They all happened in conjunction with others, and what was more, all of those efforts were for the benefit of others, not an individual. Autonomous? No, Gael, this is not correct. But I could see some of the others in the crowd nodding along. This was how easy it was to brainwash a population. A handsome smile, a dangling carrot, and the rotten stench of what their fate would be emanating from a deep hole, not one hundred meters from where we all stood.

Gael continued. "Each of us wants to decide what we want to do and when we want to do it, with no one telling us how we should dress or think or act." He paused and the silent nods of compliance turned into murmurs of agreement. The irony was lost on the masses.

"So, if we are to gain our autonomy, then we must sacrifice a small amount of time to the Porthana. Are you with me?" Gael raised his arms, and some in the crowd applauded. I looked around in disbelief. *This is how they will brainwash us.* I remember very clearly defining this moment as one in which my brain was subjected to advanced manipulation skills, of which I would not succumb to. I knew that to survive I would need to become one of the hive, but to escape I would need to circumvent further attempts from Gael, his bumbling drones, and those commanding him.

Every man for himself was the motto and creed of Gael. And he would play along with the Porthana and continue to help them so long as they treated him favorably. But he knew that the day would come when they would no longer need him, or when they might cross him. It was inevitable because no matter how much he betrayed other humans, he was still one of us. I was his leverage. At first, he hadn't riddled out how to use me, but he acquired me like a "Get Out Of Jail Free" card in the game of Monopoly. He didn't need me now, but I could potentially be valuable in the future. I was eager to solve this as well, to be able to define my own way, but I had to wait.

I waited for weeks and then months. I would be drugged each evening. I would awake in some new state of trauma or delirium. These were my days as an automaton. I functioned, I walked, I stood, I ate, I defecated. I did the basic things that my body and Gael required. Each morning brought a new set of bruises and cuts, dried blood on my hands and thighs. If I hadn't been too stoned to care I might have tried to solve each riddle of evidence on my body like a mystery. But I didn't. I had shut down, turned off the curiosity that had propelled my mind to comprehension in those first few weeks. Maybe that same mechanism that gave me a false protection actually betrayed me, if I had remained engaged and curious, I might have riddled it out sooner.

And why not stay distracted and doped? It made it easier to ignore my own pain and to casually shuffle by the pain of others. I could see their suffering in the periphery and not blink. I saw the metal clasps sticking through the flesh of some who had been experimented on, and did nothing. We did this to each other before; we have always had a habit of ignoring the pain of others. Why not continue to do so now? Men starving, women naked and beaten in the street. It was a menagerie of human hurt and we were all too scared or nervous to act. We were a docile and captive population. Well done Porthana, well done.

I let the panic and anxiety be drowned by the drugs, and when they wore off, I bit and I nibbled and I ate at my fingers until they were raw from fear. And as if on command, as if somehow sensing that my fingers were in my mouth, making them unclean and sticky, Gael would command, "Stop biting your nails, Pandora." This phrase haunted me as I was tasked with actual work, which would have been appreciated if it had not been forced on me. I was a cog in the Porth created and murder-driven machine that had become our small society in the aftermath.

Gael, the tall man with his long stringy brown hair and skin the color of thick paste, never liked to run a legitimate operation unless it could be used as a front for some nefarious activity. He liked the danger and hustle of what he could do off-the-books. Strictly speaking, I was an off-the-books human. No tracker, no living person to check-in on me. I was his best-hidden operation yet, and he kept me in plain sight. The front was that I would work during the day, but really, he was using me for what he could get away with in the evenings.

The work was in a bar, of all places. The establishment had been called The Snake Pit pre-invasion; the name remained when new management took over. Gael devised a scheme not long after I was taken into his custody to continue to keep the human population docile and complacent. He would drug them, his fellow humans, but he would do it with their consent. I guess he did have some small conscience, but it was minuscule and often worked too well with his evil tendencies. He opened a bar in the main hub between the five outlying stations where the human population was sent to toil. At the end of a hard day's labor slaving away and mining for minerals, the people would stumble into the bar dirty and exhausted. Gael would use this bar as a front to push the powered neurotoxin, the same he had been using on me, as a drug. Those looking for an escape could purchase it serving as an additional revenue stream. Gael said *they* called it HEX-P. Some asked for it in a bag and left quickly, hiding it in their pockets. Some enjoyed it with their drinks, a luxury becoming more and more expensive as reserves of alcohol would run dry eventually with no new production. Gael was rolling in food ration tickets and favors. He accumulated his wealth and displayed it well.

The bar also served as a means for Gael to entertain the Porthana leaders and sell some of the waitresses to them. I was never sold out because that would risk exposing my untracked little finger. I was to observe and stay close. I would gnaw at my fingers each evening as the doors opened, afraid each night that Gael's scheme would be uncovered. I was sure that the Porthana would not appreciate being cut out of his drug deals, and for this perceived theft he would lose his life, and I would lose the small modicum of safety that Gael had afforded. There was another level involved in this I'm sure, but I didn't figure it all out. The aliens wanted us docile, but it was also clear that Gael was breaking some rules in his actions.

Three months into the occupation I had adjusted to a new normal, but I still felt like a visitor in someone else's demented daydream. As I settled into my constant numb feeling, my fingers were fumbling to grip onto reality and with their rubbery loose inability to take hold I started to act more genuine around Gael. Although I was disgusted, I was spared. The fog of barbiturates in my system blunted my constant anger and shame so that I could carry on a halfway decent conversation with the man.

I'm not sure if I've gained any sympathy from you, and I believe that I don't deserve it. I could have done more; I could have suffered more so that maybe others might have been spared. I could have at least tried. I'm writing all of this down in the futile chance that if any living being ever reads it, this is the only way to purge the guilt, it is the only refuge from the lashes I deal myself with my own thoughts. But onward, this is the real reason I've brought you, the imagined and improbable you, to this place.

One morning at breakfast, Gael gave me specific instructions. "Keep an eye on Meryl and Whitney. I think one of them is pocketing additional tips from the Porth officers when they finish. I need to keep them in line." Meryl and Whitney were two of the waitresses at the bar, and the most popular to be pimped out. All of the women in Gael's employ were put to work in this way, to be objectified with objects, and mutilated by the monsters. Of all the waitresses, they were the only two who weren't reduced to a near-constant catatonic state so they were the only ones that could carry on a half-way decent conversation. For this I was partly grateful because Whitney had become an unlikely friend in this place, I was partly ungrateful because Meryl was akin to the rust on a door hinge, she would squeak and squeak and chafe your ears. Meryl was also a no-good rotten bitch. She tried to poison me the first night she worked at the bar so that she could step into my role as Gael's captive. (I would have willingly given up my place, but that idiot couldn't figure out how evil he was).

Whitney, on the other hand, was sarcastic and a welcome confidant, although I didn't actually trust her. I could tell her which of the regulars had the worst smell and laugh at the odd habits that I observed, but I, under no circumstances, trusted her with any personal details. Truth be told, she didn't trust me either. We could handle a discussion about the surface stuff, the mundane, the idle prattling that would allow us to pretend that this life was normal, but we would never discuss anything beyond that. Whitney was a live wire and a welcome reprieve from the all-consuming desolation. Meryl was the perfect specimen of the hate and lies that Porthana were cultivating on Earth. Upon Gael's words, my first uninhibited and primitive thought was to accuse Meryl. But I had a heart.

"Last I checked you were the pimp and I'm the silent mutt in the corner," I spoke with no emotion, without moving my eyes from my plate. I was stoned and inured to all that was happening around me. I had been eying the butter knife on the table wondering how the dull blade might deliver a swift end to my drawn-out and never-arriving death. (I could kill myself and no one else, certainly not Meryl, was allowed to make that decision for me.)

Gael smacked me with force, and I was on the ground. He continued to act swiftly with his retribution. Sundeep was still in the kitchen, he witnessed these scenes regularly, but he was silent and never interfered. I was grateful because I would have been responsible if he had been injured while trying to defend me. Thank you, Sundeep for being a witness, for being silent, and for being the only calming presence in that household. He often snuck me candies on the days when Gael had been particularly cruel. But this would be the last time I ever saw him. After that evening, he would be turned out of the house, never to return.

As I laid on the ground, observing the kitchen at a right angle, feeling the pain of Gael's latest punishment I wished for a cranial fracture, or a gaping wound that would never heal or clot. I wanted out. I wanted to die finally. My survival instinct had evaporated leaving behind a grainy compound of exhaustion and pain.

The events that would transpire that evening would ignite a fire and, unknown to me, incinerate that remaining compound, an explosive mixture.

Gael broached the subject again as he drove the regular forty minutes to the newly constructed central station where the humans were dispatched for their daily slave labor. All of their faces were slack, only barely cleaner than they had been the evening before; they were concave reflections of who they had been. I hated to see them, but I could never bring myself to look away as we passed them from the shiny black car that was my saving grace and my tomb. I began to experience the first pangs of appreciation for Gael and realized that all of the years that Stockholm Syndrome had been a punchline in my previous life, it was a real thing. (Again, I would request your mercy in judging me, if you have any to spare.) My world shrank to the size of his house where I was imprisoned, his car where I was transported and the bar where I was given the illusion of liberty. It was almost better that my reality had become so limited. If I had to experience the growing vulgarity of the world outside, the invasion, the desiccation, the erosion of our humanity, I might have lost it. I was happy to have my syndrome, although now I do wonder how the humans living in Stockholm have fared throughout the invasion.

"Dora, I need your eyes and ears tonight. If Meryl and Whitney screw this operation up it's more than just their asses on the line. It's ours too." He was so convincing when there was something that he wanted. "This could disrupt everything; do you want to experience full-blown withdrawal?"

I sat silently. My fingers went instinctively to my mouth. I didn't like to be lumped in with Gael and Meryl. I didn't like that I had allowed myself to become so addicted to the escape offered by the drugs that I was now dependent on it. I didn't like it one bit.

"Stop biting your nails Pandora and answer me. I know you're not stoned."

"When do I get to run?"

"Answer me." Gael was still staring ahead focused on the road. We were minutes from arriving at the bar.

"You said that I might be able to run. When?"

"Damnit, Dora! You have yet to prove very useful. You had better stop acting like a wounded child and start owning your choices. You can survive or you die. You can do as I ask or you can try to find food on these streets." He pressed the button to roll down the automatic window. "Is that what you want?" The stench of the streets wafted into the car. The rotting carcasses of animals and man had been souring since the invasion. While some were thrown into mass graves, most were left. Those left alive were suffering through the stench.

In this torture, we were finally all equal. Black or white or some shade in between, we were all beaten and killed just as easily as the next. The Porthana killed for no reason, other than the laugh, their impossibly deep tenor of a chortling laugh that was mutilated and modified through their thick suits. I imagined their true voices, those uninhibited by their protective suits to be extremely high pitched, and this made me laugh when they were just walking by. But when they shot at people ten feet away from me, I froze, I did not dare to laugh.

And the men and the women were equally traded and trashed. It did not matter, the Porthana's taste for perversion knew no gender, which led me to believe that as a species they were asexual, but I was fortunate to never get close enough to know for sure. The women that were used by them were just as shell-shocked as the women that were tossed around among the human men, the mercenaries and the merciless prisoners alike quickly devolved into possessive monsters. All that equality that we had marched for, was wiped out when the Porthana sent us back into the Stone Age and with it, the men regained their clubs to whack their women over the head and drag them back to their caves, unconscious and unwilling. The women could bond in their victimhood; the men didn't know what to do. As women, we had always been assigned a value and were often de-humanized, never to this extent, but our pre-Porthana society of 2015 was still very disingenuous towards gender-equality. So, the men were finally experiencing what us women already knew, and the women were their own support system. Except for me, none of them reached out to me, because they all assumed that I was willingly the prize of Gael. And they were all wrong.

I moved my hand to roll up the window. Gael snatched it and held it tight. I knew of ten ways that I could break his arm and for the first time in weeks, I felt like I might have been strong enough to do it. But I didn't. "Dora, we have to be in this together, we have to be a 'we' if you think there is any chance of survival."

I hated myself for what I did next. I will always hate it.

I nodded. I put on a half-smile and I said, "Ok, I'll keep an eye out." We were just arriving at the bar. The timing was perfect, the timing was horrible. And most importantly, time was running out. With the entirety of what was fabricated between Gael and me, this agreement was the most artificial.

Whatever the Porthana were mining for they were starting to tap the extent of the resources in this area. Each day there were more and more humans with lash marks, grotesque injuries, or reduced rations. They weren't finding any more of what they wanted, so they used their punishments as a means to encourage harder work. For all the sophistication of the invasion, their thumb-nail trackers and their ability to maintain order, they were horrible at motivating their workforce.

That was where Gael's plan was starting to work so well, but it was a dangerous precipice. Humans needed the diversion of The Snake Pit. At The Snake Pit, the world-weary humans could try their best to forget the troubles hanging onto their every limb, appendage, and breath. But if the Porthana were growing impatient with the results, there was the possibility that this entire outpost could either be relocated or just removed. I could see with each moment that Gael was looking for an out, he was a creature of survival, and he was looking for his next move.

Each day started with a thorough accounting of the remaining liquor. Gael had been able to assign workers to obtain all bottles from abandoned personal residences, restaurants, liquor stores, quickie marts. The liquor was tightly locked each night, and more importantly, no human tried to fuck with Gael. He was just as easy to pick up a gun and shoot a man down as the Porthana were. He was the perfect person to assign to his position and the worst of all humanity.

After counting the booze and cleaning the bar he would divvy out his drugs into small bags. I never knew where he obtained his stockpile from or how he was able to access it so readily. *Had he been preparing for the invasion, did he know before it happened, did he help them and this pseudo-power was his reward?* Yes, surely, he knew. Perhaps a chance alien encounter had afforded him this knowledge. Either way, he knew. If that doesn't make your blood boil then perhaps you knew too- in which case I can only hope small bits of fingernails, sharpened shards of them, collected in the pit on my teeth find their way onto your eyelashes and slice into your eyes.

There was the awkward time when we were left alone in the bar each day without any work to keep our hands busy. Each day he seemed to be on the verge of speaking to me like a person, like someone who could keep him company. Today he decided to break through.

"I could see about getting you some new clothes." His offer was direct and I assessed my current outfit. I had finally been able to clean the clothes that I had stolen with Don and Becca. They had survived with me, and while they were certainly no longer tight, they weren't as loose as they had been when I had first arrived. I was gaining some of my muscle mass back.

"I don't mind these." I shrugged his offer off my shoulders and let it fall like an errant paper on the ground.

"But, if you wanted to, I could. You should-" he hesitated, "look the part."

I looked at him directly. I could spit out some words at him. "*Yes, master,*" "*I have to wear whatever you give me,*" something obvious and rude and, I hate to say it because of what it implies, ungrateful. I held those thoughts back and pictured myself running so fast across an open brown desert. I could almost feel the wind in my hair and hear the heaving of my chest. "Okay," was the only response I gave him. But it was enough. It was progress for him and surrender for me. He was winning this war of attrition, or at least that is what I needed him to believe.

Much like every other day, we waited. We sat. I bit at my cuticles. He told me to stop. Having this "job" was helping me to compartmentalize. I could pretend that this was a normal job at a normal bar. But the undercurrent of fear was still pulsing through me. So, I bit. The skin on the fingers never peeled off like a banana, clean and even and firm. It was always ripped and jagged like when you would try to peel a grape, the skin cutting itself into thin sheets. It would peel away like the dried and cracked skin of my parched lips, inviting a bite and then quickly drawing blood. And when that saliva on my fingers would dry, there would be tiny spike sticking up from the cuticle, inviting another nibble, another bite of relief from the constant pressure and the maddening itch. I could only imagine how irritating that metal disc would have been had it been inserted into my thumb, or index finger, rather than sitting plainly in my back pocket.

As the afternoon started to turn into evening, the waitresses started to arrive. Shuffling in silently they had the defeat of occupation in their eyes, but slowly each evening they began to come around. They were able to forget while they were enclosed in the dark box with black walls that was The Snake Pit. They were able to push the fear aside for a little bit each night. They were young and robbed of a future, but for now, they were still living. Millennials, the last human generation. A generation ridiculed for their adaptability to technology and pop-culture of bright color and easy money. But what society had forgotten was that this was also the generation defined by acts of mass violence when they came of age. This was the generation that went off to fight a nameless, faceless terror and returned without their limbs or their lives. And now- this. We were almost bred for this kind of fear, like we had been primed for it our whole lives with video games and bad movies and the wars of the world around us. But now it was real and there were no mulligans, no start-overs, and no way to escape save for drugs and death.

Whitney came in and found her way over to me at the bar. She sat and chatted for a bit, only a few of the regulars had stumbled in and the night was starting out slow. She told me about how her food rations were bland and how she was hoping for some chili powder or actual peppers to be able to liven up her meals. "Well you could always get a second job, or something to supplement your income," I said in a sarcastic tone. She laughed and rolled her eyes. I knew I had to bring it up, so I just came out with it.

"Hey Whit, Gael asked me to check up on you and Meryl to make sure you're not taking extra tips. I know that you wouldn't do it, so can you help me keep an eye on Meryl." Whitney didn't share my supreme hatred for Meryl, but she accepted the task.

"You think she's taking extra jobs?" Whitney asked.

"That's what Gael thinks. I'm not paid enough to think for myself. Just keep my mouth shut and keep this bar clean." I couldn't help, but let a little bit of my frustration show through. Whitney had revealed one night that while no one knew about how Gael and I came to be together, the general assumption was that we were together before the invasion and were somehow bonded together through our survival. I had never led her to believe any different.

"Well he's keeping you safe and fed, so I guess that's not too much to ask." Her voice was sympathetic, although her words were short and to the point. I nodded and knew that I needed to keep my thoughts to myself. We, that horrible term, applied to Gael and me now. Shiver.

"Although, if you ever needed someone to talk to, you know I'm here right?" She reached out and touched my hand. I looked over at her and gave a short nod, almost imperceptible. A grubby and overweight man tripped his way up to the bar and invaded our space. "A drink!" he ordered, pounding his fist on the bar, turning immediately to take in an eyeful of Whitney. She moved her hand quickly and started to pick up her tray.

"Are you going to deliver my drink to me?" he asked her with a crawl in his voice, a lecherous tone, a hideous idea behind it. This man was a regular at the bar, but moreover, he was a regular creep. He would be found touching himself each night, through his pants, as the waitresses made their rounds. He was often drunk and stoned and reeked of the environment that was decaying around us.

"What do you want to drink?" I tried to mask the disdain in my voice.

"Whiskey!" he shouted, still staring straight at Whitney, not even looking over at me. I felt sorry for her, that she was so openly being eyed up like an item. I knew how it felt. It was disgusting.

I poured the drink and set it on the bar. "One whiskey," I stated. This gross man, whose name escapes me now, looked directly at me and snarled. He picked up his left hand and held out his thumb moving it close to his eyes as though he was using it as a sight on a rifle, pretending that what the aliens had implanted in him would give him additional abilities. He mocked a gun with his right hand and made a "pow" sound, miming that he was shooting me. He focused next on Whitney and copied the move.

I knew I was safe from his threat, Gael and his effect on the population extended some safety to me, but Whitney would be exposed. She took her tray and started her rounds. I knew that eventually, this man might make good on one or more of this spoken and unspoken threats. I was sad for her, but I was glad to have a friend. I knew that there were no humans left on the Earth that I could trust, including myself, but it was nice to have a friend. It was a small aid in working through the guilt of bringing all of this upon myself. All those that had at one time helped me had turned out to only do me harm, and those that seemed genuine were dead. Or so I thought.

The Snake Pit saw two main waves of patronage each evening. One just past sunset when the humans would come in for a drink and to forget for a while. The second wave would always come at midnight when the Porthana would clamor into the bar, demanding alcohol and delighting in any small bit of terror that they could inflict. Having seen them in close proximity for some time my eyes started to adapt, only mildly itchy now when they were near. I had finally seen them clearly and plainly. Even the shortest of the dispatches would tower over Gael when he spoke with them. And Gael towered over me. They were massive, I couldn't imagine the energy needed to propel such a life-form into existence and their impenetrably black suits seemed to encapsulate the fact that they would always be an enigma to me. I was always glad that they came in after most of the humans had stumbled out into the night. Glad that if these unpredictable aliens were suddenly angered there were fewer people to lash out on.

On this particular evening, I was watching the tables, keeping an eye on the creepy man who was lusting after Whitney, when a man sat down at the bar and cleared his throat, beckoning my attention. I looked over and began to ask what he wanted when I realized that this was a man that I recognized. His hair was a bit longer, but still standing out straight on its ends and his glasses had been repaired. It was Simon. Simon the Scientist.

I hadn't given him much thought since I had seen him lifted and taken out of the same hallway we had shared months earlier. But now, seeing him alive, I wanted to know every detail of every second that had passed since that time. I couldn't tell if he remembered me, but I surely remembered him. I felt a small sadness within me because he was still alive, and his death, likely painful and at the hands of our invaders, was still ahead of him.

He looked at me directly and said, "I wanted to speak with you, but if I must order a drink, then an Old Granddad Whiskey and Coke would suffice." I found the bottle of amber liquid with the orange and black label and poured him a drink.

"Most of the cola has gone flat, but at least the bourbon still has its bite." I slid the drink toward him. He looked at it for some time.

"Here's to modern science." He raised his glass slightly, offering up a toast to me and the empty seats beside him. "For all of the advances of our species, we were brought to the brink of extinction by an invader that came out of the sky with no warning." He took a small sip and I, with no beverage to drink, just nodded my head.

"What happened to you?" I would wait no longer.

"You heard what they called me that day? Remember?" He nodded, his head, his hands, his body seemed agitated.

"Yes, they said you were a scientist. Is that true?"

"I don't prefer that term; it seems pejorative and pedestrian. I am a socio-anthropologist."

"Oh, I see-" I had no clue what any of what he said meant, he offered an explanation.

"I studied how our ancestors formed into social groups, primitive societies. I apply those findings to the modern world to understand how people relate to one another and where groups that are dysfunctional can improve."

"So, you don't work in a lab or use chemicals," I paused, "Or metals?"

"No, not until I was dragged away by that stinking," he lowered his voice, "alien."

"So, have you been working *with* them?" I tried not to sound judgmental. But it was difficult to hide.

"No more than you've been serving them and their whipping boy," he gestured toward Gael.

I stayed silent and took his critical words. I had no excuse that I could offer.

"I've come here a few times now, I wanted to check on you to see that you were still OK. I wasn't sure if you were with them or against them."

"Neither. I'm trying to survive Simon."

"As am I. Until recently I enjoyed being in the dark as to the primary purpose of this invasion. But now that I have pieced enough information, I'm not sure if I can live with myself much longer." He took another sip of his drink, this time longer and slower.

"I wanted to see if you would help me." He had a look in his eye that seemed desperate.

"What?" I had heard him plainly, but I was at a loss for words.

"You're strong. I saw that the first day in the hallway. Physically you're strong. I need that kind of strength. And I can tell that you had evaded capture for some time, that I'll need as well."

"For what? What makes you think I could even help you? What makes you think I would want to?" I had the promise from Gael that he would let me run, one day. I had no such guarantee from this man sitting before me.

"I've seen things. They've had me running some," he spat out his words, "experiments. They've been gruesome and I have a theory. I hope I'm wrong, but that hasn't often been the case."

"So, what is your theory then? What do they want?"

"No ransom that could be offered would be acceptable to them, and no ransom that they demanded could be paid." He finished his drink with a quick swallow.

"What does that even mean? You're not making much sense." I poured him another drink and looked around to make sure that Gael was not watching. I was nervous to be seen speaking with Simon for too much longer.

"None of this makes sense Dora. I've seen people, other people just like us, submitted to the most heinous torture. And worst, those who aren't even in the labs are constantly biting their nails, leaving open wounds for infection." I hid my hands behind my back. "What's worse is that those who have had on nail polish have been ingesting arsenic with each bite." He reached for my arm, but I moved back. Simon seemed to become aware of his mad-scientist ramblings. He sat silently for a moment and took a sip of his drink.

"Let me see, Dora," he softly commanded. I offered up my hand. The tips of each finger were jagged from my teeth and my cuticles were either red from being bitten raw or covered with a faint dried blood. It was a monstrous doing, all my own. He inspected each finger and shook his head.

"This is what *they* wanted," he dropped my hand after his examination. He had paused at each finger to look at the surface, I hoped that he hadn't sensed anything missing beneath the skin. I felt anxious, as though Gael would walk over at any moment and take violent recourse for this action.

"The subcutaneous implant is more than just a means of tracking us and sedating us, it serves as a test to see how much we will harm ourselves." I pulled my arm back. I could see that Gael was now making his way around the bar and would be near us soon.

"So that is your theory?" I was still confused as to what he wanted.

"No, my theory is that we, you and me, we can escape with a quick slice of a blade." He gestured at his hand in a cutting motion, pretending to lob off his thumb. I winced at the thought.

"I'm not sure that would be a wise idea. Besides, if you have been watching me, then you know I have an additional obstacle." I motioned my head ever so slightly towards Gael.

"I know, I think his days are numbered. The Porths don't seem too pleased with him. They've caught onto his racket." He drank without moving his eyes from the glass.

"How?" The news he had shared was too scary to be able to comprehend. If Gael was a target then so was I, if he was exposed then I could also be exposed. If this man was telling the truth then I had a short time limit to act, but if he was lying, I could die just as quickly.

"I can't stay much longer. I want to be out of here by the time the Porths make their nightly visit. But consider my theory. I'll be back again to collect your answer." He threw two slips of paper on the bar, one was a crude voucher for additional rations, and the second was a crumpled church bulletin with something written on it. I put it in my pocket quickly.

"I'll have to think about this. I have my own plans to consider." I tried to seem disconnected. Simon looked at me directly, as though I was under his microscope and he was trying to riddle out how I worked. His eyes examined my face and then he stood back.

"I am a man of science, but I am a man of God as well Dora. As society has fallen apart, I realized what my preacher had always warned of had come true. That judgment was upon us all, and in seeing that the devil was among us I didn't have to see one of the aliens to know they were evil and had bad intentions; I didn't need to see them to know they existed. They were here and they were proof to me that no Jesus, no Messiah would save me at the day of my judgment. We only have one chance to escape. And that time is coming soon."

Gael was close. I knew I had to make a calculated response. "Thank you, please stop by again soon. I'll be sure to remember your order."

With that Simon nodded, understanding that our conversation was at an end. He turned and walked out of the bar just as Gael was approaching me to ask for an update on sales and any feedback on Meryl and Whitney. He seemed uninterested in the man who just left the bar, the one break that I caught in this entire mess. Simon had been invisible to him, and for that I was thankful. At that moment when I was telling Gael that the bar was a little slow, but would probably pick up in an hour or so, I was thinking that my encounter with Simon was so odd. I was so sure that would be the most interesting aspect of that night.

I was wrong.

The Porths clamored in noisily at midnight. Their stench dispersed throughout the bar, a fire that wouldn't be gone from my nostrils until the next day. They stood over the seats that they wanted, signaling the humans that were currently sitting there to move, quickly.

Each night that they came in I hated their presence, but felt equally thankful to be protected behind the bar. Meryl was always eager to serve *them*, I guess she thought one night she would be offered some kind of amnesty for her loyalty. But for what? Where would she go? In the midst of my judgment, I asked myself that question very clearly. *Where would I run, if I were free?*

The group of *them* that evening was particularly rowdy, and there were a few more of them than usual. Whitney went over to help take their orders. The first hour or so was normal. They had their drinks, they made their noises, some of which were becoming familiar to me, but they still made my skin crawl. Meryl was being her usual horrible self, gloating to me and Whitney that she had learned some of their language and was planning on trying her new skills out. I immediately knew this was a mistake, but I was happy to let Meryl suffer any consequences. But what I didn't notice was that she had also taught the same few phrases to Whitney, and Whitney was daring enough to try her hand at their language first. It was all so fast, but I can see each second in my mind so clearly now. I feel responsible, had I not been so blinded by my flat-out hatred of Meryl, I might have warned Whitney.

Meryl and Whitney took a full tray of drinks each from the bar over to the Porths. From the markings on their shoulders, I could tell that these were high-up officials, not the lowly working grunts.

Whitney took one of the full glasses and placed it on the table, leaning over in the seductive manner that Gael had insisted she utilize whenever possible. She smiled at the monsters and handed out the next few drinks. The largest of the Porths was sitting closest to where she stood. He made the usual vulgar gestures to indicate that Whitney would soon have another sale for Gael. And then she leaned over to whisper a response. I remember seeing her wild and curly hair moving as she was speaking, though I couldn't see the words coming out of her mouth.

The loud screeching of the metal table being flung across the room came first, as though the sound happened before the table even moved. In an instant Whitney was pinned against the wall, her neck in the hands of the large Porth and her legs flailing, unable to find the ground. This was the reaction for daring to speak to this alien in his own language. This was the reward for trying to be a smart human. The Porths saw us as lowly and inferior. Their alcoholic thirst for power and authority had driven them to this point was noxious, it was poisonous, and it was lethal.

The alien hurled a series of unknown words at Whitney. But she was screaming too loud for anyone to try to translate or understand what the alien was saying. "Oh God, Please God, no, don't let me die. Please God!" It was almost as if her pleas were one long word, she chanted it several times.

"I am your God" it seethed those menacing words at Whitney. I was in a panic and sank to the floor. I don't even remember making the decision, my legs just knew what to do. I didn't want to watch, I didn't want to witness, my vision started to blur with patches of black invading the light. Gael pulled me up by my arm and tried to keep me looking straight ahead. He knew that failing to look would result in further punishment. But I closed my eyes tight as her screams began to reach a new level.

Then I heard that horrible liquid sound, the sound of human matter being ripped and the oozing of blood from a wound. I could hear the splatter on the leather chairs. The sound was so much worse than I had ever imagined. And then there was a short silence followed by that horrible yeti-like howl of the Porthana. I wanted to open my eyes, but I never wanted to open them.

I heard their heavy boots as they all headed for the door, and what was worse, was the sound of something sliding on the floor, likely being dragged behind them, out onto the streets. I felt responsible. I felt as though I was just as guilty as every other person who stood by and did nothing. But I felt like I had done even less, I could have warned her, I could have told her it was a stupid idea. But I was silent. The unimaginable had happened so quickly that I couldn't even get my head around it.

Surely, I had become one of them, I had become a monster, a stranger to the human race. I felt responsible for Whitney's death, and I knew it in my mind that I would harbor guilt in my heart forever. No matter how much I tried to deny it with my words, I felt that I was the one who set the events in motion that took her life. At that moment, I knew that I still believed in a God because I feared him and the punishment that waited on the other side of this hell.

For several minutes everyone was silent, in shock. We were just wincing, waiting. But the Porthana didn't return that evening. Gael sent everyone out and told me to get a sponge to start cleaning. I shook my head violently and began to drag my sharp and mangled nails across my face, hoping to draw blood. But no blood came. No sanity restored my mind that evening. I sat in the corner and watched Gael mop up what had been the last human matter of the one person who could have been my friend in this darkness.

There weren't enough sponges or clothes or buckets to clean up the mess. And there would never be enough to clean the blood from my own hands.

PART THREE

The Fear of Man

"Until power is made subservient to morality, humanity will continue to suffer."
- Tasneem Hameed.

I had folded up these memories and laid them in a cardboard box. I was ready to have them all gather dust until the moths and cockroaches ate through the box and began to feast on these repressed terrible files from my mind. But recently, as I've been able to gaze up at a clear and often gray sky, these memories have been crawling and slithering back to me. I am in an eternal purgatory with them now, too aware to deny them, but too stunned to accept them. They've been rolling around and now they have shattered all over these pages.

The night that Whitney died was the box within the box. That was the night that I crept back over the edge again and let the unruly manner of my panic take hold. That was the last time.

Gael spent the evening cleaning while I could do nothing but look on. When all was done, he led me blindly to his vehicle. Along the way we passed by- not her body- rather it was a carcass, or what remained of it. The air of the desert night was cold, I began to shiver.

Gael walked over to her, to what had once been Whitney. He pulled the sweater she had been wearing off of her, awkwardly maneuvering her heavy dead limbs. I caught it in my hands after it was balled and tossed to me. It was still warm with the heat of her body, now quickly dissipating into the night. I accepted the sweater and slowly put it on, minding the collar, where her neck had once been warmed. The sweater was necessary. I stopped shivering, but the thick and protective wool weighed on me like a chain mail of guilt.

Neither of us spoke a word as he drove home. My only thoughts were to go directly to the cabinet where I knew he kept the drugs and to take enough to knock me into oblivion. But once we had arrived, the car was off, the garage was closed and the usual evening ritual was about to commence, I found myself unable to move. The naïve young girl that still lived in a corner of my brain kept telling me over and over again that if I went to sleep that meant that I would have accepted the events of that day and that if I never slept again that maybe it meant that Whitney wasn't dead. But the rational and hardened woman who I had become told me to move my feet and go upstairs.

I pulled the church bulletin that Simon had handed me earlier in the evening out of my pocket and before any curiosity fell over me, I ripped it to shreds and carried the pieces with me to the bathroom. I flushed them down the toilet. What good would his words do when I could be dead before I ever saw him again?

It was the first night that I hadn't been drugged into sleep for months. It was the first time I had cried since the last allergic tears fell from my swollen eyelids. And I cried at first for Whitney, but then for myself, as most humans do. I cried because I knew that my demise would be much like hers: gruesome, uncontested, and meaningless. I cried and then I slept. My sleep was uninterrupted and then I dreamt.

At first, I dreamt of freedom, of walking out to an easy morning and being greeted by a friendly dog that I could enjoy the morning playing with. I dreamt of what it would be like to feel at ease again. I dreamt of my body being my own again. And oddly, at the end of this dream, when I turned around it was Simon standing right behind me, handing me something. It was small and shiny – it was the alien tracker, the disc that was my secret.

The next morning the mood in the house had perceptibly changed. Sundeep was not there at all, Gael informed me that he had asked him to leave after breakfast was made. I was silent as I stood in the doorway to the kitchen. I was waiting for Gael's inhumanity, his callous disregard for life. I was dumbfounded when I saw that he was stoic, silent and perhaps, just maybe, he was grieving.

"So, you are capable of feeling remorse?" I remained where I was as I said the words, but they felt as though they had been spoken by the air, certainly not by me. He didn't answer, but his weak smile revealed that he did want to be more human. Perhaps that he was enjoying the brief moments of normal life that we allotted ourselves each morning to maintain our sanity.

"Well don't let the Porths find out." I crossed my arms and moved quickly to the breakfast bar after I uttered this warning. He stopped moving, this half silent conversation was moving with alarming ease. His jaw was still, and in his eyes, I could see he was trying to riddle out my last statement. The food that he had been chewing made a bulging bolus in his cheek and perfectly accentuated his quizzical expressions. It was almost funny; if anything was able to be funny anymore.

"Really, Gael? You're the muscle man. They've made it clear that they have no need for any atrophied cells. What do you think they'll do when they realize you've gone soft? They'll cut you out." I tilted my head very slowly towards our kitchen window, which faced the empty house in the lot next to ours. Ours, a funny sentiment, but I felt that this house had become partially mine. I had lived in it, I had suffered in it and I had bargained in it, which certainly afforded me some ownership. Gael finished chewing what was in his mouth, the worry on his face starting to spread like a gas in a fixed container, finding every available corner and equalizing based on the pressure. The bad boy with a soft side routine had no impact on me.

This was the Gael that I could handle. Calculating and diabolical, I could not interpret a Gael that had "gone soft", nor could I trust it. This way I knew exactly who I was dealing with and what measure of evil he was capable of. "You think time is running out?" He finally said something!

"We've all been living on borrowed time since those first satellites started crashing. There was never an end solution where we were alive and free." I couldn't believe how easy it was to finally say the words out loud that I had been battling to accept in my own mind. But it was true. Humans were extinct, only a few were still walking around, out of step with our evolutionary timeline. Dead men walking so to speak.

"So, we run?" His question was too hopeful.

"I don't know. Die on the run, die holding our ground? Which is better?"

Gael eyed me closely trying to decide. I couldn't take it, while I was getting away with my smart comments, I had a real dose of honesty to lay on him. "Have you ever witnessed someone die?" I asked him. "Not the way we've all seen recently where one moment an entire room of people is alive and the next, they are on the floor. And not the way you do it where you have someone do your dirty work or shoot them quickly. No, I mean watching them in the act of dying. Have you seen them gag and their eyes reach out to the ceiling in terror? All that you want to do at that moment is comfort them because the fear of death is universal, but nothing you say can help because the synapses don't have time to relay the message in their last few electric moments."

Gael shook his head. I couldn't believe that this memory had finally resurfaced, but it was inevitable. The memory of my parents had been so close to my consciousness since that night in the schoolroom prison. And now I was underwater, swimming in this visual memory. I had seen my mother's last breath; I had seen the end. And I had been strong-willed to survive since that moment, save for the last few months. I had found the Dora buried within, Whitney's death and Gael's idiocy had awakened it.

"Ok then, so if you want to avoid that experience, you had better think fast. I've kept up my end of the bargain, you need to keep yours."

"Your end of the bargain?"

"I do your spying and I take your abuse. I'm ready to run, Gael."

He cleared his plate and headed for the sink. After rinsing his plate, he started towards the door, but on his way, he stopped and grabbed my arm, squeezing hard. "I haven't touched you in weeks. You've been too stoned to notice."

"Meryl was the one who was stealing." I could only offer this as a response to what he had just told me. What else could I say? *Thank you?* Could I argue that I hadn't been knocked out? No. There was no other response than to give him the information he had wanted. It didn't matter which name I gave him; he would have interrogated them both. Now with Whitney gone Meryl was his only suspect left. There was no more pretense to maintain. She was guilty by association, guilty by suspicion. I guess those words made me responsible for her death too. Greater losses had already happened.

And with that our morning discourse ended. I nibbled at my knuckles and waited for our normal routine. That raw, exposed saliva coated cuticle, inviting infection was sore and stinging every day. It gnawed at me as much as I gnawed at it. With each torn and uneven rip of the skin, calling out for another bite, I indulged.

It was on this evening that Simon returned to the Snake Pit. We had a quiet crowd the night after Whitney was dragged away, bleeding, in the clutches of a high-ranking Porthana. I wanted so much to run after them and fight off her murderer. I pictured doing this in my mind over and over, but I had been conditioned to stay silent. So, I did. I was silent that night and tried to stay quiet as best I could that next night. I was a coward, I remained more concerned about my own well-being than hers. I had succumbed to the ultimate survival instinct for which I had forfeited my ability to be human. I was now only an animal, docile, and working off of instinct.

I was clearing the corner tables, trying to be invisible, trying to go unnoticed and make it through to 4 am as quickly as possible so that I could sleep away the rest of the day. I had one sober night and I longed to be sedated again, this addiction would be tough to fight. *Gael was right.* I hated thinking those words.

Simon had slipped in quietly, taking a seat in a booth, way in the back. It was as though he didn't want to be seen. When I noticed him, I figured he must have heard what happened and he would know of my inaction. If I was alive, then I didn't put up a fight. That would be how he reasoned his opinion of me. I couldn't blame him. I was so focused on his potential judgment that I spent most of our conversation on the defensive, perhaps if my mind and conscience had been clear I would have heeded his warnings sooner.

I could feel his judging eyes on me as I passed by, trying not to acknowledge or be acknowledged. I heard a low hiss coming from his general direction, "Dora." I tried to ignore him at first, but eventually, I couldn't resist and turned to look at him. He beckoned me to come over to him with a slight movement of his hand.

I moved mindlessly forward, intending to treat him as a stranger. "Yes, what can I get you," I didn't even recognize the flat and lifeless noise coming from my larynx. The words never touched my tongue, but rather slipped out like water tumbling through a wide glass cylinder.

"I have my drink," Simon pointed out. "I need to talk to you," he hissed, again in his slithering whisper.

"I have to work," I stared down at the table, refusing to make eye contact. "Gael will- he's been-," I knew that no words could explain the increased strain on my imprisonment. While others whispered behind my back and expressed envy for my favorable position, I knew that no other human could understand the tight grip that Gael had on me. The closer I came to his fire, to his rage, to his possession, the closer I came to my death at the hands of his paranoia.

I started to turn and walk away, but Simon was persistent. He thrived on the challenge of defying Gael and the Porthana. "Please," he lunged forward, almost spilling his drink, and brushed my wrist. He had intended to grab it, and it is fortunate that he did not. Too many men had grabbed me, trying to control me in the past few months that my temper was always set to boil at the physical aggression of others. I was startled by the touch of his fingertips. His action was so desperate, so hungry, I paused. I would give him another moment of my attention, and then I could return to my mindless routine to get me through the evening.

"Please, come sit down." The need in his voice stirred inside of me. Before I could stop myself, I folded onto the edge of the booth. My feet relieved at the unplanned rest mid-shift.

"With everything that happened last night, I think the time is right Dora. Gael is distracted."

"Gael is humiliated, which means he feels that he should pay the feeling forward tenfold to me." I pointed at the bulging purple welt, the freshest of my injuries, above my left eye, a gift I received for being smart while we were taking stock of the alcohol that morning.

"I've tried to explain this all before, and I didn't want to tell you too much because I was worried that you might rat me out to Gael. But I think I can get us in." Simon had an expectant look on his face, as though I could feel relief at his words.

"Into what? Into trouble? Into danger?"

"Trouble?! That implies that you accept their authority over you, they have no authority over us, Dora. They have seized hold of us, but they will never have our consent." His dogmatic words did have an impact on me, my pessimism subsided, briefly.

"It's just easier to relent," I said in earnest exhaustion. I hated to admit it, but I had given up. I was defeated. And with that, I could retain the small hope that if I was docile, if I was compliant, that I might live to see a future when I could be happy and free.

Simon waited to respond. I could see the internal debate spilling across his face, his lips slowly moving, silent words coming out, as though he was practicing what to say.

"Have you noticed a trend among the people that are left?"

His question was unexpected and I was struck by the fact that I couldn't answer. I hadn't paid much attention to anyone else since the day of the invasion. I had seen, but hadn't analyzed them.

"No, not really," I shrugged my shoulders.

"Oh, so it's totally normal that everyone is under 45, slim and attractive?"

"Maybe those are the traits needed to survive an invasion of this scale," I tried to point out that so many people had died; there couldn't have been more of a design to the Porthana plan. They destroyed so much, there was clearly only one aim, human annihilation.

"Or those who didn't fit the bill were systematically executed." Simon's words implied so many things that I couldn't begin to process them all.

"So, the Porthana intentionally gave lethal doses of aerosol poison to the exact houses with people they didn't deem fit to live? No Simon, they bombed entire cities." The wisps of white smoke that flooded downtown Tampa like a summer storm flashed in my mind.

"Yes, a mass genocide, followed by selective executions," Simon spoke so succinctly that I felt a chill run up my spine.

"Well, I guess if the Porthana knew they needed people strong enough to work their mines, then I guess it makes sense that they only kept who they needed."

"No!" Simon raised his voice. He paused and resumed in a hushed whisper. "Have you seen those mines? There is nothing in there but dirt. They kept the people that they wanted to study and breed."

"Breed? These trackers render us all infertile, Simon!" I held up my thumb as though to demonstrate my point, as though I had a tracker implanted.

"Who told you that?"

"No one, I riddled it out on my own. I saw some things on my journey out west after the invasion"

"Such as?" He pried, so I told him.

"Organs, human reproductive organs harvested and then dumped.

They're studying us," I hissed the last word. The pink and maroon organs were still too vivid in my mind.

"I know, why do you think they have interest in a scientist?" His words were like a slap on the face. *Simon the Scientist… Simon the Traitor? Simon the Zealot to be sure.*

"So, you're helping them?"

"Dora- you need to stop referring to these monsters as *'them'*."

"What do you mean?"

"I can't tell you; I can only show you. That's why I need you to leave with me. Now. Do not pass 'GO'. Do not collect two hundred dollars." His allusion to the game of Monopoly endeared me to him and also made me want to smack him across the face yelling that none of this was a game.

Simon was so passionate about the need to go with him. And he seemed safe enough. But so had Mitch, and he had turned out to be just as bad as Gael and the Porthana. Mitch had traded me in, he had sold me out, and so could Simon. While on the surface Simon seemed trustworthy, he had the means, the same human capability, of turning on me.

I demurred. "No Simon. I-" I almost made an emotional plea. *I need to stick to this plan. I don't want to die. I'm scared to leave this place, at least I know what to expect here.* Instead, I appealed to the reason and logic of his kind, scientists. "I need more proof."

"Proof?" He seemed insulted by the request.

"Yes, proof. Just because aliens have indeed descended from the sky doesn't mean that all of the UFO sightings over the years were real. Some really were hoaxes. I need proof."

I stood up and carried on my business. I cleaned the table. Simon left, but I didn't notice until he was gone and his booth was empty. His glass turned upside-down on the table, a ring of condensation working its way into the fibers of the wood table, working on becoming a water-mark ring.

Gael knew.

Of course, he knew. I should have known not to underestimate him. He elaborated on the car ride home.

"That man hasn't come to the bar often, but in the past two nights he has been there." His words were accusatory.

"I think he liked that we have his brand of bourbon." I dismissed his comments.

"No, he was there for you." Gael gave no room for speculation. "But you refused. You could have run."

"I will run on my own terms Gael. And when I run, I will be free from all men." I could feel my voice shaking. I had suddenly become angry and felt afraid of the power in my own voice. Once my lips delivered those words, I knew that they would be true one day. I just knew it.

Gael was silent for a moment. "Yes, you will be able to run. Soon."

I wanted to ask him for more information, but I didn't want to seem too eager. I didn't want to let him see me get my hopes up, and I didn't want to let myself believe that it would be that easy.

"Good, I will be sure to train my body to handle that journey. I'll get up early in the morning to do this." I explained this plainly.

"That means no drugs." At this, he moved his eyes from the road and settled on me. I could almost see the lascivious thoughts rolling through his mind. I remembered his words from that morning. He had abstained from violating me because I had been too drugged. Being sober could leave me at his mercy again. And suddenly, I understood. What he wanted was my loyalty, not my obedience. He wanted me to want to stay, he wanted me to agree, and he wanted me to be with him, not owned by him. I repressed the strong urge to cringe, to flinch, to physically reject him. No words could have undone that motion so I was careful to not let it show.

"I know," I could find no other words to give. I couldn't lie and verbally agree and I would not allow myself to refuse and therefore close the window of opportunity to escape. I would get up each morning and train. I would work. I would submit to Gael's wants. I would train again the next day and the next until I could run on my own, strong and capable of carrying myself far, far away. I doubled-down on my plan to stick with Gael. I had refused Simon and was now putting all of my efforts for freedom on the line with Gael. May God have mercy on my soul.

Each morning I went to the bathroom, locked the door, and started my exercises. The bathroom was the only room in the house with no window. This meant I could train without any risk of being seen. Gael had explained that if I was caught trying to strengthen myself, it would jeopardize us both. So, I did my push-ups on the floors. I did pull-ups with the shower curtain rod. I did my squats and crunches. I was building my strength again. My left knee was healed and moving easily. My ear had scarred over and was easily hidden if I wore my hair a certain way. I was recovered and now building my strength.

These exercises left me with muscles, but not endurance. I needed to practice running in order to be able to run. I did laps around the basement to solve for this. There was a small window near the ceiling that would have allowed the faceless Porth commander to see in if he was so inclined so I only ran at night in the basement without the lights on. I tripped a few times, but I needed to do those laps to get strong again.

I was dedicated and I endured more than I ever thought I could handle in order to achieve it. I was astounded at what I had been able to accomplish to get to that point. I had a goal in sight and I would not relinquish it. I had no idea what I would do once I was on the run and free. But I knew that I wanted that more than anything else. In my mind, I had a small thought that I would find a beautiful spot where I could feel the true essence of the Earth, where I could forget about the aliens and about science and the advances of man and feel connected to my home planet. I wanted to be in that place as a free woman and I thought that I might end it there. I would like to die as a free woman in a place where my soul will be at peace. That was my silent goal, one that I had trouble admitting to myself even. But it was there in my heart, it was what I wanted.

The Snake Pit foundered. With Whitney slain and Meryl, ahem, disposed of by Gael, the remaining waitresses needed to rise to the occasion and they were unable to adapt. One went mad and started screaming loudly in the middle of her shift. Fewer humans started showing up. Once they realized that they couldn't escape the fear of their impending doom they had no reason to visit. The Porthana continued to patronize the bar, and they seemed to grow in numbers.

Within a month there were only a few brave humans left each night and the rest of the evening the bar was full of Porthana, absolutely infested with them. Their growling speech was a constant hum, like the dull rhythm of a cricket, but louder and fuller and much more sinister. With each passing night, I became more and more aware that Gael was running out of waitresses to sell to the Porthana and worried that he might try to sell me. I kept the loose tracker in my pocket and would hold it with the tips of my fingers and pray to be released before that could ever happen. The tracker had become a talisman, a rosary for me to pray on. My fingers would brush against it as if the toxin had been replaced with a secret source of luck or fate.

Gael had also been running a major stockpile of the HEX-P powdered narcotic that was supposed to pulse through the human bloodstream when released in the implanted tracking device, the one that I had on my person at all times, but never inside my skin. With fewer humans visiting each night, he had fewer customers for his drugs, and that meant that there was a lot of "product" to be moved and nowhere to move it to.

Gael was increasingly paranoid and on one night, in particular, it seemed that all of the elements of change converged on the small patch of desert that we were inhabiting. It seems strange to say that in the entirety of the invasion and the occupation that these few moments that I have already described and will soon describe are the only ones that mattered. But when I look back now and think of that time it is only these few moments that stand in stark contrast to the blurred memories that fill the rest of that time. I've come to see life as a very precious commodity, but those months could easily be tossed aside without much loss.

On this night, many things happened. It had been a month since Simon had last visited the bar, and since Whitney had been murdered. The first event of circumstance involved a pale-faced man with rounded glasses and hair that stood up on its ends visiting the Snake Pit one last time. But this time he didn't bring everything with him that he had before. This time there was a thick bandage and a stump where his thumb used to be.

He made a raucous when he entered. The front door swung wide open then slammed back onto the frame announcing his arrival. His previous visits had been quiet, unassuming. This time he was loud and present. Simon staggered to the bar, to the spot directly in front of where I was standing. It was early enough in the evening where the few other human patrons were sipping their drinks quietly and the Porthana leaders had yet to arrive. For this, Simon was lucky. Had any of them seen what he had done, the crime he had just committed, it surely would have cost his life.

He landed his left hand on the counter, all five fingers splayed out and then, with considerable effort, he heaved his right hand onto the counter. He was careful and tender with his right hand, and gently let the bandaged edge rest on the bar. I could see his four fingers, all slightly red from the compression of the tightly wrapped gauze. The space where his thumb should have been was now a nub, a red bump on a bandage.

"I did it, Pandora!" he was trying to stay quiet, but his words were still too loud.

I was in shock at the very idea that he had cut off his own thumb. Millennia of evolution had given the human race opposable thumbs. This small distinction separated us from the animals and gave us dominion over the planet. *Without it, wouldn't we be just like the animals?* Would our other human traits such as empathy and compassion also go to the wayside as we looked to escape the Porthana.

I tried to offer a reply, but I had no rational thoughts to construct a sentence. I quickly hid my thumbs in my pockets. I may have bitten them and picked them until they were a jagged remnant, but they were still my thumbs and they were still attached. I could picture his severed thumb, laying in the dusty street. His tracker would be emitting a beep with red and green lights flashing. Or at least that was how I pictured it in my mind, in reality, it would just lay there, to be covered by dirt, slowly secreting the chemical that should have been released through his blood system, but that would never touch Simon's veins again.

"It burns like hell right now. I can almost still feel it, I still have the sensation that it is itching, that I should bite through it to stop the itching. But it is gone." Simon sat down on one of the bar stools. He began to smile. "I did it! I'm free!"

I quickly poured him a glass of bourbon. "Here, drink," I commanded him.

He picked up the glass with his left hand and took a long, gulping drink.

"I didn't use any morphine, so this should help take off the edge."

"What? Why?" I was finally able to ask the question.

"I told you, if you cut out the tracker, then they can't find you. If you cut it out, they can't just release the toxin and incapacitate you whenever they want."

"But they'll know, they'll be looking for you-" I began to search the bar nervously for any Porth officers that may have found their way in early. None in sight, yet.

"Yes, they will. That is why we must go. Now! Tonight!"

"Where? Why should I go with you?"

"Because I can help you be free. I can show you, Dora. Please, we must go, it is our only chance for survival." His eyes were pleading, but I saw a small twitch in the corner of his mouth. It might have been from the alcohol, but I couldn't trust it.

"No, I'm not running off with a man crazy enough to cut off his own thumb."

"Crazy?! No, smart. I stayed completely calm; I didn't let my nerves start to get to me. I knew if I waited too long, I would start to have adrenaline in my system, which would have triggered the reaction in the device and knocked me out. No way, had to do it quickly."

"So now you're a man with nine fingers, they can catch you and insert it into another." I had been biting at my own thumbnail for a moment and just realized it.

"Not if they don't catch me." He finished his drink and stood up. He extended his whole and empty left hand, beckoning me to join him.

"No, Simon. I'm staying. I have my own way out." I was firm on my answer, but still sad to see him leave. He seemed like a good man, but I had my own ticket out, and then it would be me on my own, not with anyone else. Not even a nice scientist who had the audacity to dismember himself. He closed his hand and let it drop to his side. He opened his mouth as if he were about to say something, but then he snapped it shut. I wonder what I must have looked like to him at that moment. Weak? Pathetic? Scared?

Stupid? Proud? I never asked him what he was thinking at that moment.

Without another word or argument, Simon turned to leave. He walked out into the windy night, putting his right hand in his coat pocket before anyone or anything could see what he was hiding. He was now a man on the run. I made a silent wish for him to stay safe. I wonder sometimes how things might have turned out if I had agreed to go with him. Would Gael still be alive? Would I still be alive? I guess I'll never really know.

Almost as soon as the door latched Gael was beside me. He had a question on his mind, I didn't need to inquire to find out what it was. His face was angry. His arms were crossed. This was a territorial matter.

"He asked me to leave with him again." I looked down at the bar, not wanting to look Gael in the face.

"I said no." I could hear him release a deep sigh, perhaps it was a relief, or it could have been his mounting frustration.

"I appreciate your honesty, Pandora." His strange accent had become muted to me now after hearing it for so long, but it was still there. His words drawn out and fluid, but still the words of the emissary of the devil.

"We have our deal, Gael." I started to wipe down the bar when he grabbed my wrist.

"Don't flinch, everything is normal, ok?" His words were muted and whispered, there was an edge, a panic to what he was saying.

"OK." I tried not to quickly look around. It was difficult, I couldn't help but sense the danger.

"Finish cleaning the bar, then come into the back room." He released my wrist, and then quickly moved towards the back corner of the bar where he would go into his office, and from there presumably the back storeroom.

The next one hundred and eighty seconds were the most terrifying and most exhilarating of my life. I am so thankful that I didn't have a tack in my thumb that could have knocked me out because in that small amount of time I was running on pure adrenaline. *Is this when he kills me? Is this when he sells me? Is this when he releases me? Is he mad that Simon was here again? What is about to happen?* There were countless opportunities behind the door. I put my dish-rag under the counter after I wiped it down and walked quickly and deliberately towards the door that Gael had only just walked behind.

The office was musty and a dank grayish green that seemed to match the smell in the windowless tiny room. The décor and the smell were inherited from whomever had owned the bar before the invasion, so Gael tolerated them both. His chair was empty, his desk was covered with some small bits of paper. Gael was nowhere to be seen in this small office. The second door in the office, the one leading to the back store-room was ajar. I could see the light coming from the store room as I advanced. I stepped through and immediately saw that something was amiss. Where a large pile of white powder had once stood, was now an empty and bare floor. The thousands of little baggies of HEX-P that had been there only the night before were now gone. I had never seen the stockpile, but the faint powder outline on the floor revealed what was missing.

Gael was standing in the middle of where the pile once was. My eyes widened, "Where is it?" I was dumb enough to ask.

Gael quickly moved behind me to shut and lock the door. "I don't know" he hissed.

"How soon until-" he didn't let me finish my question.

"I don't know, they could already know, they could have done this, or they might never find out." His words were rushing together. He was in a state of terror. My thoughts were moving at a similar pace. *Who did this? Was this retribution for any of Gael's heinous crimes?*

"Is there any left?" I asked calmly.

He removed one small baggie from his back pocket, he was too stunned to speak.

"Take half now, you need to remain calm, Gael." He had started to pace the floor. He was likely moments from triggering a reaction. At my recommendation, he licked his finger, dipped it into the bag and then rubbed the powder into his gums.

"The last thing we need is for you to trigger a reaction, then they'll know something is up." I was trying to think of what to do next.

"Dora, the second they figure it out, they could flip a switch and have me out cold like that," he snapped his fingers for emphasis.

"So, we run, tonight. We set off in different directions." My solution was self-serving, but could have potentially saved him. I was suddenly engulfed in a "we" scenario.

"No, we can't run, that will tip them off."

"So, we stay and risk being executed? Gael I am not going to die for you!" I was starting to panic, but I had the luxury of being able to.

"This was the deal that you made, Dora. You are not released yet, give me until dawn and then maybe it will be ok."

"Maybe? Maybe?!" I was starting to shout. I should have anticipated his next move, but I was being stupid and bold. This time when he hit my head, I fell against the hard concrete of the storeroom. I was out cold.

I came to as he was placing me in the passenger seat of his car. It could have been ten minutes, or it could have been an hour. I had no idea. But we were leaving the Snake Pit when it was still deep in the night, no sight of an approaching dawn. That meant we were leaving earlier than any other night. Gael would have closed up early, or perhaps he just fled without a word. I never found out; I never saw that place again.

He strapped the seat belt across me and quickly closed the door and made his way around to the driver's side. "You were going to cause a scene; I couldn't tell if people in the bar could hear you." I half believed his reasoning, but I also knew that he was a violent son-of-a-bitch and he didn't have a reason for hitting me half of the time. At this point in my existence as Gael's property, I didn't know whether to hate him or forgive him. I was so absorbed in the small corner that he was keeping me in that it did really seem that the world began and ended at his word and at his palm. My captivity had distorted my perception of what was right, what was wrong and what was Gael. I can see this clearly now that I have had more time and miles to distance myself, but at that time I couldn't see the surface from the hole that I had been placed in. I find that I keep trying to beg for forgiveness with my words. I don't deserve it.

On the ride back to his house, Gael was skittish. He kept the headlights off and in spite of his constant chastising; he was biting his nails. More aggressively at his index finger than the others, hyper-aware of the tracker beneath the surface, needing to scratch it, needing to pry it from his skin, but only being able to satisfy the urge with the pressure and biting of his teeth.

I sat silently; I had never seen Gael worried. His fear was like an unseen hand, moving in to squeeze my throat and bring me into the same head-space, causing me to panic, to fear, to worry. As we made our way back to his house, I half expected to see it on fire. A large roaring fire climbing into the night, grasping at the dark velvet of the sky. I thought about unbuckling and opening the car door, rolling onto the road and running. But I knew that Gael would run me down before I made it off the ground. I pictured many things in those few moments, none of which came true. My imagination was running wild, but it never ran in the direction of the truth until it was too late and it was unfolding before me.

When we did pull into view of the house, there was no magnificent fire. No line of Porthana soldiers barring our way, no weapons aimed at the vehicle ready to annihilate us. There was only one small eerie sign that the time had come. The three remaining houses in that Enclave were pitch black with the exception of one light. The Porth commander's house was dark and silent, Gael's house was black and gray blending in with the evening. The spare house, the house that stood as a symbol to Gael that he could be replaced had one light shining clearly. It was on the second floor in the western corner of the house. That small light might as well have been an inferno for all that it represented. Gael stopped the car a hundred yards away from the houses.

"Are we running?" I whispered, afraid that whatever was inside the spare house might hear.

Gael was silent. Sweat was accumulating on his hairline and his upper lip. He ran his hands through his long and greasy hair, stalling, thinking, mentally maneuvering. I was looking intentionally at him, waiting for a sign of what to do. He was staring at that illuminated window, he didn't blink or flinch, he just saw it and calculated.

"Gael, what do we do?" I didn't want to be anywhere near him when his punishment came.

"I- we- I" he stumbled trying to find words as though he was trying to grope for something on the floor in a dark room. He began to breathe heavily. His chest heaving up and down quickly.

"Gael?"

I was too slow to realize what was happening. I was free to panic; I could let adrenaline and cortisol flow so freely through my veins. I could let the natural human reactions accompanied by imminent peril happen, I could feel that fight or flight response kick in. Gael, however, was tracked, and his panic and fear had started to trigger the reaction. The same chemical reaction that I had needed each evening to maintain a last bit of sanity, the emptiness that I sought in order to sleep through each night, was being forced on him. I could see in my mind the thin liquid starting to seep into his system, oozing from the metal in his finger. He would be knocked out cold within 30 seconds. I hadn't seen this reaction up close before, I remembered that morning in the desert when Gavin was on edge, but I'd never seen this right before my face. It didn't look peaceful, it looked like torture. To be forcefully knocked-out, to have no freedom within your own body. I felt a small bit of vindication seeing Gael suffer the loss of his own personhood. But I could feel a sticky wetness in my front left pocket. Some goo, some grease was leaking from inside my pocket. The same chemicals being pumped into Gael were trying to get into my system through my tracker.

"Gael?" I asked again, my mind finally beginning to realize what was happening. He looked at me with his dark and unfeeling eye and stopped moving. I could have sworn that he was dead were it not for the soft rasp of his lungs continuing to pump air in and out of his system. I looked out toward the street and saw a creature standing in the driveway of the spare house. It had appeared in the time it took Gael to pass out. Perhaps his reaction had been moved along by some remote device. I had heard Whitney tell me once that she saw an entire room of people pass out on command. Then I thought of my most recent memory of Whitney and began to shake with unadulterated terror.

I'm not sure why that first thought of Whitney ran through my head at that exact moment. But it did, and I can confidently say it was a result of my human nature, my will to survive. Because remembering her observation, that is what kept me alive that night. Thinking back to that small bit of speculation, kept me from the fate that Gael would soon meet.

I looked at the creature for only a moment, until it began to move. I was thankful for the dark tinted windows and the black night with no street lights or stars in the sky. I was grateful for a few seconds of cover. I grabbed the pistol that Gael always had tucked behind his back, pressed between his pants and his skin. I held it in my left hand, finger on the trigger and tucked it behind my back quickly, hoping that this movement would be unnoticed at such a distance. I imitated Gael's heavy deep breathes and collapsed onto myself closing my eyes.

Then for the longest twenty seconds in recorded history, I heard the heavy thud of alien boots approaching the vehicle. I heard each clomp and scrape on the pavement. And in the final seconds, I heard the wheezing breathes from behind the face mask. I heard death walking towards us, and I had no way to riddle out an end to this that didn't lead to my quick and insignificant death.

Finally, the boots were close, it was upon us. I wanted so much to open my eyes and see this danger as it approached. But I kept them shut. Not squeezed tight, but gently closed, as though I were pushed into a drug-induced slumber. I heard the boots stop. I expected a fiery blast of a weapon to pulverize us. I expected a loud smack on the hood of the car. I expected a loud guttural and animalistic (hmm, alienistic) roar of dominance and power. What I heard instead was a low and hallow laughing, a mechanical laugh behind the thick and anonymous mask. I wanted to wince and brace for impact, but I willed myself to do no such thing.

The laughing paused and the boots were now moving towards the driver's side of the car. They were so close. For a moment I wondered if this thing would be able to tell that I was faking. But the serum had been released from my tracker, the damp spot on my thigh proved that. I worried that it might absorb through my skin and cause a topical reaction, I worried enough for a decade of pre-invasion years in those small moments that night.

I heard the uniform click of the door latch release and the slight brush of the night air as the open door breathed and the monster gained access to the car. My skin must have betrayed me, I felt goose pimples rise all along my bare arms. I heard a slide and a light thud and a dragging. I could feel that

Gael was no longer next to me in the car, but was now outside, being moved by the alien. I heard the boots as they made their way back this time heading towards my side of the car. I braced for the boots to get closer and closer. I heard them approach and close the space between us until there were only a few inches of aluminum and a motorized window separating us. I heard the tell-tale click of the passenger door latch releasing.

In this moment, I am truly surprised that I didn't fumble. That I wasn't stunned and immobilized by fear. I can say that I don't know what saved me. At that time, I believed no God would save me because the existence of these aliens, in my mind, negated the existence of God. Maybe it wasn't an instant of divine intervention, but rather the pinnacle of a lifetime of surviving and training. Either way, a miracle happened, I didn't shoot myself in the back with an eager trigger finger. I didn't feel my forearms cower under the weight of the loaded gun.

I opened my eyes, swung my left arm around, managed to point the gun level with my arm and fired a shot at the alien standing next to me, the car door now open and his head crouching down to meet mine. It stumbled back. I shot again and again. I hadn't stopped to consider that there could be more nearby, an infestation waiting to pounce. In the darkness, I couldn't make out the bars on the alien's shoulder, but this was the Porth Commander, our neighbor, our warden. And I had shot at him, and made contact, three times.

I saw it stumble back further until I felt confident enough to unbuckle myself, stand up and point the gun at the beast on the ground and fire, both hands on the gun.

This is why I was so damn valuable to Gael. This was what he knew might happen. Because while he was knocked out, unable to stop the reaction from the disc in his finger, I was able to evade it. I was the guard of his body, the sentry as he was starting his passage to the underworld. I was his slim chance at survival should he ever be caught and incapacitated. I was the bodyguard and the body-bruised.

I stood with the gun aimed at the alien, it had fallen back onto its back end and was now holding onto its torso, compressing the spots where bullets had struck him. I couldn't tell if they had pierced the suit and made an injury. I couldn't see any bright green or blue blood flowing from its stomach. I was curious to find out if it was red blood pumping with iron and if it would oxidize when it made contact with the air, or if it was milky and clogged? What substance kept these horrible beings moving? It was too dark for such detail and I wasn't given any time to examine it further. My curiosity was alive and well again, I couldn't say the same for my unfriendly neighbor.

A loud scream rang out from the street behind me. I spun and pointed the gun at the dark road towards the direction of the noise. I was grossly unprepared for another attack from the Porthana, but I would have been proud to die fighting.

"Dora! Don't shoot!" I heard the bodiless voice shout. It was human and it knew my name. Only a few humans left alive on the planet knew my name; I immediately distrusted this voice and lowered my weapon. The contradictions of the human experience should never stop confusing you. (Yes, I instinctively did not trust whomever was coming toward me, but I lowered that gun because it was human and I thought I might need the remaining bullets for the alien not four feet away from me. Humans I could manage with my hands. So far, the gun that was in my hand was the only thing I had seen that stopped the Porthana.)

As I heard the approach of whoever was calling for me, stumbling feet on the pavement and shallow human breaths, I thought of what they must have seen. A few bright flashes of light in the darkness, illuminating me and the alien, hunched over, but still far taller than me. And in an instant, it made me think of that dark night on a stretch of highway not so long ago. When Mitch betrayed us, Gavin was killed, and Barbie and I were captured. That night, when the sting of betrayal was clear in my mind and my wounded knee was failing me with each pounding stride, I had also been free. I felt the impossibility of my plan, my simple and foolish plan to run for freedom, sink into my bones and ligaments. I felt the hot shaft of the pistol with my hand and wondered if I should stick around to find out who was coming towards me. *Should I run now? Should I exit the entire scheme with a quick and brutal shot to my head?*

"Don't shoot!" the voice called out again, as though they were already inside my head. The voice, clearly male, was much closer and soon I was able to see a shape in the darkness.

"Don't-" it wheezed, and with one step closer I was able to see the clear shape of a man, hair sticking up on its ends, long raincoat flapping behind him, glasses barely hanging on to his face and nine fingers held up above his shoulders, an act of surrender and the universal "I come in peace." But what peace was Simon bringing?

I thought he might stop running once he reached me, but no, he ran straight at me. He grabbed the gun deftly with his right hand and pointed it quickly at the alien on the ground. It was curling up on its side, rocking itself back and forth, but it made no sound that I could hear. Simon kicked it and the alien moved fully onto its side. With the back exposed Simon fired a shot into the large square machine on the exo-suit and with a whimper the arms and legs of the alien relaxed and it stopped moving. It was dead. Humans- 1; Porthana- approximately ninety percent of the Earth population.

How the hell does Simon know how to kill one of these things? He had just done the impossible in a manner of seconds. The Porthana had been so protected by their massive size and their unfathomable quantities. We humans stood no chance against them, and yet Simon knew what to do. Simon the Scientist was also Simon the Warrior.

I didn't know what to say and as the shock of the situation began to set in, Simon wasted no time. He grabbed my arm and led me over to where Gael was laying. Gael's eyes still open, his lungs still functioning, his greasy hair covering part of his face. He looked peaceful, but even a sleeping lion can be a terrifying sight. In the darkness, he was just visible, but he was there.

I wondered if Gael would be thankful enough to let me go. *When he woke up, would he realize that I had served my intended purpose and set me free?* My horrible human hope was bubbling up inside of me and it was betraying me with each neural pathway it infected. I started to crouch down to see if I could rouse Gael. I had my hand on his shoe, lightly pushing it to one side.

The loudest sound I've ever heard deafened me in an instant. I closed my eyes and fell to my left, away from the sound, away from the smell of the sulfur. When I opened my eyes, I could no longer see any of Gael's face, and Simon was covered in blood. Not just on his hand, but all over him. But this is also where my memory splits, and often where my nightmares begin. When

I think back on it, I can clearly see in a flash that the shot to Gael's head was small, almost superficial. He had that calm and incapacitated look on his face forever. But I also remember seeing his head blown off, pieces of gray matter and slimy blood sprayed all over, the resulting reaction making me scream. I haven't riddled it out in my mind which one of these memories is real, but I think maybe I was seeing Don's brutal death again in the second vivid memory. I don't know. I have a lot of time to be my own psychologist, but I know that I saw Gael dead.

Before I could think about whether Simon would shoot me, enslave me, save me, or abandon me, I succumbed to the raw shock and passed out. At least it was of my own volition and not because of a stupid metal disc.

I dreamt in the final moments before I awoke. But the dream was just a replay of what had happened. Gael was burned by the Porths, we were both isolated and on the execution list for the Porthana. And then gunshots. So many quick gunshots. *Simon, the Social Scientist, the Timid, the man gone mad who had cut off his own thumb, had come to help? Had he come to finish the job? Had he come to force me to run away with him? Had he come to rescue me? Had he come to imprison me as well?* As these questions about Simon flooded my mind my eyes shot open and met his stare. Across a dwindling fire, he was staring intently at me, lying on his side, the weight of his torso resting on his arm, the one without the missing thumb. His small eyes, shielded by his glasses, didn't move as I awoke. The dying flames reflected on his spectacles and gave a brief illumination to his face.

My head was heavy and my body was tight. I tried to sit up, but found that was difficult. I felt a dry thirst in my lips and scanned the expansive dark sky for some sign of where we might be.

"Don't move too much, Dora," Simon spoke softly. He lifted himself onto his knees and crawled towards me. As I tried to sit up once more his hands were on my shoulders, his knees beneath my head, now cradling me and keeping me still.

"Why? Where are we?" My demanding questions were weakened by the fog cascading and pooling in my skull, the thirst in my throat, and the months of alien occupation that had left me senseless and confused on a continuing basis.

"We're outside of the city limits. Headed east through the Mojave. We'll rest for a bit longer before we head out." He stroked my hair and calmed his words to soothe me. I felt like I was a house-cat being pet by a patient master. I didn't like being the house-cat.

"Why did you take me here, Simon?" My frustration came through in my words.

"Should I have left you to finish off the alien and then face the punishment their kind would offer you? Should I have left you to resuscitate Gael, only to find that he would have readily sold you out for a chance to live?" His voice was stern, like that of a teacher. His patronizing was annoying, but his justifications seemed logical enough.

"How can those things insist on punishment for murder? If there was a universal justice system, *they* would all be condemned by now." I tilted my head and met his eyes.

"The irony isn't lost on me, Dora," he finished his words then offered a soft "*shhh*" to keep me quiet. I followed his instructions this time, closed my eyes and drifted a bit. I could feel his hands stroking my hair, I could feel his hard knees and the dirty denim that covered them on the pressure points behind each of my earlobes. When I woke again, I was only thirsty, not groggy. I was thinking clearly and all that I wanted was-

"Water!" I wheezed the word as loud as I could.

Simon had left the fire fully die down and now in the absolute darkness, I felt my head lowered to the ground and heard his boots sliding in the dirt as he moved around the camp that he had set up.

Soon a cool trickle of liquid covered my face and I moved to catch the stream in my mouth. Warm water, warmer than the desert air around us. But it was water, it tasted clean and pure. The stream stopped and I heard a plastic bottle it had come from crinkling in his hands.

"We only have a few bottles Dora so we have to reserve it for now. We can both have more at daybreak." My eyes were adjusting to the night, my pupils dilating to fill the entire size of my irises. The light offered from the stars above began to give a shape to Simon's figure moving back towards me. He sat down next to me as I managed to sit up, this time not suppressed by a heavy head. I wanted to know how he had found these provisions in Gael's car. *Did he stop to pick them up while I was knocked out? Had he been planning this trip or was it all on the fly?*

"You passed out, I had to put you in the car quickly. You didn't hit the ground when you fell, but I may have hit your head when I closed the car door." His examination and explanation were almost comical. I could almost hear the embarrassment in his voice. I let out a small giggle.

"That explains one thing," I reached to the crown of my head and patted it softly. My hair was in a large disarray, had Simon let my hair down? I maneuvered it into a make-shift bun and let it sit on top of my head.

"What else needs explanation? We're heading out at first light east through the Mojave."

"I remember that part, Simon, I don't know why we would head back east, but I'm sure you have your reasons."

"I do, very good reasons in fact."

"OK, well I appreciate you taking me to safety, but my own plan is to head north. So, we'll just have to part ways in the morning." I liked the taste of freedom on my lips. When I had first set out from Tampa, that first day, I had been so afraid to be alone, now it was the only thing that I trusted.

"No, Dora," his words weren't brusque or demanding, they were cool and subtle as if to say "*oh no*" not "*hell no*". I felt his hand reach up and caress my face. I was receiving the house-cat treatment again, although now his hands felt cool and smooth, a welcome reprieve from the heat of the night air.

"I can go where I want to Simon," my defiance was clear even if thirst muted my voice. I had been through enough of other people trying to control me. I wanted to do what I wanted to do and would let my stubborn indignant nature kill me if I needed to prove my point.

"I know Dora, and I know that you have wanted to be free, but I know things," the desperate tone to his voice matched the shakiness of his palm, still on my face. I was silent and let him continue.

"Please, stay with me? I don't want to be alone," his voice broke, and I wasn't picturing the Simon who had been strong-willed and had cut off his thumb, I wasn't picturing the Simon who had killed Gael. I was picturing the man who was being dragged down the hallway on that day when I was betrayed and sold. I pictured the scared and helpless look of shock on his face after he had been beaten and kicked by the giant alien. And that moment of weakness, remembering how afraid he had been and how afraid I was, made me rethink and question my own plan.

"OK, I'll stay for now. But I'll go when I like." I was firm, but the words were melting as they left my mouth and I leaned my head further into his hand. And there it was. For the first time in months, I wanted to be touched. I wanted to be held and cradled. I wanted a man to protect me and possess me. Gael and Don had both tried to control me with their hands, they were hard and cruel. But Simon's hands were soft and tempting. Surely, he felt the same need that I did, surely, he was a better man than those two. *Surely, my assumptions and human rationalizations were bound to fail me.*

We slept side by side on the hard and cool earth. As the horizon faded into a cool lavender and broke out into a bright red we woke, took our small sips of water and got into the car. It was the car that had been driven by Gael not twelve hours earlier. It had been the vessel that had carried me from one point of captivity to the next. But now Simon was behind the wheel and headed east.

"So where are we going?" I finally asked as the morning sun was striking straight ahead of us, starting to pierce our eyes, making us wince and hold our forearms out as a small means of protection from the light.

"East." Simon was plain and direct.

"Yes, but where exactly?"

"I don't think you'll like it, but I need you to make this work Dora." His honesty was not in the least bit comforting.

"Where are we going, Simon?" All charm and warmth from the previous evening dissipated in the energy between us.

"I think I know where *they* are based out of for their North American occupation."

I didn't respond. He was right, I didn't like it.

"If we can get in and somehow-"

"Disarm an entire army of sadistic aliens aimed at enslaving and studying our entire species?"

Simon had no response to this. Simon the Silent.

"Had you actually planned this out? We should be trying to get as far away from these things as possible and you want to go into the hub of their operations?" I was a shrill and nagging woman in that instant.

"What, so we just hide forever Dora? We let someone else figure out a plan to fix this?"

"Yup!" I had no problem sitting out this round and letting someone else do the dangerous work. I hadn't been like this before, but now I was cold and calculating. I was thinking about my own survival. Damned if I did care enough to act, damned if I was too scared to help.

"No Dora! We have to do something; we have to at least try." He gestured with his left hand, and that motion reminded me of what he had done already. The man had already cut off his thumb, he was committed to this cause. This also made me think of the thin disc in my own pocket.

"And die in the process? What good will that do Simon?"

"No good, it will do no good. But at least our conscience will be clean."

"I can live with a bad conscience Simon, at least I'll be alive."

We sat in silence for some time. And then I found a bullet to shoot into his moral argument.

"How can you lecture me about a clean conscience when you killed Gael?"

Simon let out a deep and heavy sigh. His eyes still focused on the road ahead as he tried his best to explain.

"If we had left him and he had woken up, he would have been captured easily by the Porthana and his death would have been slow and torturous. It wasn't an easy choice, but it was the most humane."

"You don't know that; you don't know that at all. He could have escaped, he could have had a chance," I wasn't sure where my anger was coming from, or why I was so ready to protect and defend Gael. I was glad that Gael was dead, elated, but threatened by his absence. How was the death of Don, who had abused me for two weeks, so readily accepted than that of Gael, the man who had enslaved me for months? Was I becoming inured to my own pain, buying into the rhetoric that my life was only worth what my body could be used for?

"Oh, would you prefer to be back with him being forced to do God-knows-what every evening just to earn a few scraps of food and a black eye?" Simon had reached his boiling point. His words were correct, not a single one was untrue. I held my tongue and looked out the car window. I didn't want him to see me as I felt my face get red and hot, my eyes start to water. It was all true, I had been a piece of property and felt no worth for myself. I was ready to defend Gael because he had been my primary food source, the only person to offer shelter. His price had been my soul and my humanity and now that the transaction was complete, I didn't know where to begin starting to find myself again.

Simon made no apologies, and neither did I. We sat in silence as he drove, the desert passing by us and the mountains behind us now growing smaller and smaller in the side-view mirror. As the wind whipped across the barren land it sprayed a thin satin sheet of hot dust over us, covering us and concealing us from what was all around us: aliens.

At mid-day, Simon pulled over at an abandoned gas station. From the looks of the rust on the gas pumps, it had been long forgotten before the invasion. Simon looked in the garage bays for any gasoline and eventually found some tubing and managed to siphon what was left in the underground wells into the gas tank of the car. I worried that the gas might be too old and could damage the vehicle, but it started just fine.

I worried that the rest of the day would be spent in silence, but Simon handed me some food: two wrapped beef jerky sticks and a Hostess cake. I accepted and gave my thanks. He nodded and continued to look ahead at the road.

"Are you going to eat?" I asked when I noticed that he didn't have anything set aside for himself.

"Nah, I'm not very hungry."

"Oh," I sensed that it was something I did or said that repressed his appetite. My human tendency to think primarily of myself was still alive and well. I pulled open the wrapper of the Hostess cakes, bright yellow and fluffy. I handed one of the cakes over to Simon.

"You should still eat. Your body needs something." I tried to be firm, but was still timid. His latest rebuke had been too true and I knew I couldn't stand another dose of that truth.

Simon accepted and devoured the cake in a matter of seconds.

"When we stop again later, I'll redress your bandage for you, you don't want it to get infected." I nibbled on the beef jerky as he continued to drive.

"Thank you, Dora, that would be," he paused, causing my eyes to shoot up to meet his, "very nice."

"Okay, then," I found myself nervous and excited. I didn't necessarily want to see the giant sucking hole where his thumb had once been. But I felt electrified to think of touching his arm and his skin. For all of the contact that I had with Gael, the slaps and punches, the unconscious molestation and rape of my body, I felt nothing but repulsion. I was nauseated to think of all of the places that man had touched me. But to think of Simon the Scientist, Simon the Savior letting me touch his arm I was on fire. Alight with desire and not sure how to handle that feeling.

After a few more moments, Simon broke the kinetic tension and energy between us. "Since we're on the run together," he emphasized the word. "I have a small confession to make."

"Go ahead," I encouraged him, somewhat curious, but mostly nervous. Not nervous in that I was scared of what he might tell me, but nervous because his hand was so close to mine. Attraction had been a human feeling that had been banished in the past months, but suddenly it was alive and well and I didn't know what to think of myself.

"I had to know that you wouldn't be tracked or followed Dora. So," he let out a deep sigh, "I'm embarrassed to admit it."

My eyebrows stitched themselves together without my permission, my lips drew themselves into a flat line. I knew that I was not going to like what he was about to say, I was beginning to wish for an uncomfortable silence again. Every time Simon spoke, he seemed to only have bad news.

"I checked your fingers and your palms when you were passed out, but I couldn't find your trigger. I was going to cut it out for you, but I couldn't find it."

"You were going to cut off my finger while I was asleep?"

"Yeah," his response was timid and nervous.

"And what did you think I would have done when I woke up? Thank you for permanently maiming me?"

"Well, you would be able to stop biting and itching so that would have been a relief." Simon wore the guilt of his plan on his face.

"Oh, so that would have made it OK?" I was so frustrated at the thought of another man trying to make decisions for me. He was just like the rest, but he hadn't gone through with it, so perhaps he had a chance of not being a total asshole.

"But I couldn't find it Dora, so I didn't do anything. They must have put it deep beneath the skin." He waved his hand in the air dismissing the idea, batting it away like a patch of cigarette smoke.

"Well thank goodness for that."

"So, where did they implant it? They must have done something very experimental to get yours so deep. Do you still have the urge to scratch it all the time?" The scientist was coming out to play and investigate. He had so many questions, I wondered how long he had been dwelling on them, picturing the procedure, imagining faint scar lines beneath my clothes.

"Yes, I still bite my nails like the rest of us," I showed him my ripped and raw fingernails.

He smiled as he looked at them. I wanted him to reach out and inspect each finger, hold it in his hand, to heal it with his mouth. But he didn't do that.

"So, where did they implant it then?"

"I'm not telling you," I replied instantly.

"Why not?"

"Because I don't want to wake up in the middle of the night to find myself dismembered. Thank you very much."

"I won't do anything about it, I just figured we could make conversation about it."

"Well Simon, since you inspected my hands thoroughly when I was asleep, I bet you have your own theories as to where else it could be. You'll just have to keep searching." I couldn't help but tease him. His face was so sweet and calm, and for some unknown reason, I was willing to trust him and entice him. This feeling was so unexplained, and in spite of my recent experiences with the male gender, I was revolted by my own arousal.

Simon looked directly into my eyes, staring, searching, observing, experimenting, calculating. I half expected him to pull the car over right then and there and start to search my body. But he didn't, he refocused on the road ahead and kept driving. We were silent for a few moments before discussing where we had originated and how we had survived the invasion.

Simon had been living and working in New York City. He had been on a research trip to South America and was returning to New York when it happened. His layover in Atlanta was supposed to be two hours; in the period of time between landing and when he was supposed to take off again, a fleet of marching Porthana descended upon the airport. He saw them coming down the tarmac and looked around to see if anyone else was seeing what he was. The way he recounted the tale was chilling, it reminded me of the thunderous feet I heard, obscured by lethal mist in my sunny Floridian paradise.

Simon said that he picked up his carry-on bag and headed to the ground transportation area. He heard the first gunshots as he was driving away in a stolen vehicle. The canisters of the aerosol neurotoxin were released all around him, so he shut off the air conditioning and drove for a full day without cracking a window or opening one vent. He told me that he had sweat through his entire outfit from the heat and his panic.

After a day of driving he cautiously exited the stolen car at a strip mall in northern Alabama and found some new clothes, and a new car to steal. He headed north towards Illinois, but met up with a group of humans in Kentucky. A shiver ran down my spine to think of how close he had been to where I was at that time. How easily he could have come across Don and his horrible schemes to monetize me and drug Becca. Would Simon had saved us?

Simon was hesitant to join the band of wandering survivors in the Bluegrass State, but he quickly assimilated into their group and because of his intelligence became the de-facto leader. The group decided to keep on the move so they headed west, this time working their way to Nebraska, then Colorado before they were all captured.

Apparently, it was one of the members of this group who told the Porthana that Simon was a Scientist. He had been sold out by one of his own. I remembered what Mitch did to me. Clearly one of our universal human tendencies is that being part of a group of people must require that someone is betrayed.

Simon told me that was how he ended up in that hallway when Barbie and I were dragged in. He said that we looked shell-shocked. I laughed at that comment and said that was an understatement. I told him my story and left out the parts about Don and his sadistic plans. Bad enough Simon knew what Gael did to me, little did he know that Gael was merciful and let me drug myself out of the pain.

As Simon listened, I thought again about the reason he had given for shooting Gael. Perhaps Simon was merciful as well. Simon the Strong. Simon the Merciful. Simon the Smoldering.

As the sun started to strike the rear-view mirror and set directly behind us, Simon pulled off the road and started a campfire. He asked me to help with unloading provisions for the night, water and some crackers and beef jerky. He had only a few pieces of jerky left, so I opted for crackers to start. I set out the blankets that had been our campsite the night before and spread them out evenly and smoothly on the ground. I didn't want to be too presumptuous so I set one on the far side of the fire, and the other on the opposite side.

I offered to re-dress his wound, but Simon insisted on cleaning it himself and asked me to find some kindling for the fire. When I returned, his bandage was much less bulky and the absence of his opposable digit more noticeable.

As the fire crackled and we talked about the most inane things from life before the invasion, it was easy to almost forget that they were out there. We were just two campers on the road, telling fireside stories. If we had a guitar, we might have started to do sing-a-longs and contemplate roasting marshmallows for s'mores. It was a night free from worry and anxiety, free from fear.

But eventually, we could no longer avoid the topic. Simon said that he was scarred from what he had seen, what he was told to do by them. His eyes were still and his face calm. He was retreating back into the shell, the one that the Porthana had put all of us into.

"So just what did *they* have you do?" I dared to ask.

"You don't want to know Dora. You wouldn't feel safe out here with me if you did." His voice was somber.

"Less safe than you admitting that you were going to cut off my hand last night?" I couldn't help but try to force us back into the equilibrium of a few moments earlier when we were light and without worry.

Simon laughed at my joke. "Speaking of which, you never told me where it was." There was a devilish guile in his face.

"I told you, you'd have to try and find it." My thoughts immediately went to my front pocket, but I didn't let myself blink or give it away. I knew where my tracker was at all times, I had a mental lo-jack on it, rather than it keeping tabs on me.

Simon stood up, towering over the low and small fire, towering over me as I sat on the ground, and he circled the fire before sitting down next to me. He sat a respectable foot away and looked at me, trying to see through my skin to find where it was. I liked his eyes on me. I liked guessing at what he might be thinking. I liked the anticipation and the heat of it all.

He gestured for my hand and I extended out my right palm towards him. He took each fingertip and pressed and rolled the skin, palpating, looking for something to stick out. But nothing did. I enjoyed knowing that he would never find it, I liked being in control.

After my right hand, he inspected my left hand. He searched upwards on my forearms and finally, after exhausting the obvious options said, "So if it's not in your hands, where is it?"

I shrugged my shoulders and offered nothing but a smile in return.

"You do have one, right?" his left eyebrow was raised, his curiosity was boiling.

"Yes," I tried to keep a straight face. The nervous tension was becoming too much to handle.

Simon looked at me for a long moment. The fire was burning much lower now, with neither of us tending to it. An ember snapped loudly and crackled in the pit of the flame. That sound, sharp and loud, was enough. He was upon me; I was upon him. We were on each other, our mouths and hands unable to be still. His hands were searching across my skin for anything he could grab hold of. My hands were in his hair and across his back.

The night surrounded us as we continued to search and experience each other. The desert wind cooled our bodies as we groaned and collapsed. The night shielded us and gave us one last chance to explore our one true human need.

As dawn was breaking across the horizon, I rose from our make-shift bed.

Simon, still sleeping heavily, had pulled his blanket over to my side of the fire after our needs were satisfied and slept with his arms around me.

I crept silently a few feet away to dress. I ran my hands through my loose and oily hair. I wanted to shower and clean myself, but I was finding an odd familiar comfort with sleeping on the ground and living on the land. I pulled on the shirt that had been my second skin since the afternoon, seemingly a lifetime ago, when I was thrown from a car on the plains of Texas, hooded and captured. My pants were dirty and wearing at the knees. I buttoned them and enjoyed a moment of silence staring out at the impending sunrise.

The previous night had been a welcome delight. I could feel Simon's whole hand grab at my sides and press into my skin. The sore ache from the bruises that Gael had left dissipated with Simon's hot touch. I had no concern for what this would do to bond Simon and me together. But it felt nice to be in control. I could have said no and that would have been it. But I wanted him so I had him. I liked the freedom of that choice again.

I felt my mouth start to perk up into a smile, a faint and hesitant one, but a smile. It was so foreign, like hearing my voice speak in a language I had never learned. I closed my eyes and felt the warmth of the hazy yellow sun on my face. My thumbs, my poor gnawed thumbs, were hanging on the loops of my pants. I made a small and easily breakable promise to myself to stop biting my nails. It really did feel as though the troubles of the occupation were as far away as a distant planet. We hadn't seen any signs of life, alien or otherwise. I longed to stay in this barren and empty land forever. But just like this habitat, nothing could last very long in the dry and arid desert.

With this brief and honest moment, I ruined it. I ruined it all.

I moved my thumbs from the belt loops and placed my hands into my pockets. I was relaxed and calm. I could hear my lover starting to rustle just behind me. The day was shaping up to be beautiful. But then the fingers of my left hand were alone. Puzzled, I dug my hand further into my pocket. It was empty. I reflexively checked my right front pocket as well, but it was also empty.

I moved to check my back pockets, but I knew already that it wasn't there.

My little metal disc, the unimplanted tracker, was not where it was supposed to be. In the many months that it had been my saving grace and small talisman of torture, I had never lost track of it. Ever since Mitch had explained that this should be my one true secret, I had accounted for it each and every day. I always knew where I was. It stayed on my person at all times, or in my mouth. Maybe it just felt like I had some control and that is why I had kept it so close. I could think that I had some upper hand. But now, it was not in my pocket and I knew, like a secondary instinct, that this was bad.

I could hear Simon moving behind me, so I stayed with my back to him for a moment trying to recompose my features. I couldn't seem panicked or worried in front of him without inviting suspicion, but I was panicked and I was worried. I trusted Simon enough to be alone in the desert with him, miles from anyone or anything. I trusted him with my body. But I didn't yet trust him with this fact.

I tried to find that calm smile, the one that I had so briefly just a moment before and turned to face Simon. He was almost completely dressed and shaking the dust from his hair. I walked back to our small camp and reached for the water bottle; two swallows left in it.

I took my share and handed the bottle to Simon. I could taste the free-radicals and melting plastic with that last sip, released from the container after hours of desert heat. I started to put together our camp and folded up the blankets. I was hoping that my trigger would drop to the ground and that I could quickly scoop it up without Simon seeing. No such luck.

I handled the blankets and walked them back to the trunk of the car, inspecting the ground as I walked. Thankfully that trigger wasn't in my thumb because I would have surely set off the intended reaction with the level of increasing adrenaline in my system. I tried to keep my breath calm, but I couldn't keep it all in.

"Everything okay?" Simon asked.

That damned perceptive scientist.

"Yeah, just getting everything ready to go."

"Oh, you just seemed a little off," he was right on the money, but I didn't want to admit it.

"No, I'm fine." I sat down by the cold ashes of the fire.

"So, you're not weird about last night?"

Right, Dora, he can't read your mind. "No, not at all," I actually fully smiled. It was the most unusual feeling. In all the things that I missed in the occupation, I missed smiling and being carefree. I missed being- human.

"Good," he smiled back. It was such a foreign sight; it was so disarming. I hadn't seen another person smile in what seemed like forever. He sat down next to me, so close that our legs almost touched. "So, we have enough gas for us to keep driving for a few more hours. I don't know if there is anything up ahead in terms of fuel so if we run out, we'll have to continue on foot."

"How much further is it?" I didn't want to speak of the place we were headed to. While we were waking and readying it was almost as though we were aimless nomads, no goal in sight. But Simon did have a goal. To take us into the heart of where the Porthana were coordinating their efforts. Simon the Scientist. Simon the Brave. Simon the Fool-hearted. Simon the Reckless.

"Another full day-and-a-half drive. If we have to walk though it could take a week. We'll need to be careful along the road."

In spite of the strain it would surely have on my feet and knees I wanted the longer option. I wanted to be in the wilderness and on the run longer, but I partially just wanted this endeavor to be over and done with. Perhaps with more time, I could convince him that we should just run. My muscles were in shape and ready for a fight, ready for a journey. But I didn't want to use them this way.

As if he was able to sense what I was thinking and wishing for, he offered an alternative view. "The longer that we are out on the land with no water and food, the less likely we are to survive. Also, we increase our risk of being caught."

I nodded, understanding the reality of survival. "So, let's hope for some gasoline." I shrugged my shoulders and stood, ready to be on our way.

"That still leaves us with the risk of being tracked. I liked your solution for finding the tracker, but it still left me-" he paused and laughed at the joke he was about to make. "-empty-handed."

"I think if they were tracking me, they would be on to us by now." I tried to ignore the fact that I now had no idea where it was. I had lost my tracker. I had no clue where it could be and I felt completely naked without the piece of metal that I had grown to hate.

"Dora, we need to get rid of it." He spoke evenly and sternly. There was no fun air or hint of excitement. It was a matter of fact, if I could be tracked then I was the biggest threat to us both.

I tried to look away.

"Dora, I know it's not a pleasant thought, but every second you risk them triggering a reaction that could knock you out." He gestured with his hand, his thumb-less hand.

I looked one more time at the ground, hoping that it would appear in the campsite.

"Every second that they can track you leaves us both at risk."

"Why are you so worried about being captured when your plan is for us to travel to where they are headquartered?" I didn't mean to snap at him, but he did have some pretty fucked up logic. As I was reacting with my words, I saw a small glint of metal in the ashes of the fire. Or did I? My mind was so ready to find my tracker, like a Tolkien character desperate for the metal, that I must have imagined it.

Simon was taking angry measured breaths, clearly frustrated at my hard-headed response. I quickly crouched low and ran my fingers through the cool embers, my hands becoming sooty and gray with each swipe. The object that caught my attention was no object at all, but actually a gray stone. I must have looked like a crazy woman, swooping and scrambling on the ground. My mind had been tricking me, and this was the way that I noticed it.

"Looking for this?" I looked up towards Simon.

Sitting at the tips of his fingers, like a precious stone on a pedestal was a thin and small metal disc. Simon the No-Good-God-Damned-Son-Of-A-Bitch!

"When-" I started to compose a question as my mind ran through the infinite number of scenarios where I might be able to still be alive in the next thirty minutes. I felt that I was in peril, I felt that this revelation could bring me no good fortune.

"I found it this morning; I knew what it was right away. I've seen enough of these implanted." Simon tossed it up in the air and caught it, as though it were a dime or a nickel or a piece of currency.

"Did you ever put them into someone?" I thought back to how Mitch, who had inevitably sold me out, had initially refused to participate in my torture. So maybe Mitch hadn't been half-bad after all, but he certainly wasn't half-good.

"No Dora, but *they* still made me do things I'm not proud of. When were you planning on telling me that you weren't being tracked?"

"I wasn't," I responded feeling moderately ashamed at my cold answer.

Simon's first response was a head-jerk with a question on his face. "What, you didn't trust me?"

"You just told me yesterday that you were planning to cut off my fingers when I was passed out!" A clear lover's quarrel with much higher stakes, we were either scaring away or attracting all manner of desert wildlife. Our voices were loud, probably carrying on the wind, muffling and mutating, but still flying away across the expanse.

"Well, I wouldn't have had to resort to that if you had just told me about this!" He threw the disc out into the open desert.

My eyes widened and without thinking my feet were moving. I started after it. I couldn't see where it landed, I didn't even hear it land it was so small, but I was moving towards it.

"What are you doing?"

"I'm getting it back!" I turned to answer as I continued to walk away.

"Why?"

At this question, I stopped.

"Well, because having it with me, but not in me has been a valuable thing."

"How so?" Simon the Adjunct Professor was present.

"Gael kept me alive, sheltered and fed because I was valuable. That disc was why. I could pass for being tracked, but I wasn't really being tracked. No one knew, absolutely no one. And that has been why I've survived so long."

Simon considered my answer.

"Well now I know, so it's no longer a secret." Simon shrugged casually at the loss of my last true vestige of individuality. Now I was just another untracked human, perhaps I was still rare if not unique. "And the two of us traveling together untracked and untagged gives us more of an advantage than you still keeping it around."

I tried to consider every possible way that he could be manipulating me. I hadn't come to expect much from other humans after these long months. All I had seen was a small bit of kindness in an endless sea of extortion and lies. Humans have an amazing capacity to hurt one another. It seems that is the most basic element of our nature. In any situation a power will be created or consumed, one human subjugated under another. It was in our nature long before the skies opened up and revealed the beasts of the universe. They may have enslaved us, but they also exposed how we were merely civilized animals walking on hind legs. Strip away the rules of society and we all crumble, we self-destruct, we disregard, we bite at each other.

Simon may have been scanning my face for the recognition of his words. Would I comply? Would I agree? Would I be passive? Would I be difficult? And perhaps his motives were simply to be rid of any chance of detection.

"Okay," I said tentatively, trying out the word like I would have tried on a dress in the life that had been eviscerated by the alien occupation.

And so as we drove away, towards an empty gas tank and a certain foreboding doom, my trigger, my tracker, my once prized secret that had spent long hours wearing thin the materials of my pants pockets and wallowing in the dimple of my tongue would lay flat on the desert floor until the Good Lord rose or the expanding Sun swallowed the Earth whole.

The gas tank did run empty. We walked for fifteen miles before we found another abandoned gas station. By this time, it seemed impossible that it could be any hotter, but we didn't dare speak that thought and curse ourselves to any additional degrees on our skin. As we started to see the edge of a thick forest approaching, we could make out the hollow fiberglass sign, like a beacon of hope for stranded and thirsty motorist calling us forward. But the pathetic remains of the gas station only seemed to be laughing at us. Should we collect as much gasoline as we could carry and galumph back to the car to get it started and drive it to the station to extract more fuel? Or should we simply accept that fate had stopped us from our optimal plan and that we would now have to face a choice?

As we sat on the cement median between the long-ignored gas pumps we chuckled at the irony of our situation. Simon suggested that we scour the convenience store attached to the station for any remaining food scraps. The windows were shattered and it looked picked over, but there was always the hope of a stray Twinkie or some other food that could survive any nuclear winter or two.

We found some protein bars and a neon green sports drink. We didn't bother to speculate as to whether it had been created that color or if time had turned it to be that color. We had made rudimentary shoulder slings with our camp blankets that we had carried on our backs and I cradled our newly discovered goodies in my drop pouch like a mother cradling a newborn.

We headed along the road walking without any intention of hiding ourselves. We were calm and easy as we strolled, holding hands at times, not holding hands at others. Simon and I were two rogue cells in an efficient killing system. We were the start of a potentially cancerous growth. Simon the Scientist and Dora the…. Well, the first word that comes to mind is "Dora the Dead," but that was really the first time that I felt myself start to come alive again in small and simple ways. We had moments where we forgot what we were running from and running towards and shared sweet exchanges of words and other goodies from our tongues. Simon was the guide and I followed him willingly. No drugs needed on this ride.

We extended our walk by one day. After three days of hiking up into the mountains, we decided to take a rest for a full twenty-four hours and not leave our little camp. Simon was aware that we would make our descent into the cradle of our desolation soon. Our blankets were wearing thin and they were stained with mud, small twigs and barbs were catching onto the errant strings and the seams were loose.

In our firelight evenings, we remarked at the familiarity of telling old campfire stories or singing folk songs. Simon regaled me with some theories from his dissertation, a document fated to never be finished. He pulled from his memory some details about the Greek myth of Pandora and her renowned beauty. I saw through his act, but decided to let him in one more time.

These memories are vivid and fleeting and they only make the actions that we were both destined to take that much more bitter. But we savored the human luxury of time and that was the last and most beautiful thing that I will accomplish in this life. Extending our little affair for another twenty-four hours may well extend my life by years. This bit of happiness in the scariest place imaginable, an Earth run by the Porthana, is what I often long for, and never find, each evening.

We had to leave our sheltered camp. Our walks now were intentional. We were quiet, walking so that the balls of our feet touched the ground first, instead of the heel. We crouched and hid in the conifers, and as old habits die hard, I bit my nails to fill the tense moments when Simon would run ahead to check the road beyond where it curved to make sure there were no natural or alien surprises waiting. We felt the cool air of our altitude on the roads that we walked. We hurried through and huddled together for warmth. We shivered, and we scurried like hungry and scared mice. And for the first time in a week, we were scared.

As we ventured from the paved road and cleared the trees, we saw a long open plain before us. We would be exposed and without any means of hiding, but unlike our jaunt in the desert, we were now closer to the hive, the throng, the epicenter of our captivity. We both strode bravely, Simon getting excited and more determined as we approached the cylinder.

Yes, in the distance we could see a large glass cylinder, rising skyward, shimmering in the sunlight, connecting the ground below to the unknown and unseeable sky. How did this even get here? Did they lower it into our atmosphere? How could no one see this being built if they had planned the invasion among us? For a transparent object, its purpose and origin were milky and unclear. Simon increased his pace; he was eager to arrive and enact whatever his plan was. I grew increasingly nervous, unsure of what Simon thought we two small and feeble humans could do against the teaming masses of Porthana. *Shouldn't we turn around now?* At least we might have a chance of a quiet life in the wilderness. I wanted to voice my concerns, again, but I didn't want to risk Simon pushing on without me and leaving me alone. I wanted to be independent, but I wanted it to be of my own choosing, not because I was being left or abandoned. A social tendency of my species, so sue me (oh wait, court is adjourned forever, too bad bucko!)

The mounting tension was palpable and within a matter of hours, we had closed the valley that had separated us from doom. And like most good human females I had been trained to not whine or complain, to not question or intercede. I was docile, I was silent and obedient. Perhaps some of Gael's control still weighed on me, the tentacles of his influence pulling from my skin slowly, dragging with each footstep that separated me from that reality that was now dissolved.

We were twenty paces from the cylinder, it was not apparent at first sight, but it was the size of a city block in diameter. Simon finally broached the subject.

"What will we do when we exit?" His question was unexpected.

"When we exit? Simon, what is your plan for when we go in?" I couldn't curb all of my sarcasm and frustration.

"I don't know, but I hope to find a way to stop them." He was searching for words.

"I thought you had a plan!" I needed no time to find mine.

"I have some ideas, and if they are correct then we certainly have the upper hand."

"Simon?!" There was no question, but my voice called his name out as though he had spoken in another language and I was asking for a crude translation.

"So, to keep us focused on making it out, what will we do when we exit?" His question seemed absurd at the moment. He had led me across many miles with no plan, but the determined will to enter the metaphorical lion's den and now he wanted to know my plan for where to go next. Now?

"North. Head north and survive." I was careful not to include a 'we' in that sentence. After leading me for days across the country on foot with no plan, my patience for Simon had sublimated, vanished into steam and carried out on the wind. Perhaps I should have vocalized and visualized a happier ending, then maybe it would have happened.

"That's as good a plan as any," he added with a nervous laugh. He smiled at me cautiously, as though he had sensed my errant thoughts of frustration with him. I smiled a guilty smile, the kind that you offer to show that you were sorry, but that you knew you had been caught. That was the smile that I offered. He pushed his face forward and kissed me. "Let's go," he was moving quickly, I ambled to catch him.

With the technical grace of a gorilla, we found our way into the cylinder through a well-camouflaged access panel, painted the cool and muddy brown of the plains, but unable to mimic the feel of the ground and wispy grass under our feet. We dusted off the double doors and pried one side open. The hinges were cool and young, no age had rusted them yet or caused them to whine. We were both grateful, but exhilarated. We were in.

Through a cool tunnel, we could see the ambient light that was allowed into the cylinder as it touched the wires along the walls and reflected off the small pools of water in unpredictable patches on the cement floor below us. The path was short and we were under the expansive sky contained within the cylinder quickly, looking out at the ground where we had just been crouched. I felt more exposed now that we were on the inside than we had been on the outside.

I could see Simon surveying the long way up the cylinder as the ground below us, the metal paneling and mimicked tall grass, began to shake and I could feel the micro-movements of my body being carried… down. It was the feeling that would put a puff of air into my gut when I was in an elevator, it was familiar, but so alien in this reality. Simon reacted, his arms about him for balance and on guard, he looked like a primitive man, reacting to the thunderous footfalls of the saber-toothed tiger. He was on alert; his protective instincts were subtly attractive. His distracting seduction would kill me, I was sure of it, and I was ready.

After a slow churning ride 16 feet below the surface the platform stopped. *Had we been found? Had we activated a security system? Would a door soon open to reveal a small army ready to attack us?* Five seconds of still silence was too long. "Simon?" I whispered, risking the cataclysmic chain reaction that my near-silent words could unleash if that was all it took to signal an attack.

But no such attack happened. Simon moved to the edge of the circle and touched his left hand to the wall, he moved about the circumference looking for a switch or a side-panel or a lever or anything familiar. He passed in front of me and then behind me. I heard the even and crunching sound of his steps pause; he had found something. Each second was more terrifying than the one before it. There was no stopping the adrenaline and cortisol in my system, it was in control and I had to trust that it would keep me safe. I decided to trust Simon to take the lead, I was happy to be the follower. I turned to see what had caused him to stop, there was something under his hand. I moved closer to where he was standing. There were two palm-sized knobs, one faintly lit in green, the other in red. Simon moved his hand over the green knob and it glowed brighter. When he moved it away, the green light dimmed and the red light intensified.

"It seems so intuitive, right?" Simon asked, although I could sense that he anticipated no answer from me.

"What?" I asked, having heard him clearly and not needing him to repeat himself, but I was still confused by the question.

"Green means go and red means stop right?" Simon followed up with another question.

"Sure," I answered. He looked at me for a second longer than was necessary as he pressed the green knob, the panel in front of us opened. He continued to look at me as we stood in front of the open doorway, we looked away at the same time. What he was trying to communicate to me with his eyes I did not ascertain. I thought it was just fear and apprehension and the bond that we had created with our bodies. I was wrong. He had been trying to relay a message via a telekinesis that neither of us had within our power.

Simon led us into the hallway that was poorly lit by circular lights spaced every three feet. The tubing and wires that were secured to the bulkhead were tight and clean. There was no steam emanating from an unknown vent. My illusion of what the Porthana headquarters should look like was too focused on science fiction movies. This space was clean and orderly, what else would be expected of the species that coordinated a simultaneous invasion across the globe?

Simon crept softly in front of me, his back crouched and curved, I followed his lead. A few steps in he reached back for my hand, I took it. I wasn't afraid of being left behind, but it was just another human reflex.

A few paces further he stopped suddenly and pushed me quietly against the wall, his breath was urgent and he quickly flipped so that we were shoulder-to-shoulder, flat against the wall behind our backs. He had heard something and now I could feel it under my feet. Something big was coming, something with a hefty weight was moving and working its way across the same floor that we were standing on. I was somewhat surprised that we hadn't encountered one of *them* sooner. It was inevitable to find an alien in the alien headquarters, right? *Right?*

Simon was busy surveying the hallway around us, I was making myself useless and trying to decide what I wanted my last human thought to be before I was murdered. Simon released his hold of my hand and ventured across the hallway towards another set of those mysterious knobs. Once he was upon them the faint green and red glow started again. At this discovery I was curious. Motion detected door releases? *That's advanced. (Duh Dora! Of course, they're advanced, they flew in their fancy spaceships with sophisticated biotechnology, but the doorknobs are what strikes you as advanced?!?)*

I took action, for the first time since we started this adventure, and without any prompting, I joined Simon. We passed our hands over the green button and the door opened. We stepped through quickly and watched for the door to close.

It was pitch black. I could see nothing, but I could sense Simon next to me. We may have evaded detection in the hallway, but we had no idea whether danger or safety was in front of us. *Why this room, why this door, why underground?* I crouched down low to the ground to feel what was in front of me. I heard Simon move, I heard his breath next to me on the ground. We crawled for a few feet, but I noticed that my eyes were adjusting, my pupils dilated and began to find the forms of the shapes around us.

I could start to see that we were in a storeroom, there were boxes around us like skyscrapers in a city grid. Simon fumbled next to me. *Had he tripped? Had he been grabbed? Had he found something? Had he lost something?*

I looked in the direction of the noise and soon my eyes were under the acute pain of bright light flooding through open pupils. My face soured and tightened and pursed in the invading light, illuminating my least attractive looks. Simon had found a source of light and had pointed it directly at me, he quickly lowered it upon the sight of my sour-puss face.

"This box," he bumped his elbow against the box beside him, "is full of them." The circular light was the same shape and intensity of the lights in the hallway. He passed the light from his hand to mine. I held it up to the top of the container so that Simon could find another. He grabbed three, one for each of our empty hands. We stood and began to assess where we were. And then I saw one, I saw thousands ahead of us. My heart stopped beating for a second and then resumed a pounding at no speed I had ever encountered before in my life. They were so close, they had to see us. We were caught.

Simon hadn't seen them yet; he was checking the boxes to his left. I wanted to bring his attention to them, but my vocal cords were scared flat. I felt that my throat was so tight, had my adrenaline controlled me, forcing me into silence in this most terrifying moment?

"Siii- Sii-S" I tried to finish his name. I concentrated on keeping the lights in my hand. *Don't drop them, don't drop them.* My left hand shook, jiggling the light. This is what caught Simon's attention. He turned and began "Yeah, Dora?" at a regular volume. I was so mad at the volume of his voice.

"Lll—loo-look Si-Siiii" I stammered like a pile of mush and human capabilities.

I couldn't point to them without raising my palms and moving the lights in my hands again. I just wanted to be so still that I would disappear and find myself in a safe place. He must have seen them because he threaded his arm through mine and began to gently tug at me, pulling me backward. He positioned himself right behind me and with the small movements of his hands we navigated into the crook between two bins and squatted on the floor, lights down.

He moved his mouth so close to my ear that he barely had to make a sound for his words to be clear to me. "We hide for two more minutes to get our control of the situation. Then we stand and continue forward. We aren't giving up or going down without a fight, Dora." I nodded, but he couldn't see that. I wanted to say "okay," but I was afraid of my words. I wanted to point out that if attacked we had nothing to fight with. But I was silent and took charge of what Simon instructed me to do. I tried to control my breath and calm my heartbeat. It worked, a little. I was too terrified to have much success with that endeavor, but I tried.

Simon must have been counting the seconds in his head because he gently rubbed my shoulder and whispered so faintly, "Let's go." He stood and I followed. We held our palms down, the lights in our hands provided just enough illumination to find our way. His right hand created a claw around the light, with no thumb to hold it in place. I thought about how his fingertips must be burning up from the heat of the light. Both of my palms were already sweaty and overheated, I wondered how soon these lights might slip and cause a loud noise that would alert all of the aliens crawling in this facility to our presence and bring them to this exact location.

I was surprised that the aliens that had been directly facing me not a few moments earlier hadn't moved towards us yet. Simon crouched and moved quickly towards them. He knelt behind another storage bin and I followed. I could make out the shape of him, his head peeking over the top of the bin looking at the Porthana just a few meters from us. I tried to keep my breath quiet, I focused on being as small and invisible as I could be to avoid detection. And then I realized that the only breath I could hear at all was Simon's and my own. I didn't hear the clunky and disjointed breath of the Porthana respiring and oozing through their exo-suits. I didn't smell the sweet and stinky odor that emanated from them. I could only smell the dirty and human smell from Simon's skin, his manly stench now so familiar, but still distinctly human.

As Simon peeked and crouched, I stood up and walked over to the Porthana, now just three feet away, two, one. I reached out to touch the arm. I could feel Simon behind me, reaching for my other arm, the one closest to him, to try and pull me back and stop me.

But I had already touched the hard material of the suit and there was no recourse. The suit swayed a bit, as though it was dangling from some tall and unseen hanger. Simon was now behind me; he had dropped the lights and now his hands were on both of my elbows, holding me back.

"They're just the suits," I hissed, no longer afraid of the volume of my voice. "Simon, they're just the suits." He released me and moved further to examine them himself. He touched another one of the suits. Then another. He finally came to a third and gave it a solid kick. He had his first-hand proof and emitted a short laugh. It wasn't a laugh of joy, but rather a "we thought we were about to die, but now we may have at least a few more minutes" kind of laugh. It was sweet and unapologetically scientific. Just like Simon.

After the exo-suit scare, we regrouped. I couldn't stop the thoughts in my head because for the first time since we set out on this suicide-plan I had realized that we would be lucky to make it out alive. I began to understand the gravity of the situation, the force remanding me to this cursed planet, we would be severely outnumbered and probably no one would know of our death or where our bodies would be buried, if they would be buried at all. We were martyrs already, just not dead yet, and without an audience to cry out over the injustice of our pain. But hadn't that applied to every human massacred in the past few months?

I looked at the empty suits again, refocused and refined in my panic. *We'll see them for what they really are. See the face of our universal enemy plain and naked.* Knowing that they were out of their suits in this place, I wondered what their tentacles would look like, nude and exposed. What puss and seeping organic material would come out of the skin? Would it even be skin or just a muscular bulbous mass that covered their body? I pictured the worst and most ugly being I could think of, but my imagination was nowhere close to reality, once again.

As I mentally prepared to face our enemy, Simon went on inspecting the bins around us. He found one that was labeled with male stick figures. He opened the lid then quickly slammed it shut. He shook his head and muttered, "Biological samples." I was so grateful that I didn't have to see what Simon had seen or smell what he had smelled from that box. But a shiver, a cold and spinal shiver, ran down my back. The Porthana were indeed studying us, mutilating our bodies and collecting pieces at will for their own use.

I was afraid to open any of the bins myself, but I wanted to help with Simon's effort. I was also hoping that near the exo-suits might also be an arsenal of weapons. We had been nakedly unprepared for any kind of fight, I wanted to have something on our side to help us for when the moment of our capture arrived.

And like an addict stumbling across a cache of heroin, I found three containers near the far side of the storage warehouse. Simon was close by, but still ten meters away. I opened the first bin and saw bags upon bags upon bags of white powder. HEX-P. I had found a supply of it. I wasn't sure how it could help, but I grabbed two baggies, full of the precious powder, stuffing them into my bra. I smiled for a second at the surprise I anticipated on Simon's face when he realized that my breasts had somehow grown a full cup size in the matter of a few minutes.

"Simon," I said plainly, calling him over. As he made his way to me, I opened the next two boxes, they were full of canisters. The aerosol HEX-P, the kind that I had seen in action on the day of the invasion, now sitting calmly in a little box. I wanted to scream as I thought of how many people died because of these canisters. How many people suffered as they aspirated the chemicals? I saw Simon approaching and thought of the stump on his hand, forever without his thumb. I was ready to kill me some aliens, but I knew that with their exo-suits on the chemical would do nothing to them. I hoped that they were all exposed. I hoped that they were all naked and unprepared. I was ready to give them a taste of their own death. I was ready to murder them.

Simon reached me as I pulled out two of the canisters. His eyes were wide in disbelief. "Dora, you'll kill us before you kill them," he was indignant.

"Not if they aren't wearing their suits," I pointed to the rows of empty Porthana suits. "We can take a good amount out with us on our way if we have to." The whole murder-suicide angle was becoming the most likely. There was an infinitesimally small chance of both of us making it out alive.

"Dora, what if it doesn't work on them at all?" Simon asked the most obvious question. It was the question that I had quickly tossed from my mind as my murderous pep-talk was playing in my head. But it was so true, that it didn't need to be asked.

"At least we'll try then," I swallowed the stupidity of my plan and put a canister in my top, nestled above the cloud-like packets of the powdered HEX-P in my bosom. Simon, first silently watching me place the lethal aerosol directly over my lungs, began to dig into the bin as well. He grabbed for two other canisters and attached them to his belt. He attached another two onto the belt loops of my pants. We were laden with poison now, death swinging from our hips. We were modern day human cowboys ready to roll into alien-town. (My inner self-talk was really going at this point; we had found a potential weapon and I was drunk off of hope.)

The weighty substances felt clunky on my body, I was so nervous that one of the canisters would begin to shuffle, then fall and explode. We were very close to death, and we had just made it that much easier to die. Although I found a small comfort in the idea of dying by our own accident then being captured by the Porthana. *They would vaporize us or probe us if they captured us, right?*

We had worked our way across the storage room for thirty minutes. Now Simon was focused on finding the next way out, surely, he didn't want to go back the way that we came, and the room was massive enough that he presumed there would be another point of entrance or egress. Our small lights were minuscule and didn't carry more than a few inches around us, creating a soft halo. We couldn't see the other side of the warehouse clearly, but we could hear. And as Simon was checking the walls with his left hand again, slowly dragging it across, looking for a way out, we heard a door open. The door we had initially entered in was opened and then shut. We heard thick boots on the metal floor, heavy and full of intent. I began to panic and Simon started to move much more quickly to find a point of exit.

With great luck he found the green and red knobs within seconds, he pressed the green and we slinked through the door as it was still in the process of opening and he pressed the red button on the other side. As the door began to close, he grabbed one of the aerosol cans on his hip and threw it into the storage room. One can used. Hopefully, one alien dead.

We found ourselves in a hallway, but a very different one than the one we had seen upon our entrance. This one had cool steely blue tile floors and white walls with clean white recessed lighting. To our left was a dead end, and to our right was a window, looking out over the plains. We had gone underground, but somehow, we were still looking at the daylight we had recently left. Perhaps it was a live feed to a screen that mimicked the outdoors. Perhaps we had been in a time-space warp within the warehouse. Perhaps my brain was too fried to try and comprehend it all.

Simon and I walked toe to heel, quietly hoping to avoid detection, but this dead-end hallway had only one door. It was as though we had been pushed into taking that exit to lead us here. Perhaps we had intentionally been left alone so that we would find this hallway. Next to the door, the only one other than the entrance to the warehouse now swimming with HEX molecules in the air, was the familiar two buttons. Simon waved his hand and they began to glow, light green and light red.

I started to see what Simon meant when he first encountered them. "Almost too intuitive," was my long-awaited response. He looked over at me,

I looked back at him. This was it. We were about to uncover something, we were about to die, we were nearing the end of our short-lived freedom.

There is a point in every great story where the reader becomes frenzied. I recalled this sensation many times in my life, my life before the invasion and captivity. There would be a suspenseful moment, mostly at the rising action before the denouement, but sometimes it would be earlier in the story if it had been told well. At these moments my eyes couldn't devour the words on the page quickly enough. I found myself skipping ahead to get to the next patch of dialog, in desperate need of knowing what happened next.

And if the story was really good, if the mystery had been well laid out, I would often step back and think, "what just happened" and then force my brain to calm down and read every detail that I had skimmed.

That was how I felt standing before that steely-blue door. Simon and I stood there, shoulder to shoulder, for only a fraction of an instant, but for me, the door could not open soon enough. I wanted to fast forward to the moment when I would be face to face with the Porthana leader. Their leader had to be behind this door. It made logical sense, though I had no evidence to support it. Behind this door would be the queen bee, the sultan, the raj, "the man in charge," the maestro, the great orchestrator of the human annihilation. I was ready to be face-to-face and pull the pin from the canister. I was ready to murder the being responsible for a human genocide. A transformative journey over the past several months had brought me to the brink and now I was a murderer, if not by deed then by intention. But I knew it would be worth it. And that door, pressure-sealed and covered in a matte finish, could not open fast enough.

I will provide one disclaimer here. If you do not wish to know the truth, if you are content to believe that Simon and I are successful in our mission, then read no further. If you are scanning, searching, reading ahead at this point and desperate to know the truth, then continue on, but only if you can accept the consequences and allow your perspective to be flipped. The door is opening, a hiss of air escaping as the seal to the doorjamb releases and the door slides smoothly along a hidden track, enveloped by a sliver of space in the bulkhead wall. Read on if you will, but you have been warned.

There was a man.

Standing on a platform that was to our left as we entered the room, facing a vast open window with a view of Earth, there was a man. His skin was pink and flush, and flanked on either side were more men. Behind this man, with gray hair highlighting the temples of his face were his guards. These guards were all wearing the now familiar exo-suit of the Porthana, and on their heads were the masks that had become the faces of my nightmares, the dark void that I had come to associate with the aliens. The masks were ceremonially removed and these guards, now revealed to all be men and women, held their masks to their side, their faces were bare and plain to us.

Simon's anger was palpable. He was a man of ideals, and the humans in this room were clearly the engineers of human destruction, they were the wicked and the wretched. They were traitors. "You!" he thundered. Had he known the man standing in the center, with his curly salt-and-pepper hair and thin lines framing his face?

"Oui, my name is Claude. You have been trespassing in my station for the better part of an hour. I would say 'welcome,' but you are not welcome here." This man, Claude, was the clear leader. The way the other men in the room moved and positioned themselves around him, he was clearly the person in control, the man with the power (something they all sought to earn one day).

My mind was silently spinning, gently pushing into my mind thoughts of every single encounter. The arguments spewing and shouting from Simon's mouth were a dull background noise as my head ached and filled with denial. *No, it had been two smelly and ugly aliens who had tried to implant a trigger into my thumb in that decrepit hospital, right? Right?*

And that is why I had been concentrating so hard on that exact moment, that hot and exhausted moment on the plains of Texas, when I was first thrown into direct and close contact with the Porthana. I was distracted by the constant bickering of my captor and his drugged companion; I was distracted by the smoke and mirrors of the entire invasion. And the slip in the hospital, the human bickering and the mistake that led me to handle and hold one of their trackers. The blaring alarm had distracted me again from realizing that only humans could have made that mistake. Maybe that is why it took me so long to realize. I was distracted, and I had been duped.

Should I have known then, on that hot afternoon on an abandoned stretch of highway? Should I have observed some contact or habit that was distinctly human that could have predicted this moment? As Simon began to hurl insults and accusations, I tried to calculate this in my head. Shouldn't I have noticed sooner? No. It is far easier to believe that an alien species would inflict this upon us than it was to swallow the thick and heavy truth that it was a self-mutilation all along. These Porthana, these backward men, have been exposed.

I had stopped my mind from ripping apart every last piece of my sanity in enough time to tune-in to Simon's latest interaction with Claude.

"Eugenics? Human experimentation? How could this be sanctioned?" Simon gestured heavily with his arms.

"Sanctioned? You still operate under the assumption that a governing body needs to grant permission for everything. We have no authority to report to, we're men on a mission, and we took what we needed in order to make that happen."

"Who knew then, before it all started, who knew?"

"The people in this facility and the sister facilities in other continents." Claude gave a plain and honest answer. To me, that meant one thing, and one thing only. We would both be dead before we left this room. A secret this big, a corruption this deep would never allow for it.

"And what have you gained from all of this?" Simon spat out his question.

"Well, with the population dwindling, we've eliminated most of the undesirable genes, although we have lost more than a few of the positive traits, but no doubt our team here will help to re-introduce those characteristics back into the genetic pool." The guards placidly smiled at each other. Everything was on schedule and on time in this warped world.

"But the research, the observation, Simon I'm surprised that you of all people can't appreciate the value of the scientific data being collected." There was so much appalling and wrong with every word this man spoke. And the worst part was that he pronounced data like "dater", his manner was too cool and removed. I hated that he made any kind of implication towards Simon.

"No, I cannot appreciate any of this!" Simon was the man I knew he was.

"But we're finally gaining an understanding of raw human nature. Seeing our species without the mores of our society. What small hives have tasted cannibalism; what murders have gone excused when the world thinks no one is watching?" I wanted to hear no more. And it seems that Claude was tired of explaining himself to us.

"You won't get away with this? We can't be the only ones who know? We can't be the only ones who are mad?" Simon was emphatic, but the guards began to slowly shift, moving to circle us. They were coming in for the kill.

"No matter, no one will believe you. A crazy deranged person on the loose ranting about a conspiracy theory is always easily forgotten." Claude smiled as he waved his hand, flicking away an imaginary undesirable molecule.

"We'll find a way to tell the world, to expose your scheme."

"I'm sure that you will try," Claude was quick to respond. I remained silent. I couldn't participate in a conversation with this man.

"This leaves us with a problem. This system works because the remaining population believes we are alien, foreign, and they can excuse our methods because they do not know that we are human. So, you cannot leave this place with this knowledge if you are against us." Claude's words were finite and firm. That was the ultimatum, beat 'em or join 'em.

After a pause, the two guards that had been flanking Claude moved across the room and stood behind us. One guard for each of us. "You can join us and live, or you can deny us and die. That is the choice."

I looked over at Simon. We had known this all along, but had refused to think it, whisper it, or say it out loud. And this is where the last shred of humanity in each of us differed. Looking into my eyes he gave an almost imperceptible shake of his head. I moved my chin up and then down slightly.

He hissed, "If you accept them, then you are complicit in their extermination of our species."

"If I don't try to live to watch them all burn, then I'll never be able to make them pay," I shouted these words with my eyes. Simon knew what I was saying.

We were at an impasse. The only thing human in him was his dogged determination to uphold his ideals. Simon would not compromise and yield to Claude, even if he knew he would never truly belong to them, and that he would work every day to defeat them from within. And I had only the human need to hope for the future left. I hoped to see Claude and his crew die, to see them all hang and then help rebuild the world. This was all that we had left. Our animalistic need to survive had driven us this far.

And so, Simon spoke the words, "two pistols please, we'll take care of this ourselves."

"The Romeo and Juliet exit eh?" Claude's vile mouth emitted the words. "This makes for an interesting addition to our studies." I wanted to vomit from the mixture of neurotransmitters, adrenaline, and repulsion moving through me.

The guards that were behind us presented each of us with a gun, the pistols were steely and cold. I couldn't help but start to cry. Finally, in all of the confinement, imprisonment, and abuse I was crying. I was at the end and I couldn't avoid it. Of all the hate I felt at that moment, hating myself for missing out, hating Simon for bringing me to this moment, hating stupid Claude and his sadistic plans, what I hated most is that Simon and I would just be numbers, just another test subject meeting their unnatural end. I hated that feeling. We were pushed down to our knees. I looked down at the pistols, I couldn't even think through the motions of how I could kill myself with it. Of the months and weeks I had spent thinking I was ready to die, ready to be released from the pain of what this existence had brought, I found a bubbling within me, a willingness to fight and try to riddle my way through it all. The body really does fight death until the very end.

On my knees, tears lightly rolling down my cheeks, it felt like there was no rush, but that we must be getting on with it. Simon leaned forward and pulled my head near him. He took the gun and my wrist in his massive right hand and positioned it to his heart. He did the same with his. We would kill each other, I understood what he was positioning us for. But he must have known that I wouldn't have been able to kill him. I was trying to figure out how I could move my hand so quickly to fire a perfect shot at Claude before being taken out by the guards. Or should I shoot the next in line and Simon would shoot Claude? *How could we communicate this with the time we had left? How could I steal one last moment with him? Why hadn't we discussed a plan?*

Simon leaned close to my ear, but his private words escaped our proximity, the most horrible men in the history of the world heard them. "Don't cry my dear," he pulled the fabric of the sling around my shoulders up to my face and wiped my cheeks. I took it with my free hand and began to wipe more deliberately at my eyes, hiding the sadness on my face from Simon and those watching us.

Each of these seconds seems so sweet that I must linger on them for a while longer. I am not ready to completely dispel them from my memory.

I looked directly into Simon's calm eyes, he was looking intently into mine, the only part of my face that was visible. His academic mind a relic, a leftover pearl from the centuries of civilization brought down in a matter of weeks. What wonderful bright thoughts had been wiped out, never to be collected or considered by our planet, thrusting our collective mind into atrophy and trauma?

He nodded and spoke clear instructions, "On three, okay?"

I nodded.

"One," he said softly. I closed my eyes. I couldn't bear to look at him. I wanted to clear my mind. I wanted to think of a cool and peaceful patch of grass, I envisioned a mountain range waiting for me in the north that would always be waiting, for I would never arrive.

"Two," I hoped that Simon had done the same, but I felt his free hand on my arm, caressing my skin, moving upward quickly and reaching into my shirt.

Seriously! The arrogance of men to try to take and take and take from me until my last moment. I was briefly appalled until I felt the slight pull and tug. He had ripped the canister out and pulled the pin, releasing the aerosol. I never heard the word "three," but I did feel the muzzle of a gun that was pressed into my chest pull away and I did hear the gunshot. With my nose and mouth covered by the same fabric that had been drying my eyes I opened them quickly to see the panic as the men on the platform and around us began to twitch, Shots went off as they lost their balance, ricochets were bounding through the thick and hazy air.

Too stunned to cry, too terrified to move. Simon was dead on the ground, his head blown away by his own hands. *Off with their heads, all of those men who tried to control me: purposefully, accidentally, even with the best of intentions. Off with their heads. None of these men are safe near me.*

I moved quickly, though I felt slow and sluggish. My imperfect mask was letting through some of the aerosol. My eyes were stinging, although if they hadn't been reacting to the toxin my blind rage and anger and pain would have been enough to keep me stumbling until I found the door. I slammed my hand on the green button, opening it and ran to the door for the storage facility. I opened the door and closed it quickly. I had only a few moments before some kind of alarm was set off, perhaps it already had, calling for a search for the lone human female roaming the hallways.

In my stupidity of not realizing the truth, I began to doubt my instincts for a fraction of a second. Hadn't I been captured and recaptured following those instincts? Hadn't I been betrayed and sold out? But then again, my instinct had been to not come to this place and that would have been a huge mistake because I wouldn't have learned the truth, but it would have been the best choice because Simon would still be alive.

The gears in my head were spinning so fast and trying to find a solution. I kept the blanket over my mouth and nose, feeling the same sting of the aerosol toxin in the warehouse because the canister Simon had released in this room was still dissipating. I needed to be able to breathe and move and hide. I headed toward the obvious solution and did what I had to in order to survive.

The suit was heavy and burdensome. I hated each millimeter of my skin that made contact with it, but it was my lone security in the mass murderous scheme overrun with humans hiding behind the evil mask of the Porthana. I had slipped into the suit awkwardly, but I was quick and my fingers didn't fumble as I held my breath and heaved the bulky mask over my head. I was tall, uncomfortably tall and with my first step I noticed a mechanical whir and whizz beneath my heels. Spring-loaded stilts. And at my fingertips were five circular wires, ripe to be grasped and pulled, worn like rings and controlling the extended mechanical arm. I was six and a half feet tall with hanging long arms to match. *Those evil geniuses.*

I donned the suit and the attitude of those traitors and ran. I was right under their noses and they didn't see me. I had been correct that some alarm had been raised. There seemed to be a mass search in all directions which left me within the reach of the horrible human claws for a bit longer. I was careful to blend in during the first two days that I had contact with- *them.* Those monsters that murdered everyone, that pushed me to the edge, that were responsible for Simon's death.

I cried each evening after I found a place to hide, my stomach empty and my muscles sore. The suit was unforgiving and uncomfortable. While I was on the run, I never took it off, afraid that I might nod off for a few minutes and be discovered. Hiding in the brush and fallen leaves that gathered under glorious trees I hid, the perfect world feeling my metallic and unworthy exo-suit pressed against it. Each morning when I woke, I became more and more determined to find a real shelter. I did find some abandoned hotels and motels along the way once I crossed the Canadian border. (I knew I was in Canada because of all of the faded signs for gas listed prices by the "litre", not the "gallon.")

My first evening in a hotel I removed the suit completely and saw the hollow and dewy look to my skin. Maybe I was turning into an alien, I certainly didn't recognize myself. Filled with self-loathing and repulsed by the reality that was settling in, that all of my pain had been sanctioned by some rogue group of men and women. I wished I had been focusing more on what Simon had been shouting at Claude, it might have explained more about how this all started and what their end-goal was. But I had been reeling from our discovery. After some vacant time, where I stood in front of the mirror and let the minutes slip away easily, I broke the glass in front of me. I slammed the mirror so many times because I didn't want to see. I didn't want to see myself or any others or to have seen what was in that station. I left a wake of broken mirrors in my path as I traveled on foot through Canada.

This is what I have figured out in my exile. I have no proof other than what I've seen and the proof in my heart. It all fits together now. We were being studied and had been selected for the greatest redistribution of wealth in human history. Not a wealth that could be used to trade for goods or services. A wealth of healthy genes. Intelligence, beauty, endurance, adaptability were all the qualities that they desired. A mass genocide from an alien invasion was the perfect diversion to follow through on what had been started decades earlier.

I struggled for weeks trying to understand why Simon shot himself. *Was it because he thought that odds of survival would be better if only one of us made it? Was it his unfailing morals that wouldn't allow him to live with the knowledge of the greatest ongoing deception in human history? Was it his belief in my ability to constantly hope for an escape?*

Simon the Clever. Simon the Cynic. Simon the Selfless. I missed him too much to think. I crossed far fewer miles each day than I should have, but I went further and further with each step.

Each night brought a new set of nightmares so I slowly dipped into the powdered HEX-P to keep me asleep at night. Should a Porthana, because I cannot even think of them as men, find me and kill me in my stoned sleep so be it. I made my way far enough north that the only living things I have seen are wolves and birds, a few ground-dwelling animals, but not much. I stumbled across a dwelling in the woods, well designed with lots of glass and beams. I made my new home cozy, but kept my suit nearby in case I was ever found.

I endeavored to write this all down when my stores of powdered HEX-P began to run low. I was hoping that my attempts to record it would absolve my conscience and allow for easy rest, but I'm not sure that I have succeeded there. I will live my lonely days as long as I can.

And that is what it all came down to. Humans hating humans. Humans raping, beating, using, murdering humans. The carnality of our species working against itself. I should have known no alien life would ever seek us out. If friendly, they would be wise to stay away. If sinister, they could sit back and let us destroy each other. We've already trashed our planet to the point of melting, a soup of raw elements, sulfur, and ozone, dripping down and then splattering into the cosmos. Who would ever want to interfere with the perfect damage we were already doing? Who in the known and uncharted space would want to deal with this?

I invite no pity. And take whatever wisdom you will from what vain attempts I have made to detail my ordeal. The most terrifying thing in the universe is not the unknown, the other, but rather what is known to dwell within each of us, boiling beneath the surface. The human race is the most violent and dangerous: other life-forms beware of our planet.

Should I have spent more of this paper eulogizing the men, women, and children that were lost? Perhaps, but then this story would never end and I would spend the rest of my life writing down as much as I could to try to honor and remember the people that I knew, but that would never do them justice. I have told this all to you to bring justice. If someone is reading this, if someone finds this in the rubble that surrounds my corpse one day, please know that all of my attempts to restore my humanity have been a tireless effort. Please know that the real danger is within us all and choose your own manner of escape. Life is too short to spend another moment imprisoned by the will of another.

I know that eventually a person will come across my camp and I may die on that day. I could hear a twig snap or a rustle of duff on the ground. I might even be completely off guard or maybe swindled by some resilient and nomadic humans. I expect that my death will not be natural or peaceful. But at least I will die free. I will be free from the anxiety of society, the oppression of this knowledge of the Porthana plan and the constant urge to bite my nails.

THE END

ACKNOWLEDGMENTS

My amazing support team, family, friends, and fans have made this and all of my books possible. Thank you to my wonderful editor, Debbie Williams, for all of her patient guidance. Thank you to all my fans who have read each of my books and continue to ask for more.

M.K. Williams is the author of multiple books. You can follow her for more in-depth information on these books at 1mkwilliams.com. To receive updates on upcoming books, please take a moment to subscribe.

If you enjoyed this story, please consider leaving a review for Nailbiters. Each review helps other readers discover this book. Thank you for your support.

Looking for more to read about the world of The Project Collusion Series? Read the follow-on story for more about what happened to Dora next in The Dora Diaries. Visit 1mkwilliams.com/project-collusion to claim your copy today.

Preview of ***Architects***

Three years after "the outbreak," Hunter is part of a dwindling crew stuck at sea. Until he is assigned to a small mission to restore their supply pipeline. Once ashore, the mission goes sideways. Fear of the virus that wiped out the global population, roaming packs of survivors, and an ominous Reaper rattle Hunter's grip on reality.

What really happened to the world and how much did Hunter's superiors know about it?

The long-anticipated second installment of *The Project Collusion Series* is here. Fans of *Nailbiters* have been waiting for the answers to their questions, now they'll know how it all started. You'll want to read this one with the lights on.

Part 1: The Sit In

I can't tell you; *this is how it all started.* I don't believe any person, dead or alive, can. But I can tell you how I got here. This whole thing started from so many different places and the root cause has existed as long as mankind. This path is towards nihilism, creating our own ultimate destruction. But you're not here for the philosophical theories about the why. You want to know the how, the when, and the who behind the destruction. I can tell you what I know.

Let's just say that I didn't know everything that had been going on. Not until recently. An assignment from the captain, a suicide mission, sparked off this whole thing.

"Hunter," I heard Captain Gomes bark at me through the intercom that made his voice sound nasal and distorted. "Get up here now."

No need to explain where 'here' was, no need to clarify further. The ship had maybe one hundred people aboard and I was the lone Hunter. I didn't appreciate the accusatory glances of my shipmates as I passed by. Each wondering what I did, what I was about to be told. I recalled one similar trip to the principal's office in elementary school. The mortification and unease mounted with each step as I approached the bridge of the ship, high above the deck with a view of nothing except dark blue below and pale gray above.

I hesitated for a moment before opening the door and stepping over the knee-knocker. Once I was there, in that room, I would know what new crisis would be thrown at me. But for those few seconds, I was in the glorious unknowing; the time when this could still be something positive, maybe even welcome news. I took a quick breath and went in.

"Captain," I greeted him briefly when I spotted Gomes hunched over one of the monitors towards the back of the bridge, closest to his private office.

"Hunter," he started in immediately, standing up firmly and squaring his shoulders, a habit drilled into him by years of procedure. At an impressive six-foot-ten inches Captain Hector Gomes was one of few people who managed to make me feel short at six-foot-five. "Another supply shipment was attacked, never arrived at the depot on land, nothing for Roz to fly back."

Roz was our helicopter pilot on the ship, and she was also the only one who regularly went to shore. We all looked at her with a mixture of fear and reverence. She was brave enough to go there, but she could also be carrying some pathogen with her.

Gomes continued, "We need to figure out what is causing the disruption. It's happened too many times in the past three months for this to be anything unorganized. We need to find out who is behind it and eliminate the problem."

"I did notice our rations were getting rather bland," I offered in my own particular brand of speaking. I wasn't military. I wasn't part of his crew. I was a refugee on this vessel, and I had resisted the vernacular that was foreign to me for the three years I'd been aboard.

Captain Gomes had been upset with my non-compliance at the outset, but I think he either got used to it or he was told by PeeC that my particular skill set afforded certain exceptions. Or maybe we were so far removed from people and procedure that it didn't seem to matter much anymore. But with everything that happened, it felt as though procedure was what would keep us all sane. Either way, he had softened to me and what would have earned one of his soldiers a quick rebuke for being so informal was met with, "Yeah, tell me about it."

"So, what do you need me to do?" Aside from my observation regarding meals, I didn't know the extent of the problem. With this new information and the rations that had been issued in the past two weeks, I inferred that we hadn't received a new shipment for at least a month. But I'm the biomedical engineer; I'm the science guy, the tech nerd. I don't touch the logistics. If what the captain had just said was true, the situation was likely more dire than I could have imagined. Even with a small population of about one hundred on the ship, The Pricus Capricorn, without new supplies more intense measures were likely on the horizon.

"Well, the crew is dwindling," Gomes started. My mind flashed on the image of something moving quickly in my peripheral vision, a blur of black and gray out of my porthole window, followed by a near-silent splash. I winced at the thought. The crew was indeed dwindling, people losing their minds, the sea looking all the more inviting each day. The captain continued, unphased, "I need as many of my trained team to stay on board to keep this thing afloat." He smirked and leaned up against one of the consoles, relieving some of the weight off of his boots. "Based on who I need on board and who can do the task on shore, you're it."

So, who can you expend in case this goes south? "I don't have the training for that kind of mission." I had this argument with him in the first few months on board. He knew this, sending me ashore was tantamount to a death sentence.

"None of us had any kind of training for this." He shook his head and considered his next words carefully. "We think that the attacks on the shipments can be stopped with your little invention." Gomes didn't notice, but his right hand went to his left forearm.

"And if I am attacked onshore, who will be able to help you with it?" I countered. I knew the power I had; I knew I was the only one left who understood the technology and could interpret the readings.

"If you don't go, we may never get another supply shipment onto this vessel. You want the life of every crew member on your conscience?" He narrowed his gaze at me, willing his mental picture into my own mind of the ship drifting afloat, unmanned, and only inhabited by the corpses of a starved crew.

He knew exactly what button to push to get me to jump. "Fine, I'll go," I turned to leave, my mind was already racing with the violent ends I would meet onshore. Disease, or attack from survivors, now rabid with only their primal instincts to guide them. "We'll do a briefing at 2000 this evening. You leave tomorrow at 0600."

"Meeting at eight. Board at six. See you then," I muttered on my way out, my last defiance as I knew I would likely never return to the ship.

I held it together for as long as it took me to get back to my bunk. I tried to calm myself, turn my inner thoughts from my inevitable demise to the promise of success. *Visualize success, visualize a positive outcome.* I had to have some kind of memory of what that felt like buried somewhere deep in my mind. I ran through the same mental route I had carved over the long months on that ship. My own warped form of meditation. A word association exercise:

The first visual in my mind was from my college days. *Rushing to class, running down historic streets where the upturned bricks in the sidewalk almost tripped me up. Some poking out. Some crammed back down but always jiggling when your foot struck them. You were at risk of twisting your ankle. You had to mind them, unconsciously, you avoided the loose ones. I don't ever remember stumbling, but I recall that I learned to sidestep one nasty section at the exit of my favorite pizza shop.*

If we had to play the game "Desert Island," the food that I could eat every single day is pizza. No toppings, lots of toppings, doesn't matter. Piping hot pizza with cheese melting off it. Piping, why is it called piping? Hot like steam pipes maybe?

Well, now, I've gone and done it. Steam pipes, PVC pipes. The ceilings in every corridor of the Bunker were lined with pipes. They went every which way, following us as we hustled to our laboratories. Sometimes I would picture an invisible cable reaching from one pipe down to the crown of my head, like I was a trolley car and I was being guided along my route.

Bunk to cafeteria to lab. Lab to Rattray's office. Office to cafeteria. Cafeteria to Rec Room, Rec Room to Bunk. It was a fun little mind game I would play sometimes. It doesn't work here. The pipes on the ship are too wide and bulky, too utilitarian to ever play host to my little daydreams.

The little hash marks on the wall next to my berth do play though. They remind me of cave drawings; perhaps I should go back and attach eyes, appendages. Would that help my psyche to make them alive? To give life?

No, they would turn on me in my sleep. They would fashion Clovis point spears and attack me when I least expected it. I cannot animate them. I've already had two nightmares this month, each time I wake up in a sweat. As my eyes adjusted in the dark, I thought the hash marks were really scratch marks, someone clawing at the wall, itching at something beneath it. No, no more little mind games to pass the time.

I had been keeping a journal of these dreams for months. I was in the habit of journaling and writing down my thoughts and experiments, so I added a new practice to include these vivid dreams. Dr. Simmons was the only psychiatrist on board and had been inundated with discreet requests for treatment. I heard through an unofficial network of other passengers that there was an opening. What with all the jumpers, her schedule was clearing up.

The journaling helps a bit. It makes me feel like I am doing something. Survivor's Guilt. She joked during our first session that it had infected everyone on board, but I didn't get the joke until a while after it ended.

She is a reputable doctor, but I'm sure all of the stories that she has heard so far have all been the same. Every person here had to watch from afar as the world burned; the flames not visible on the coastline, but still, we knew what was happening on land.

I thought that perhaps my story would add some new excitement to her routine, or I could just lie, make something up. But the truth is already unbelievable as it is. It's not every day that you meet someone who knows that they are culpable for an apocalypse.

Earlier that week, or was it the previous week, I had been telling Dr. Simmons about my worries, neuroses, guilt. "They called me up to the bridge yesterday," I said to the ceiling as I laid on the empty bunk in her cabin. She had no bunkmate so this served as her makeshift office. On my first visit, she told me that we could just sit and talk facing each other. But I preferred to lay on my back, speaking to the ceiling. She told me every time that this wasn't psycho-analysis. But I couldn't break the habit.

"I heard," she replied without further prompting. Of course, she had. Everyone on the ship could hear those announcements. No way to not hear them. We were referring to the last time I was called to the Bridge to help read the flashes on the screen, the flashes that I created.

"They're going to send me ashore, I just know it, and then I'm dead." I had expressed this exact worry to her multiple times. Every time it felt fresh and new, as though the words still had the potential to explode back at me, finally becoming reality. No amount of saying it out loud dulled the effect.

"Maybe they will send you ashore, but why would that necessarily mean you would die? You've survived this long, haven't you?" Dr. Simmons always answers my worries with questions. She never tells me anything new. I like that though. I don't think my brain could handle anything new.

Now that I have my orders from Captain Gomes all I want to do is pound down her door and say, "I told you so." But that won't change the captain's mind. It will only make me feel slightly better. Validated in my paranoia.

I knew that my time on board would be ending. I could just feel it. My days of staring at the gray walls and finding myself lost within a tangle of passageways would soon be at an end. I always assumed I would find myself overboard, just another one of the mentally weak scientists who went stir crazy without projects to tinker with. Of course, I didn't believe any of the bulletins they gave as the cause of the disappearances of late. People were starting to lose it. Everyone aboard was starting to go stir crazy, agitated. There were strong dividing lines between the soldiers and the refugees. The ones who had earned their spot on the ship and the ones who had earned everyone a one-way ticket to misery.

Our place here, my place here, was based on timing. They weren't going to keep me on the luxurious cruise ship in the middle of the Pacific that I happened to be aboard when the outbreak happened. It was arranged that the top scientists would be picked up so that they would help with the situation. But no specimens were ever provided. Instead of my story being that I took the opportunity so that I could help, I just took the out so that I could live a protected life on this vessel.

The paramilitary team was welcoming at first, but they made it known that they didn't think much of us egg-heads. Where they had physical strength, tactical awareness, and the first priority on the ship, the scientists had theories, and laboratories, and our skills were no longer in high demand. They told us that the disease had already spread too quickly and that at this point every country had entered into a state of martial law. No need to start developing a cure, most of the population was already dead or dying. Best for us to hunker down and wait for the all-clear. But the all-clear hadn't come for three years.

I began to speak out, having the audacity to ask when we could leave. I had indeed lost a small piece of my sanity, but the thing with your mental health is that you can lose a bit here and there, but you don't know which bits are the most important until you've completely unraveled.

"Maybe the team that is supposed to give us the all-clear was infected. We need to send out a search and rescue team!" I remembered my first conversation – or argument – with Gomes.

"Rescue? Rescue them where? You bring them aboard and they could infect us all." The captain made his response clear. I tried to connect with his lieutenant, Nelson Chang, to see if he might harbor the same concerns that I did; see if I could convince him to break rank. I was shut down, and ever since then, I've been awaiting the day that he would try to call me out, to get me off the ship. And that day had arrived.

After wasting idle moments back in my bunk, throwing soft items at the metal walls and feeling no relief, I stormed out and worked through the maze to try and find Dr. Simmons. The last of my colleagues had all found their way over the railings in the past few months, leaving me with no one else to talk to except the good doctor.

I tried to politely knock on her door, but my hand refused and curled into a fist, pounding instead. Demanding an immediate answer. She didn't respond. I pounded again. Did I scream out her name? I can't recall. After I tired myself out, I charged back to my bunk.

I tried to have a conversation with the Doctor in my mind. What questions would she ask, what platitudes would she offer? Hunter, why don't you tell yourself a new story? I could try to convince myself that this is what

I wanted. I'm going to leave the ship.

That could work. But I would remind her that I knew this was coming all along. There was a conspiracy among the crew to slowly pick off the scientists one by one, to eliminate us, punishment for our crimes, and to save food for the rest of the soldiers. She would tell me that conspiracy theorists are often wrong. I would ask her a question, finally. "*What do you call a conspiracy theory that turned out to be right?*"

My feet thumped against the hallway. Everything about life on the Pricus Capricorn was loud. Every surface was metal. Conversations echoed. Light footsteps sounded like a pounding march. Engines whirred on and off, steam whistled, and then subsided. There was always noise on the ship. I added my fair share to it.

When it was time, I headed to the meeting to learn about my onshore mission. I entered the small conference room off of the command center. Lieutenant Nelson Chang was fiddling with the remote control, trying to set up a visual presentation. He was extremely lean, almost frail, compared to the rest of the crew. All of them were supposed to be ex-special ops soldiers. I never would have figured this guy for that line of work in a million years. But perhaps that was his advantage when he was on the front. The ability to look weak and draw people in was his distinct skill.

I sat down in the seat closest to the exit. I was being forced ashore against my will. I wasn't about to put on my chipper face and pretend that I wanted to be at this briefing. Chang acknowledged me as he reset his computer.

He finally got the display working correctly as two other crew members arrived. Dr. Jordan Michaels and Specialist Ansel Dawes. They didn't appear to be too pleased about being there either. Both men had been on the Pricus when I had arrived three years earlier. They had worked with Captain Gomes for years prior to the outbreak. I was shocked that he would put people I considered to be his most valuable team members on a suicide mission, but I didn't let that show on my face. *Maybe this mission isn't completely doomed*, I thought as Chang began.

He started with aerial shots of the helipad where our supplies were to be picked up. Then another of the supply depot further inland. There were older images as well as fresh ones the Connect glider had taken earlier in the day.

"We have limited information on what has happened to the supply line and limited time to explain, so I'll just dive in. You are not authorized to discuss any of this until you are on the ground tomorrow. Nobody on the ship can know what I am about to tell you. Our supply lines were interrupted three months ago. We've been living off of our reserve store of food and MREs. It's almost empty." He paused for a moment; his mouth twitched. No more food meant starvation. I nodded to signal that I understood the full gravity of the situation. Michaels and Dawes did the same. *Three months.* That was way longer than I had even anticipated.

"The three of you will start out at the helipad depot and work your way inland to the supply depot. It's a good sixty miles, so we expect it to take a few days on foot. We suggest you follow the road but stick to the trees."

"Where do you think the disruption point is?" Dawes cut in with the first question.

"We haven't had any communication with the team at the supply depot for six weeks. Their last contact let us know when the supplies left, part of our routine. After that, nothing. No supplies at the helipad. We think some of the local survivors tracked when the trucks rolled through and set up roadblocks. Our team has gone silent, so it's possible they can't safely communicate with us to establish a new route-"

"Or they're all dead," Michaels interrupted.

Chang took a deep breath. "We don't know for sure. The crew in the supply depot had sent us some of their concerns about the locals."

"You think they were attacked?" I jumped in as well. These onshore headquarters were all secure underground facilities. Buried miles into the earth, they were fortresses. They could wall themselves off and survive for years if they needed to. They'd already been surviving for years, providing us support and shipping food to the coast. Within each of these onshore headquarters were command centers for their region, medical facilities, barracks, and machinery. They could continue to produce plant protein from internal greenhouses for a hundred years. Or, in the case of the facility in question, package it and send it to the crew on the Pricus.

"We're not sure, that's what we need you to find out," Chang said in an exasperated tone.

"Well, what did they report to you about the locals?" Michaels asked.

"Some chatter around vigilante organization," Chang let the anger in his voice show, he was losing control of the briefing. Chang and Gomes were all about maintaining control. I noticed the vein on his temple start to wiggle with tension.

"So, you don't think it could be another strain of the outbreak?" I followed up. Michaels and Dawes looked over at me. Their eyes confirmed it, they were thinking it too. We had been safe on our ship, away from the biochemical weapon, insulated by miles and miles of ocean.

"We don't know." Chang didn't try to sugar coat it.

"But you think it is more likely that they were attacked than infected?" Dawes tried to get him to confirm a theory.

"Yes," Chang said and advanced to another slide. The screen lit up with several clusters of blue dots. "We know there is a small population in the area. Our latest check-ins from other depots around the continent tell us that the infection has died out, all who remain were either quarantined or immune. So now that the world is nearly empty, we've returned to small bands of tribes and wandering groups of nomads."

"Why don't we just go ashore if the virus has died out?" I wondered why the obvious solution to the supply problem wasn't being discussed.

"If the supply depot was attacked, we don't want to have this ship, the crew, and the technology we possess attacked, killed, or stolen," Dawes answered this question and glared at me across the table for daring to ask.

"So, if the coast is clear, we may get to the depot and just tell you guys to come ashore?" Michaels chimed in.

"Your primary mission is to re-establish the existing supply lines. But, to the questions you have all asked, keep us apprised of your position and any contact with survivors," Chang was using his authoritative voice, he wasn't making eye contact with any of us. He needed to deliver his information to us like he was feeding data points into a computer. But we were human; we didn't operate that way.

"How many are there?" Dawes directed the question at Chang, but he was too busy picking at his fingernails to look up.

"Ten thousand," Chang said.

"In all of British Columbia?" I asked.

"On the continent." Chang pursed his lips at this comment. This information caught all of our attentions. I saw Michaels and Dawes look up at him out of the corner of my eye.

"We think there are maybe twenty to thirty survivors total in the region you'll be in. Hunter will have remote access to the Calm program to be able to manage any issues, should they arise."

Now it all made sense.

Dawes. Michaels. Me.

Muscle. Medical. Miracle.

"We haven't had a massive breach since late 2015, about six months after the outbreak," Chang jumped back into his briefing. He advanced his slide to photos of one of the regional headquarters. I remembered them from the first time I saw them. Our regional headquarters near Coeur d'Alene, Idaho was attacked by two survivors. They set off cans of the Cease aerosol and shot up the place. It was a grim day. It was the day I realized that trying to help the world survive wasn't just about stopping the toxin anymore. It was going to be about stopping humanity from ending itself. A grim reminder of why the one hundred members of this crew might not be able to handle thirty hungry and rabid survivors on land.

A shiver ran down my spine as I thought back to the headquarters attack. We had all been working around the clock to stop the riots and insurrections. Losing a huge staff of trained soldiers and half of our executive team was a big blow. I didn't want to be the one to step in our supply depot and find the grisly scene repeated.

"If this was another breach, we may have no choice but to spray the area," Chang said with a grim face.

I opened my mouth to object, but Michaels beat me to it. "You're telling me there are maybe ten thousand people left on the entire continent of North America, and you want to spray and kill potential survivors if they attacked our supply depot?"

The idea sounded barbaric. An attack on them to even the score? We would lose the rest of the population quickly if that continued. "Do we really want to try to rebuild the world with a bunch of murderers and thieves?" Chang responded sharply.

Isn't that what we already are? I thought to myself, smart enough to not let those words pass my lips.

Michaels crossed his arms and leaned back in his chair. Clearly, he had heard enough. Dawes had resumed his thorough inspection of his cuticles. Chang dismissed us back to our bunks, reiterating his warning that we were not to repeat any of these details while still aboard.

Right, right, I thought. *Keep up the illusion.*

...